She was breathing fire into him.

It was a shock to the system, a blazingly erotic full body slam. He felt as if he'd been plugged into an electrical socket. She was soft fire, this woman in his arms.

He slid his tongue against her teeth, and they parted for him. He plunged inside, tasting her heat, feeling her yield. Her hands were burning him alive, and she was breathing fast through small, delicate nostrils.

Suddenly Craig groaned, reminding himself that Ginger Brenan was not a woman with whom he could dally. Otherwise, he was likely to find himself standing at an altar, wondering how on earth he had come to be there.

Still, he couldn't seem to extricate himself from her sweet, hot burn....

Dear Reader,

Welcome to Silhouette **Special Edition** . . . welcome to romance. Each month, Silhouette **Special Edition** publishes six novels with you in mind—stories of love and life, tales that you can identify with—romance with that little "something special" added in.

This month, we're pleased to present the conclusion of Nora Roberts's enchanting new series, THE DONOVAN LEGACY. *Charmed* is the story of Boone Sawyer and Anastasia Donovan—and their magical, charmed love. Don't miss this wonderful tale!

Sherryl Woods's warm, tender series—VOWS—will light up this Thanksgiving month. *Honor*—Kevin and Lacey Halloran's story—will be followed next month by *Cherish*. The vows that three generations of Halloran men live by create timeless tales that you'll want to keep forever!

Rounding out the November lineup are books from other favorite writers: Arlene James, Celeste Hamilton, Victoria Pade and Kim Cates. This is truly a feast for romance readers this month!

I hope that you enjoy this book and all the stories to come. Happy Thanksgiving Day—and all of us at Silhouette Books wish you the most wonderful holiday season ever!

Sincerely,

Tara Gavin
Senior Editor
Silhouette Books

ARLENE JAMES

HUSBAND IN THE MAKING

Silhouette®

SPECIAL ▼ EDITION®

Published by Silhouette Books New York
America's Publisher of Contemporary Romance

SILHOUETTE BOOKS
300 East 42nd St., New York, N.Y. 10017

HUSBAND IN THE MAKING

Copyright © 1992 by Arlene James

ISBN: 0-373-09776-X

First Silhouette Books printing November 1992

All the characters in this book have no existence outside the imagination of the author and have no relation whatsoever to anyone bearing the same name or names. They are not even distantly inspired by any individual known or unknown to the author, and all incidents are pure invention.

®: Trademark used under license and registered in the United States Patent and Trademark Office and in other countries.

Printed in the U.S.A.

Books by Arlene James

Silhouette Special Edition

A Rumor of Love #664
Husband in the Making #776

Silhouette Romance

City Girl #141
No Easy Conquest #235
Two of a Kind #253
A Meeting of Hearts #327
An Obvious Virtue #384
Now or Never #404
Reason Enough #421
The Right Moves #446
Strange Bedfellows #471
The Private Garden #495
The Boy Next Door #518
Under a Desert Sky #559
A Delicate Balance #578
The Discerning Heart #614
Dream of a Lifetime #661
Finally Home #687
A Perfect Gentleman #705
Family Man #728
A Man of His Word #770
Tough Guy #806
Gold Digger #830
Palace City Prince #866

ARLENE JAMES

grew up in Oklahoma and has lived all over the South. In 1976, she married "the most romantic man in the world." The author enjoys traveling with her husband, but writing has always been her chief pastime.

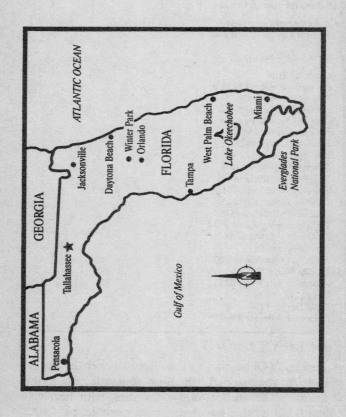

Chapter One

Ginger sank the small hand spade into the dark, sandy soil of the flower bed, then abandoned it to sit back on her heels and smile as the now-familiar Jaguar swung into the drive of the house next door. The sleek, black car came to a halt beneath the columned overhang that jutted out from the angular front of the white brick-and-glass house, and the tall, good-looking man she had glimpsed so often over the past several months stepped out of it. After pausing to remove his expensive, mirrored French-style black shades, he walked around the low-slung car and opened the passenger door, bending slightly to slip his hand beneath a decidedly feminine elbow. Ginger felt a flash of disappointment, but then the passenger sent a small, dark shoe to the ground and slipped out of the car to stare up at the soaring windows that stretched from the flower beds to the steep peak of the shingled roof. Small and delicate with light brown hair that straggled down her back, she was only a child in a school uniform consisting of a gold blazer over a plain white blouse and a navy blue A-line skirt that skimmed her knees.

Recognizing a woebegone air about her, Ginger studied the child. Frail and pale, she looked to be about thirteen, perhaps fourteen, but from the protective way the man draped his arm about the thin shoulders, Ginger guessed that she was younger. She was young enough, certainly, to need a mother; yet in all the months that the house had been under construction and the many times the man had come to survey the progress, Ginger had never seen a woman with him. Even the child was a surprise. What, then, was the story? The most likely explanation, of course, was divorce. The poor little thing could well be just another disillusioned child with a part-time father setting himself up in digs suitable for visitation, yet something about the man himself told Ginger that this was not the case.

Perhaps it was the easy, thoughtlessly confident manner in which he carried himself. He had the air of a man who had done well in life, and he seemed proudly self-contained and whole, as if he had never given away a piece of his heart and had it sent back to him tattered and bruised. Unusually attractive, he was tall and solidly built with muscular legs and arms made for athletic excellence. Even as he escorted the girl across the drive to the door of the house and slid his key into the lock, he demonstrated the innate, fluid grace that came hand in hand with athletic ability. Moreover, the squared planes of his face were smooth and symmetrical, the features regular and well-defined, the ears fitted evenly to the sleek, dark head. She had wondered over the months what color his eyes were and if the wide, chiseled mouth softened when it smiled. Soon she would know.

It was Thursday. She would give them Friday and the weekend to settle in. On Monday, she would officially welcome them to the neighborhood and satisfy her curiosity. They lived next door, after all. They shared a beach and a pier on the small, blue lake from which Whippoorwill Glade took its name. It was inevitable that they be friends—and maybe more. She smiled, intrigued with the idea that he could be *the one*, and picked up the spade again, deftly turning the earth.

Just as deftly, Ginger turned her mind to the task at hand. What should she plant in this spot? She had been trying to decide all morning. The possibilities were almost endless, for everything grew lush and strong in the friendly Florida climate, and she had a remarkable green thumb with which to assist. Humming a popular tune, hands working the soil, she went over a long list of plants in her head, seeing each one perfectly, noting the care needed and mentally fitting it into the artfully executed landscape of her front yard. Something busy, she decided. Gardenias? Yes, they would make a pretty display there next to the curb, with their dark, waxy leaves and creamy, fragrant blossoms. Gardenias, then. She could almost smell them now, their heady perfume wafting through her memory like a happy melody. When she realized the melody was a traditional wedding march, she laughed aloud and found herself thinking again of the tall, dark man next door.

He would look so fine in a gray morning coat, especially with her on his arm. Wouldn't it be something if he actually turned out to be her future husband? And why not? Some man, somewhere, surely would, and if this man didn't, it wouldn't be because she had failed to keep her eyes open or make herself available. Quite the contrary. For some time now, ever since she had been honest enough with herself to admit that what she wanted most in life was a husband and family, it had been her habit to investigate the possibilities with every likely candidate who crossed her path. She supposed the theory was unscientific at best, but somehow she had always believed that she would know right away when she had found *him*. That being the case, she should know before long if her attractive new neighbor was *the* man for her. She savored the moment, for in her experience it was the most exciting part of the whole exercise. For now, the possibilities were limitless. If only they would remain so, but too often, much too often in the past, they had not, and she knew that she had only herself to blame.

Somehow, she never seemed to get it right. Men were always attracted by her looks, but then they got to know her and their ardor invariably cooled. Her brother, Will, said that she was guilty of a certain arrogance, so sure was she that she could attract the man of her choice, but Frederick, doting father that he was, claimed the problem lay within the male psyche. His daughter was simply too intelligent for the average male. Few men could keep up with her. Indeed, Frederick insisted, even intelligent men were intimidated by Ginger's quick mind, talent and inherent honesty. Perhaps there was an element of truth in each observation, but deep down Ginger knew it was more than that. She was lonely in a way that only the right man could remedy. She so wanted to be in a caring, committed relationship with a special man. She wanted, in fact, to be married, to be married to a man about whom she could be passionate, a man who would be passionate about her.

Was Craig Russell that man? She intended to find out, but somehow she had to do it without turning him off.

She chewed her lip, wondering if she ought to make an appointment with her hairdresser. He'd been wanting to add a red tint to her honey blond hair. Red, apparently, was all the rage—for the moment. She briefly pictured herself with flaming bright hair, but then pushed the image aside. What was wrong with her? One thing she had learned over the years was to be herself. Granted, she meant to be the very best that she could, but the days of trying to remake herself physically were long gone. Highlights and shadings were one thing, changing the color of her hair outright was something else. Besides, maybe Craig Russell preferred blondes or better yet, maybe he wouldn't give a flip one way or another what color her hair was. Maybe he'd love her just because she was Gingevine Brenan. Now *that* would definitely make him the right man. And the right man was all she wanted.

Craig Russell eased back in the Hampton-style deck chair and crossed his long legs, his coffee cup balanced carefully in his left hand. Settling in, he smoothed his tie and sipped at the scalding coffee before reaching down for the Orlando newspaper lying on the deck beside his chair. This was perfection, and he intended to savor these extra twenty minutes before work that he had bought himself by moving to Whippoorwill Glen. He had bought more than that by building here, he reflected.

The house itself was everything he had hoped it would be: four large, airy bedrooms, each with its own well-appointed bath and access to the redwood decks and beach front; formal living and dining areas designed for easy entertaining; a large, homey kitchen at the very center of things, complete with skylight, bricked planters, computer center, sitting area and breakfast nook; and best of all, a den big enough to accommodate his weight machines, desk, comfy "male" furniture and the large-screen television recessed between ceiling-to-floor bookcases. Yes, the house was perfect, and the neighborhood was one of the most secure in the Orlando-Winter Park area. Plus, it was close to the corporate office of Russell-Solis Construction, one of the largest bridge-and-highway construction firms in the eastern United States. But most importantly, Jo's new school—posh, private and for girls only—was exactly right for her. No more would he worry about rowdy, careless, unsupervised teens stampeding through his home, throwing Jo into shock and the house into disarray—and Aunt Maggie into fits of interference. Yes, this was the serene haven for which he and Jo had been looking. After three moves in the space of ten months, he and Jo had at last come home. The difficult adjustments were made. The peace had been won. He was a contented man, and Jo was as happy as high-strung, delicate Jo could be, which was not saying much. He worried about her, had worried about her since their mother's death nearly four years earlier.

For the moment, he put the worries out of his mind and allowed himself to bask in the soft Florida morning. He sipped his coffee and surveyed the placid blue lake surrounded by pristine white beaches and banked by large, tasteful homes and styled fauna, everything from palm trees to pine trees, hydrangea to ivy, clover to swamp grass, but not in or near the lake itself, which was important, given the explosion in the wild gator population. Here at Whippoorwill Glen there were no reedy, marshy places for alligators to hide, and therefore, little possibility of Jo suffering a repetition of the ghastly incident that had prompted their first move. Eventually, he might even buy her another little dog, once she was wholly convinced that it wouldn't be eaten the first time she let it out of the house.

He blamed himself for that whole incident. Not wanting to frighten her unnecessarily, he hadn't warned her about the danger of leaving such a tiny pup on its own near the water's edge. After that, she had begged him to find them a place that was not surrounded by, near to or on the edge of water, no easy task on the Florida Peninsula. Nevertheless, he had managed to take a lease on what had seemed a suitable place, only to find himself and Jo overrun by a whole neighborhood of loud, pushy, undisciplined teenagers. They weren't bad kids, just used to being given the run of the place, and Jo was no match for them. Time after time he'd come home to find her locked in her room with a book while "the gang" emptied his kitchen cabinets, monopolized the television and covered the place with empty soda cans, candy wrappers, potato-chip crumbs and the occasional residue of a fishy-smelling tobacco. "Homegrown," one of the boys had confided, at which point Craig had gotten tough and ordered them all to stay away.

He had been more comfortable after that, but Jo had quickly become the butt of snide remarks and derision both in the neighborhood and at school, and he found to his dismay that he could do little to protect her. Had the new house not already been under construction, he'd have moved her right away, even though it would have meant paying out the lease, but Jo herself had chosen to stay.

"At least I don't have nightmares about alligators coming after me here," she'd said.

If only Aunt Maggie had been so sensible, they'd have had a better time of it, but Maggie never missed an opportunity to predict doom and failure. She had been sure that every moment they remained in that "unsavory environment" was the moment Jo would "snap and go wild," as if sad, shy Jo could do such a thing. Still, Whippoorwill Glen was a much better environment for a girl like Jo. Yes, they were going to be happy here. He felt certain of it. Not even Aunt Maggie could argue with his choice this time.

Self-satisfied, Craig glanced at his watch, assured himself that ten more precious minutes remained before he had to leave for the office, and drained away the last of his coffee. He was trying to decide whether to get up and venture to the kitchen for a second cup or just sit and soak up the clean, morning air while he had the chance, when the ringing doorbell prevented him from reaching a decision one way or the other. He sat up in surprise and turned toward the glass wall of the pale living room as if the unexpected visitor would merely materialize there. Only the second muted peal of the electronic bell got him to his feet and moving across the deck. His long legs carried him across the sand white carpet of the living room and onto the tan terrazzo of the entry hall and finally to the door. He reached for the ornate brass handle, depressed the latch and tugged. Forty square feet of four-inch-thick, handcarved teak swung open to reveal a small, voluptuous woman in short, faded denim overalls behind an enormous basket enveloped in dark green cellophane.

A smile curved her pretty pink mouth, and she cocked her head to one side, her hair lying sleekly against her neck and shoulders. It took a moment to realize that it was wet, as were two growing spots on her chest.

"Hi! Gingevine Brenan. Call me Ginger. Mind helping me with this?" She held the basket by the handle with both hands and as she thrust it toward him, her smooth biceps trembled with the strain. Quickly, he placed one hand between hers and bent to shove the other under the basket. When she let go, he nearly dropped it. The basket and its contents must have weighed all of fifty pounds. He put up a knee to help him balance it while he brought both arms beneath and around it.

"Sorry," he mumbled, puzzled by her strange appearance and the stranger request. "Uh, where do you want this?"

She put her head back, husky laughter bubbling out of her throat, and the two wet spots on her chest grew wider and rounder. He realized suddenly that she was wearing a wet bathing suit beneath those cutoff overalls and her ample breasts were forcing the moisture into the heavy denim at the points of contact. He forced his gaze up to her face, and she gave him a mincing little nod of her chin that clearly signaled she knew exactly what he was thinking. Craig cleared his throat, but before he could speak again, she lifted one small, graceful hand and laid it against his shoulder.

"The basket's for you, silly."

"Me?"

"Uh-huh. Invite me in, and I'll show you what to do with it." She gave his shoulder a gentle push and he pivoted aside, clearing the way for her, but protesting at the same time.

"I—I think there's some mistake. I didn't order any—" He broke off, his gaze falling on her wet seat—and a very nice seat it was, too. She tossed a look over her shoulder, sparkling lashes fluttering, and he knew he'd been caught again. "I mean, I don't even know what this is!"

She was studying his entry hall, running her hand over the smooth, white plaster walls. "Leaves," she said.

"What?" Exasperation made Craig's voice strident, but she seemed not to notice.

"Dried leaves. An arrangement of dried leaves and twigs would look wonderful here. You know, pale earth tones with just a smattering of red and, yes, a touch of summer green, I think. I'll see what I can come up with." She cocked her head as if to say that she couldn't possibly make her meaning any clearer, then she turned and walked down his hallway into his living room.

"Now see here," Craig began, thinking that she was some loony who'd walked in off the street, and she instantly reappeared, her nose wrinkled in obvious distaste.

"Kind of bare, isn't it?" *Bare?* His wonderful new living room was *bare?* She shrugged. "Well, never mind, I have lots of ideas. One thing's for sure, the place needs plants, lots of plants. I'll speak to my nursery man."

"You'll speak to whom?"

She turned aside into the kitchen, exploring. "Oh! A dream kitchen! It's perfect!"

Craig stepped into the doorway, his arms full of heavy green cellophane, to find her twirling around in the center of *his* kitchen floor. In that instant he forgave her her lunacy, his irritation vanishing in her sheer joy over this one room. She stopped and beamed at him as if he'd done her some sort of favor. Suddenly he was beaming back and wondering what on earth he was supposed to say next. Finally he shrugged as best he could with his arms weighted down, and said, "What was your name again?"

"Ginger, that's short for Gingevine, Brenan. *Miss* Ginger Brenan."

He didn't *miss* the emphasis she placed on the title. Looking her over, he wasn't unhappy to find her unmarried. She was a small but delectable piece of woman, round but taut and in all the right places. Her limbs were longish for her size and prettily shaped. Her bare feet were smooth and petite, and her hands followed the same pattern. By the sunshine falling through the skylight overhead, he could see that her hair was lighter than he'd first thought. It would dry to a leonine color, a dark, golden blond, something very near the shade of the large, guileless, tawny eyes set deeply beneath delicate brows in her oval face. Her skin, and he could see a good deal of it, looked like butterscotch, and he wondered idly how it would taste to the tongue. She smiled, as if having read his thoughts, and he jerked his gaze away, again discomfited.

"Ah, Miss Brenan—"

"Ginger."

"What?"

"Please. We're very casual here in Whippoorwill Glen." At last, a clue. "Then you live here."

She laughed. "Of course. I'm the welcoming committee. Officially."

Understanding. "Oh! Then this . . ." He glanced at the bundle of dark green cellophane.

"Is for you!" she finished for him, her tone implying that the whole thing had been plain as day from the beginning. Suddenly she was excited. "Bring it here," she ordered, walking to the natural-oak breakfast table. He was delighted to comply. The thing was absurdly heavy. He placed it in the center of the table and she immediately tore into it, peeling back the layers of cellophane until it resembled a huge, rather grotesque green flower, its center filled with fruit, tins, boxes and jars. She started identifying the contents—in alphabetical order.

"Apples, apple butter, bacon, bananas, banana bread, beef jerky, cantaloupe, capers, caviar, cheese, cheese and more cheese, cherries, cherry preserves, chicken salad, crackers—" she paused for breath and plunged on "—dates, date bars, espresso, French roast coffee, grapes, grape jelly, guava jelly, ham, herbal tea, kippers, maple syrup, mayonnaise, mustard, oranges, orange marmalade, orange pekoe tea, peaches, pineapple, rye bread—" another breath "—strawberries, sliced turkey breast, strawberry candy, strawberry preserves *and* water chestnuts. Where's your daughter?"

His mouth was hanging open. She'd listed over three dozen items. And what had she said about a daughter? To cover his confusion, Craig searched for something clever to say and wound up babbling. "Uh, uh... my, my. No sardines?" She wasn't the only one who could be irrational. He pinched the bridge of his nose, trying to recoup. The woman seemed, oddly, dismayed.

"Do you like sardines?"

It was a very careful question, and he had the crazy feeling that much depended upon his answer. He dropped his hand and shook his head. "No. I don't like sardines at all. I just couldn't think of anything else that might have been left out of that basket."

She gave a huge sigh, for all the world as though relieved. "Good. Uh, not that I couldn't handle the idea of sardines. That is, in the welcome basket. I would hate to have left out something you really love, you know?"

He didn't know. He stared at her. Who was this woman? No one had ever looked less like the *official* welcoming committee to him than this... Ginger? He ran a hand over his face.

"Do you . . . live close?" he asked, managing a conversational tone.

She cocked her head, grinning, and lifted a finger to point. "Next door."

Next door. Well. "I—I see." He remembered suddenly to check the time. Only five minutes left of his precious peace. He cleared his throat again. "I hate to rush you, Miss . . . Ginger, but I'm afraid I have to ask you to leave."

Her grin slowly died, but she made a concerted effort to perk it up. The effect was abysmal. Obviously, he had hurt her feelings. Immediately he backpedaled.

"I'd love to visit with you," he said, and her face instantly beamed. "Another time," he added carefully. "You see, it's almost time for me to get Joan to school and then—"

"Joan!" She fairly seized the name. "Is that your daughter?"

His daughter? Craig shook his head. "I don't have a daughter. My sister, Jo, ah, Joan, lives here with me."

"Your sister? That little thing?"

"She is rather small for her age."

"And how old is she?"

To his amusement and chagrin, the woman pulled out a chair from the breakfast table and sat down, crossing her bare, tawny legs. Despite the cheek that took, he had to *make* himself look away. "Seventeen," he said through his teeth.

"No! It can't be. She looks closer to thirteen."

"Yes, so she does. She's rather frail, actually."

"And why is that?"

Craig reached for patience. "I don't really know. I suppose being orphaned—"

"Poor darling! But that's you, too, isn't it? Her parents were your parents."

He smiled a little crookedly at that. She was perceptive. "Joan, being younger, has naturally suffered a greater loss."

"Oh, I don't believe that at all. I know I'd be devastated if anything happened to my parents, aggravating as they are at times."

"Well, but you're probably a good deal younger than me."

"I'm twenty-six," she volunteered happily. "How old are you?"

He was taken aback, but the answer was already in his mouth. "Thirty-six."

"Ten years!" she crowed. "That's not so much. Why, my mother was a quarter of a century younger than my father. Cost him a cool half million to get shed of her, too."

Craig barked a short, unexpected laugh. She did say the most outrageous things and was not unaware of it, if her blush was to be taken at face value. And what was his reply to be to such a revelation? So sorry? Has he made up the loss? He said nothing at all, and Ginger Brenan got up out of her chair and walked forward on her tantalizingly bare feet.

"I'm talking too much," she said silkily. "It's a bad habit, and I don't mean to delay you, it's just that I think it's so sweet—you taking on the responsibility of a baby sister, I mean. Not every single man would do that. You are single, aren't you?"

He arched an eyebrow. So the little minx was interested, was she? This could be entertaining, not to mention convenient.

"Yes," he said, "I am single." A movement near the doorway into the bedroom wing of the house caught his attention and he glanced away from *Miss* Ginger Brenan's classically featured face, spying his sister. He felt an absurd and immediate sense of disappointment, seeing her there in her dowdy school uniform. "Joan!" he called, guilt imbuing his voice with extreme pleasure. "Come meet our next-door neighbor. Miss Brenan, my sister, Joan. Miss Brenan's the, uh, official welcoming committee for Whippoorwill Glen. L-look what she's brought us." He searched his mind for an appropriately witty description and came up with only, "No sardines." He laughed and added, "But everything else!"

Joan came and peered closely and found something she liked, lifting it out with her delicate, pale fingers. "Strawberry preserves," she said gently, holding the jar aloft. Ginger Brenan smiled and stepped forward, lifting a hand to stroke Joan's mousy brown hair. To Craig's surprise, Joan accepted the single stroke with calm ease, then swiftly lowered her gaze. "It's very kind of you, Miss Brenan. Thank you."

"Oh, don't be shy," Ginger coaxed warmly, slipping an arm about the slight girl. "We're going to be great friends, I just know it."

Joan's eyes flickered over the woman in what was for her a frank appraisal. "You've been swimming," she said simply. Ginger Brenan laughed, and this time it was a tinkling sound, not at all the husky, seductive music she'd manufactured before.

"I go for a swim every morning," she said. "Maybe you'd like to join me one day soon?"

"Thank you," Joan said, "but I don't much like the water."

"Well, maybe we can change that. A morning swim is wonderfully invigorating and a lot healthier than coffee."

Joan actually laughed, something in her responding to this warm but rather obvious woman. Craig felt a prickling of surprise. It was unlike Jo to respond so quickly, and why with this woman, this very provocative, very inviting woman? Ginger Brenan was not the sort of female that other females cozied up to. She had too much presence, too much self-assurance and too much innate sex appeal of the sort that attracted every male on the planet. Other women would naturally see her as competition; their first reaction would be either mistrust, animosity or outright jealousy. But what was he thinking? Jo was too immature to sense what kind of female Ginger Brenan was. Nevertheless, the confidence the woman displayed would usually be enough to put off his easily intimidated little sister. Or was there more to Ginger Brenan than what he could see? Craig honestly didn't know what to think, but his instinct was to separate his sister and this woman, to separate them and keep them separate. Selfish as it might be, for his own peace of mind Ginger Brenan had to leave—right this minute.

He reached for her arm, using a deliberately light tone of voice to both cover and reinforce the strength of his grip. "Thank you so much for coming," he said, pulling her toward the door.

She sent him a resigned, almost sad look, and suddenly he was very aware of the feel of her skin. It was cool and creamy, but with a definite heat beneath it, like icing on a still-warm cake. Unresisting, she allowed him to steer her through the door.

"Goodbye, Joan," she called, somehow projecting the words without raising her voice.

Joan's meek "See you" followed them into the entry hall.

Firmly, Craig took up the farewell. "Sorry we couldn't visit longer, but Joan and I must be going now. Convey our thanks to the neighborhood, will you? We want to meet everyone, of course, when time permits." They had reached the end of the hallway, and he looked down into Ginger Brenan's upturned face. Golden brown eyes held him, warmed him, not a flicker of uncertainty or resentment in their glistening depths. Would she protest if he attempted to kiss her? The question shocked him. Good Lord! And with his sister right in the other room! He cleared his throat hastily. "Goodbye, Miss Brenan."

Her eyelashes lowered, and her pretty pink mouth curved into a smile, her cheeks bunching into small, golden apples. "You haven't told me your name."

So he hadn't. Barely concealing his impatience, he made short work of it. "Craig Russell."

She nodded and lifted the lids on those big, dangerous eyes. "I still think you're sweet," she said softly. "And kind of cute, too."

Cute? Why did that make him want to shake her? Something in her tawny eyes told him that she knew what he was thinking and why. He didn't like it. He didn't like it at all, and yet she was the most blatantly sexual being he'd ever encountered. Male that he was, he most definitely responded to that. She thought him *cute,* did she? Only "kind of cute," he recalled. He would show her cute and more, given the opportunity. She seemed to smile at his thoughts, and a thrill of anticipation shot through him. She turned her head and opened the big front door, then looked pointedly at his hand on her upper arm. Abruptly he released her. Too abruptly. She laughed in that breathless, husky way again.

"Goodbye, *Craig.*" She went out the door and pulled it closed.

He tarried, thinking about that husky laughter and the two wet spots over her breasts. He had always liked large breasts. Suddenly his palms itched. Amused, he rubbed them lazily against his thighs. And then he thought of Joan. There could be no dalliance of which Joan was aware. He'd known from the beginning that when Jo came to live with him, his sex life, such as it was, must be severely curtailed, and it had been, not only for her sake, but his own. He wouldn't give Aunt Maggie more ammunition. That woman could complain about winning the lottery, and when she lit into Craig, Jo blamed herself. It was a messy knot of cause and effect and had been since his mother had died. Craig shook his head, wondering how his mother and her sister, Maggie, could be so different. But that was a puzzle without solution. He pushed it—and Ginger Brenan—out of his mind, turned and strode down the hallway to the kitchen. Glancing at his watch, he grimaced.

"Come on, Jo," he said, rounding the corner into the kitchen. "Get your—" He stopped, staring at his sister.

She stood with the jar of preserves folded against her chest, the lid in the hand of the arm that cradled it against her. With the forefinger of the other hand, she had dipped a great glob of strawberry goo from the jar, and as he watched, the bright sweetness disappeared between her pale lips. Smiling, she closed her eyes and slowly extracted the finger. It was the first look of real pleasure he'd seen on his sister's face in a very long time, and it cut him to the quick.

She had such little pleasure, such little happiness. He made up his mind all over again to be good to her, to protect her, to somehow *help* her, even if he didn't know how to do any of it. For a moment he felt deep gratitude to Ginger Brenan for bringing that jar in her ridiculous basket. He hadn't even known Jo liked strawberry preserves. What else did his sister like? He determined to find out. Stepping forward, he cupped her small, pointed chin in his hand.

"We're going to be happy here, cupcake," he told her solemnly. "Honest we are."

Her mouth curved into a thin smile, then she looked away, breaking contact, to return the lid to the jar. "It's a great house," she said. "And you were right about the lake. It isn't scary at all."

"I'm glad you see it that way."

She nodded and set the jar on the table, turning her attention to the basket. "And I think I like our neighbor," she said. "It was sure nice of her to give us all this stuff. Just look at all this!"

Craig frowned but kept his voice neutral. "Actually, the whole neighborhood was responsible for this. Miss Brenan just happens to be the one who brought it over."

"But she's nice, don't you think?" Jo said, pawing through the basket's contents.

"I don't know what I think about Ginger Brenan," he said, but then Jo turned a questioning look at him and he regretted the lie. Quickly he changed the subject. "No more chat. We've got to get a move on. Don't want to be late."

Jo smiled and moved away from the table, nodding at the jar of strawberry preserves. "You'd better put that in the refrigerator while I get my books."

"Sure."

She turned and walked away in that coolly possessed way of hers, an old woman caught in an adolescent body. Craig picked up the small jar and cradled it in his hand. Instantly, Ginger Brenan came to mind. He saw her reach out a hand to his sister and stroke her hair, and then he saw the heavy-lidded look of her eyes and heard her husky voice saying, *I think you're sweet, and kind of cute, too.*

He carried the jar to the refrigerator, opened the door and deposited his charge on a clean, empty, glass shelf. What was Ginger Brenan going to be to him? he asked himself. He was an honest man, honest with himself, anyway. Ginger Brenan was a provocative, sexy woman. She could be good for his ego and his appetites, unless he had totally misread her, and he didn't think he had. On the other hand, she could be bad for his peace of mind. Involvement with her would be a great risk to Joan and to the serenity of his home. Next-door was simply too close.

It was a shame, but he could see no recourse. Ginger Brenan should be kept at arm's length. It needn't be difficult. He had played cool and aloof with other women. All that was required was a display of indifference. One could even be polite and manage it. Having settled it with himself, he put the matter out of mind. The thought never occurred to him that Ginger Brenan might be different from any other woman he had ever known or that she might even then be making a decision the exact opposite of his.

Chapter Two

The dumpy middle-aged woman gave Ginger a curt once-over and seemed to make up her mind. Ginger smiled and extended her hand anyway.

"I don't believe we've met. I live next door. My name's Gingevine Brenan."

The woman sniffed, shifting her weight impatiently from foot to foot, and slid her palm across Ginger's in the most cursory of shakes. "I'm Maggie," she said. "Mr. Russell's aunt. He's not home yet, and Joan's busy with her studies. Did you need something?"

The woman's small, wrinkle-encased eyes were hostile, her puffy mouth turned down in disapproval. Ginger had seen the look before, and it still puzzled, still wounded. She kept her smile in place. "I was wondering what time Mr. Russell is expected home."

The woman folded thick arms against the garishly striped blouse she wore over knit pants that were both too short and too wide in the legs. She cocked her head, her brittle, poorly cut, steel gray hair sticking out at odd angles. Her eyebrows had been shaved and drawn on well above the normal arch with a dark brown pencil. "I really couldn't say" came the tart reply.

The smile, at last, wavered, but Ginger was determined to remain pleasant. It was in her nature to do so, and she had learned long ago not to play against type.

"Might I leave a message then, please?" Her voice was smooth as silk, sweet as honey.

The woman scowled. "I'm not a servant," she said dismissively.

Ginger sighed, accepting defeat with grace. "Very well. Thank you anyway."

The door was closed before the last word was even out. Ginger rolled her eyes and turned away to stroll back down the drive to the sidewalk. Truth be told, she was less disturbed by the woman's surly manner than by the treatment she was receiving from Craig Russell himself. He wasn't ignoring her exactly, just not responding, and that puzzled her, because the electricity between them had positively crackled at their first meeting. Then suddenly he had turned cold, and she had only a single clue as to why. Joan had described her brother as being almost obsessively busy with that construction business of his.

Sweet Joannie. That was one member of the family who didn't seem to mind sparing Ginger a moment to talk. She was lonely. Ginger wondered if Joan's busy brother could see that and then she guessed that he couldn't. Ginger, on the other hand, definitely empathized. A good portion of her own adolescence had been achingly lonely. The majority of the other girls at her school hadn't seemed to like her and had apparently engaged in enough character assassination to convince the boys that she was an easy mark. As a result, she'd had few dates and fewer friends. Her mother had accused her of not trying hard enough and of "misreading" the intentions of the boys she had given the benefit of the doubt, so Ginger had redoubled her efforts, but the harder she'd tried, the more she had met with social failure. Ginger had come out of high school convinced that something was very wrong with her. It was a notion under

which she had labored for several years, constantly bent on
self-improvement, until she had realized at last that nothing had been wrong with her in the first place, at least not
physically.

She still remembered the night it had all come clear. Fresh
out of college and looking for a suitably challenging position, she had been surprised to run into Shelly Spees, one of
her chief detractors during those difficult high school days,
on a job interview. She was even more surprised when Shelly
had expressed delight at their meeting and urged Ginger to
join her that evening for drinks. The intervening years had
been good for Shelly. She'd turned into a truly lovely young
woman. But Ginger had known those same years had been
good for her, too. She had seen to it. And so she'd accepted
Shelly's invitation with only a bit of misgiving. It had turned
out to be one of the best experiences of her life. Shelly had
been mature enough and good enough to apologize and detail her reasons for reviling Ginger in high school, and the
reasons themselves had provided their own revelations. It all
boiled down to one thing: jealousy. Those who had not been
jealous of her looks had been jealous of her intellect. Shelly
confessed to having been jealous of both.

From that day on, Ginger's outlook on life had been al-
tered for the better. At last she had come into her own, and
the past five years had been happier than any she'd ever
known, which was not to say that they had been altogether
satisfying. That was why she was so convinced about the
direction in which she should now take her life. The one
thing missing in her life was a strong personal relationship
with a man, but how could she achieve that strong personal
relationship when she kept turning off man after man with
what Will called "arrogant intensity"? But she didn't have
to keep repeating the same mistakes. She was capable of
change. She had, after all, tried her hand with sufficient
success at several different professions, and she was smart
enough to know what she wanted as well as what she
needed. She was extraordinarily bright, bright enough to
recognize a bit of herself in a certain lonely girl, which
brought her back to Joan Russell.

Ginger had decided to take the girl under her wing. She needed help finding herself, someone to point her in the right direction, someone to encourage her, someone who understood what she was going through, and who better than an experienced, concerned next-door neighbor? Meanwhile, she was determined to get Craig Russell to notice her, *really* notice her. She had a feeling about that man, a warm feeling, and she couldn't help wondering why he held himself aloof. Well, they would just see how easily he maintained that disinterest. She wasn't about to give up just because a rude relative wouldn't say when he'd be home. Her bedroom had a splendid view of the front yard. She'd just curl up with a good book and wait for a glimpse of Craig Russell's car. If things went as she hoped after that, she might even have a word with him about an ill-mannered aunt.

Resolved, Ginger turned down her own walkway and crossed the narrow yard crowded with a curving maze of low shrubs, flower beds and rock gardens. The front door was unlocked, and she let herself into the low, pink brick house that was her private haven. Awash with pale, cool shades of lavender, blue, pink and yellow and strewn with the lush green of indoor plants, the house boasted marble floors and sturdy bamboo furnishings. She had knocked out the walls to obtain the large living/dining area and set three pairs of French doors along the back wall to open onto a vine-covered deck beyond in order to create the illusion of limitless space. What remained were two bedrooms, one large and one small, a single large, well-appointed bath between them, and a unique kitchen that also doubled as her office. The kitchen, entry hall, bedroom and bath were on the front of the house and together equaled the size of the living/dining area. Both her bedroom and the kitchen opened off the entry as well as the living/dining area.

She went to the kitchen first and checked the fax machine that resided next to the word processor on the bar she had appropriated for use as her desk. A message had arrived from her editor. It was good news and bad news. A world-famous gourmet had consented to write the foreword for her latest project, tentatively titled *An American Guide to French Cooking*. Unfortunately, one of the major suppliers of many of the ingredients she wished to include in her source guide had denied her the use of its trademark. Ah, well, there were other sources. They'd just have to be ferreted out. She acknowledged receipt of the message and promised to call the next day, then left the kitchen, with its shuttered cabinets and large work spaces, for the living room.

Dead center of the large open space scattered with long, cushioned bamboo couches and dining sets stood a narrow wooden crate measuring four feet by eleven. Picking up her wrecking tool, Ginger pried off the front of the crate and tore away the protective paper that had been wrapped around the painting and frame inside. It was perfect. The three-inch-wide whitewashed frame set off the muted seascape exactly as she had envisioned when she'd ordered it. The painting was her best work, she decided with a critical eye, and would complement the room just as she'd intended. Perhaps painting with a specific space in mind would bring the necessary commercial value to her work if she decided to try that avenue again, not that she would ever be another Manet, she admitted honestly.

Satisfied with herself, she hurried off to the bedroom to change and await the appearance of Craig Russell's Jaguar.

This might be her only chance, she reminded herself. She knew what she had to do and hoped desperately that she would be able to pull it off, but even if she did, there were no guarantees that it would work. Craig Russell didn't strike her as the type who liked his women helpless and servile, but that didn't mean he would want them aggressive and forthright, either. But how else could she discover if fate held more in store for them than simply being neighbors? Surely he would understand that she had to investigate the possibilities. Or would he?

Craig pulled his suit coat out of the car with a hooked forefinger and draped it over his shoulder, wondering what he was going to make for dinner. He really needed to hire a cook, but he hadn't proven adept at engaging domestic employees. He had no trouble with brawny, foulmouthed steelworkers, concrete suppliers, heavy-equipment operators, surveyors, engineers or the dozens of others required to build an eight-lane highway or two miles of supported bridge, but he'd found maids and laundresses oddly intimidating. Luckily, he and Jo did not require a great deal of help. Jo was a neat person, and he had lived alone long enough to know that it was necessary to pick up after himself. His cooking skills, however, were minimal, but he didn't suppose they'd starve to death if he delayed hiring a cook for a while longer. It was a pity that Mrs. Peck hadn't been inclined to continue working for them after they'd made the move to Whippoorwill Glen, but he understood that she didn't want to make the daily drive from her home in Kissimmee, which brought him full circle. What was he going to do for dinner?

Before he could address the issue in more detail, something white snagged his attention, something moving on the very edge of his field of vision. He turned his head and inwardly groaned. Ginger Brenan, dressed in white shortshorts and a pink T-shirt with spaghetti straps, was coming up his front walk. She couldn't possibly be wearing a bra beneath that skimpy top, yet her full, heavy breasts jutted out firmly above her small rib cage and even smaller waist. He felt the visual impact of that lush figure in the pit of his belly and set his teeth against the answering response of his body.

"Hi!" She came to a halt near the rear of his car, slightly breathless, as if she'd hurried to catch him before he could escape into the house. He allowed himself to return her smile.

"Hello."

She pushed the heavy weight of her long, wheat gold hair over her shoulders with brushing motions of both hands, all the while talking. "I hate to be a bother, but I wonder if you could help me for a moment."

He immediately started with the excuses. "Joan's waiting for her dinner, and I have to—"

"I can take care of that," Ginger interrupted smoothly. "I've a wonderful bouillabaisse in the refrigerator that just needs heating. I'll trade it for a pair of extra hands and ten minutes of your time."

It sounded like a more-than-fair exchange to Craig, but the reaction of his own body to this woman reminded him that caution was needed.

"I don't know if Joan likes bouillabaisse."

"She'll like this," Ginger assured him. "I happen to be an excellent cook. I'm just not strong enough to hang a wall-size painting by myself."

So that was it. Must be an awful big painting if she was willing to trade bouillabaisse for help in hanging it. Maybe he ought to think this over. It shouldn't take too long to hang a painting, even a large one, and it would save him the effort of providing dinner from scratch. Add to that the fact that seafood was his favorite meal, and the proposition was sounding better all the time. What was the big deal anyway? Bang a nail, hang a painting, take home a pot of fish stew, and even if the bouillabaisse wasn't as good as Ginger said, it would still be better than anything he could put together. Craig flashed her a grin, signaling acquiescence.

"Great!" She turned and moved back the way she'd come.

"Ten minutes," he warned, following at her heels.

She shot him a look over her shoulder, all tawny eyes and ruby lips. "Joan's waiting for her supper," she said, letting him know that she understood.

When they reached the front door of her house, Ginger opened it and walked in, leaving it for him to close. He did so, looking around him with appreciation. The floor was white marble veined with gray and pink. The walls were gray, the woodwork white, and a huge collage of seashells hung beside a tall potted fig tree and served as a focal point. Taking his time, he walked past French doors that opened onto a large airy bedroom with pale pink carpet, white wicker furnishings and walls painted a delicate shade of violet. Bed and windows were draped with diaphanous fabric the same shade of pink as the carpet, and the bed was piled with many pillows in a number of pastel shades. The coloring was feminine, but he noted a surprising lack of ruffles and flounces. The overall effect was one of softness with clean lines and cool colors.

Turning away, he crossed the hall to a second set of French doors and looked in on a smallish kitchen appointed with bleached woods, shutters in place of cabinet doors, and countertops made of small, square, glazed tiles in the same pastel shades as those in the bedroom. There were plants everywhere, pots hung from the ceiling, and baskets of dried herbs, pasta and wooden utensils were scattered around. What really caught his attention, though, was a counter covered with computer equipment. As he stood there, a bell rang and a fax machine clattered to life. Ginger appeared just as it spit out a sheet of paper. She looked at it, shrugged and tossed it aside.

"This way," she said, sweeping past to lead him into the largest single room he'd ever seen in a private home.

It looked like a hotel lobby, but with the addition of glass-topped bamboo dining tables sufficient for seating sixteen. Again, there were plants everywhere, many of them in huge, white ceramic pots. The walls and woodwork and floor were identical to those in the entry, and the many fat cushions and pillows softening the unstained bamboo furniture echoed the pastel hues he'd already seen. A closer inspection revealed many small objects of art sitting around: tiny sculptures, bowls, some small easeled paintings, several unusual clocks, pieces of driftwood and a number of interesting lamps. Then there were the rugs, all beautifully woven in those same cool pastels. He marveled at the bounty and the clean, uncluttered look.

"Incredible," he said, forgetting Ginger was even there until she slapped a screwdriver into his hand.

"Thanks. I like to think of my home as a good example of who I am and what I can do."

"You're an interior decorator, then?" It seemed a logical conclusion, but she merely lifted an eyebrow.

"Among other things."

"Such as?"

It was then that she directed his attention to the painting. She hadn't exaggerated the size of it, and that accounted for part of its impact. A seascape, its clean lines muted only slightly by the softness of the hues, it was an arresting study of solitude depicted in a vast expanse of ocean, pale sky and light, the focal point of which was a single gray-tipped gull scudding low over the distant horizon. In size, color and content, Craig reflected, it was perfect, so perfect that it might have been painted for this very room, and then it came to him that that was the case. He looked up at Ginger Brenan in surprise.

"You did this."

She nodded, turning a critical eye down at it. "I wish everything I did would come out so well."

"You mean it doesn't?"

She laughed, but Craig was serious. Everything he'd seen so far attested to her taste as well as her talent. He ticked off her accomplishments aloud. "Well, let's see. You garden, you decorate, you paint, you obviously know your way around a computer, you pack a mean goody basket, you look great and you tell me you cook, as well."

"Actually," she said, cool as lemonade, "cooking is what I do best, that and write about it, which is what the computer equipment is for."

Write about cooking? He lifted the screwdriver with a shrug. "I don't understand."

She gave him a look that put a dunce hat on his head. "I write cookbooks," she said, "and the occasional magazine article."

He was dumbfounded. A woman who looked like this, painted like that and created her own cool, beautiful haven, not only cooked, but cooked well enough to support herself writing about it? That bouillabaisse was sounding better all the time—and so was Ginger Brenan. All the more reason to hang that painting, grab the bouillabaisse and get out of there. Screwdriver in hand, Craig eyed the wall. A pair of holes had already been drilled through the plaster and into the wall studs. A step stool was positioned below the one on his right, and two shanked screws were lying on the floor in front of the painting.

"I'm going to run into the kitchen," Ginger said, "but I'll be right back to help you position the painting."

Nodding, Craig dropped his coat and bent to snatch up the screws, one of which he deposited in his shirt pocket alongside a black-and-gold fountain pen. He stepped up onto the stool and got on with the job, twisting the screws into place with a wrenching motion of his wrist. It was hard going. The wall studs were hard as stone, but he had the screws in place shortly after Ginger returned. He stepped down off the stool, and she moved instantly to the near end of the large painting. He went to the other end, leaned the painting away from the wall in order to get a look at the hanger—several strips of aluminum and a thick wire attached to the frame—and got a good grip on his end.

"Ready?"

"Ready."

"Up we go."

It took a bit of maneuvering, but they had it positioned safely within moments.

Ginger backed off to take a look, pronounced it perfect, and produced a pair of glasses and a pitcher of bright red liquid. "With my thanks," she said. "I'm warming the bouillabaisse in the microwave. Why don't we sit for a minute?"

The tall, red drink looked inviting, and the aroma of the warming bouillabaisse told him that it was definitely worth waiting for. Craig took the glass in hand and found himself a cushion on the end of a bamboo sofa. Ginger did likewise, choosing the opposite end of the same sofa. He sipped. Cherry wine cooler? He didn't usually drink, not since Jo had moved in with him.

"Very good," he said. "Your own recipe?"

She shook her head. "It came to me through a family friend in Spain, but I have made some substitutions."

He took another drink. "Excellent. So, umm, tell me about cookbook writing."

"It pays the bills," Ginger said, then almost with embarrassment, "Not that I need it to. My family is what you might call well-off. Still, one wants to make one's life count for something."

"You seem to have made yours count for a lot already."

She grimaced. "Not really. It hasn't been as easy as you might think. An art degree doesn't open as many doors as I once supposed it would. Oh, I paint, but not *really* well."

He didn't argue with her. What did he know about art? Probably about as much as she knew about construction. "Interior decorating seems a logical alternative," he said.

She sighed. "You'd think so, wouldn't you, but I was about as successful at interior decorating as I was in advertising."

"No go?"

Her mouth curled into a wry smile. "Mr. Russell," Ginger said, her tone indicating frankness, "I won't pretend that I wish to be ugly, but a woman with my looks does encounter certain problems, especially within the business world."

Craig smiled into his drink. Well, she wasn't coy, and for some reason that pleased him. He sipped and lowered the glass. "How so?"

She crossed her long, slender legs, pulling his eyes unwillingly to the silky expanse of smooth, golden skin. He took another drink, a long one this time, and she leaned forward, beginning her story.

"I once thought I'd be a great painter," she told him, "but I knew before I left college that I'd mistaken enthusiasm for talent, so I sought to put my degree to work in another way. Advertising seemed logical, and it wasn't difficult to get a job, but before long I realized that I was still destined to be seen and not heard. You see, the corporate male still tends to view a woman with my particular looks as a mindless sex kitten. They were all too busy trying to get me out of my skirt to hear anything I might have to say. So I moved on."

She took a drink, and Craig could see the anger she still felt in the quick, short movements she made bringing the glass to her lips, taking a sip, then straightening to swallow it with a toss of her head. He didn't doubt what she had told him, didn't doubt it all, and despite himself wondered just how difficult it would be to get her skirt off her. Blanching, he made himself look away and concentrate on the conversation.

"You were saying you moved on?"

She nodded.

"To what?"

"To teaching." She stood and carried her glass to one of the sets of French doors that looked out over the deck and the still, blue lake. "I like children," she said. "I'm good with them, and they're good with me, but parents are another story." Her tone had taken on a softness that emphasized rather than hid the bitterness of her words. "A single woman with my looks *must* be free and easy with her sexual favors. She couldn't possibly be a fit example for innocent little children." Ginger shot him a cryptic look. "The school principal stood beside me, though—he let me know how terribly misunderstood he was at home, too. I couldn't make myself go back the second semester." She shrugged and wandered his way. "After that I managed an art gallery for a while, but women didn't care to buy from me, and a lot of the men seemed to think they were buying more than paintings and sculptures." She stopped beside Craig and looked down at him, a smile curving her sweet mouth. "That's when I got into interior decorating."

"With similar results, I assume," he commented, trying to relax beneath the steady gaze of those tawny eyes.

"Females found me too decorative," she said dryly. "Males wanted me to concentrate on decorating their bedrooms."

He felt the tightening in his groin with genuine dismay and wished she'd move away. "S-so you chose the anonymity of writing cookbooks."

"Not exactly. It's something I sort of stumbled into."

"Ah. Well, it seems to have worked out."

"Yes," she said, "but somehow it's not enough."

He searched for a reply to that, but nothing came to mind. He straightened and crossed his legs, fighting the reaction of his body to her nearness. What in hell was she thinking? He lifted his glass, draining it. She reached out and took it from his hand, setting it with her own on the glass top of the low bamboo table before the couch.

"I like you, Craig," she said. "I knew I would the first time I saw you, and I want to get to know you better. Tell me," she went on, dropping down onto the couch beside him, "why aren't you married?"

He was having difficulty concentrating. When she had plopped down beside him, she had shown him clearly that she was not wearing a bra, and he imagined that he could see the soft outline of her nipples beneath the thin fabric of her shirt. "D-did you say—"

"Married." She seemed amused. "Yes, the dreaded *M* word. Is that it? You disdain marriage? Or is it something else?"

He was thrown off stride. Her lack of subtlety was shocking, even for a woman whose looks and flamboyance guaranteed she wouldn't be taken seriously. He was certain that he could come up with something equally shocking, if only he could manage to think clearly, but she was a terrible distraction close up. He gulped.

"I—I haven't had much t-time for that sort of thing," he said, moving forward out of the need for self-preservation. "And speaking of time—"

She reached out a hand, foiling his escape with the heel of her palm pressed firmly against the ball of his shoulder. He felt the touch all the way to his groin, where his body knotted and hardened instantly. He moved back into the corner of the couch, feeling trapped.

"Now, Craig," she said in a purring voice, "that's no answer, and I really want to know. A man like you is usually snapped up quick, so I have to wonder what the problem is."

"P-problem?" he managed. "What p-problem?"

"There has to be a reason why you're not married," she said, leaning toward him. He gulped at the sight of the deep cleft between her breasts. She slid her hand along his shoulder to the back of his neck, and suddenly he knew he'd better start talking—and fast.

"I work a lot. I work an awful lot. You can't build up a business without working a lot. A-and there's Jo. I have to consider Jo."

"I like Joan," Ginger said, curling a leg beneath her and moving closer, so close, her breasts brushed against his arm.

"She— What?" He was throbbing, the blood pounding in his ears. He pushed his gaze upward, away from the neckline of her skimpy T-shirt, up the smooth column of her slender throat and past the jut of her firm little chin to her mouth. Her lips parted, showing small, fine, white teeth.

Oh, hell, he thought, knowing what was coming and wanting it far more than was wise. Her hand slid up into the hair at the back of his head. The other came to rest on his chest. *Hell and damnation.* He felt as if he'd explode as she leaned across him and pressed her proud breasts to his body, her mouth lifting toward his. He was both horrified and elated, so that even as he recoiled, his arms came around her and his eyelids shuttered down. Then suddenly she was breathing fire into him.

It was a shock to the system, a blazingly erotic full body slam. He felt as if he'd been plugged into an electrical socket. She was a soft fire. She was almost in his lap, her upper body pressed against him as her mouth plied his with galvanizing thoroughness. Then it occurred to him that she could *be* plied as well, and he threw himself into it, bending her back over the arm he'd clasped about her waist. He slid his tongue against her teeth, and they parted for him, so he plunged inside, tasting her heat, feeling her yield and cling to him. Her hands were making wide circles on his back, burning him alive, and she was breathing fast through small, delicate nostrils. His heart was thudding so hard it seemed to shake them both, and he said to himself, *This is really happening. Seduction, pure and simple.*

Unbidden, a picture of Jo shimmered before his mind's eye, and Craig groaned inwardly, knowing how shocked she would be to see him kissing the next-door neighbor, but he couldn't seem to extricate himself from the sweet, hot burn. Ginger Brenan was hanging about his neck now, all but reclining as he bent over her, and he forgot all about Jo, thinking instead of what it would be like to lie on top of this woman and press into her soft woman's flesh. He slid his hand beneath the hem of her T-shirt and upward to skim the fullness of her breast, feeling her stiffen and jerk as if with an electrical jolt. Abruptly, he dropped his hand to her waist and probed the waistband of her shorts with his fingertips. She came up and out of his arms like a shot that ricocheted from one surface to another. Her eyes were wide, wild, and she gulped breath, rocking from side to side on the balls of her feet.

"Oh, God," she said. "Worse than I thought."

Worse? Was she nuts? He'd show her worse. He reached out for her, but she scampered away. Now what game was this? He pushed up awkwardly to his feet and moved toward her, noting with satisfaction that she seemed as disconcerted as he felt.

"Listen," he said, his voice gruffer than he'd intended, "I'm not interested in games."

She lifted her chin. "Good," she said, "because I'm not interested in games, either."

He could hardly credit that, given what had just happened, but maybe it was best if they just stopped right here, unless . . . "If sex is what you want—"

"No! I mean, yes, under the right circumstances."

He nodded. "That's what I'm getting at. I'm flattered as hell and *very* tempted, but I have to think of Joan."

"Yes, I know," she said. "You're a fine man. I can tell by the way she speaks of you, and, of course, not every man would take on a teenage sister at this particular stage in life. I've thought of that. Then there's the house, what I've seen of it. You've tried to make a home, a place of safety for your little sister. I like that." She held that chin aloft, but her voice was quavering, and that puzzled him. He cocked his head.

"Thanks, but where exactly is this going? I suddenly have the feeling we're not about to embark on a very discreet but torrid affair."

"That's right," she said. "I'm not interested in an affair."

"No?"

She shook her head. "No."

He lifted both eyebrows and shrugged. Weird, coming on to him like that then shooting him down, but he supposed he could live with it, as long as there were no repetitions. It was a disappointment but probably for the best, and he was just about to tell her so when she opened her mouth and scared the hell out of him.

"Actually," she said, her voice flat and her gaze brutally, frightfully honest, "I'm looking for a husband."

Chapter Three

"Whoa! Whoa-ho! Time-out! Not me, baby. No way! I am not, I repeat, *not* in the market for a wife!"

Craig Russell crossed his arms in front of him and brought them down in a chopping motion as he paced back and forth in front of the sofa. Ginger stared up at him, thinking how typical he was. Trust a man to react this way. Wrap yourself around him and even if he isn't interested, he'll still be pleased, but give him a little honesty and he pitches a fit like the overgrown little boy he undoubtedly is. She let him work it out of his system, her resolve solidifying.

"Be careful of the rug," she said gently. "I wouldn't like you to fall."

"Why, it's crazy!" he declared, ignoring her warning. "It's nuts, right out of *The Twilight Zone!* You don't know me well enough to want to marry me!"

"You're absolutely right," she told him soothingly. "It's far too soon to be certain. But you must admit you're prime husband material."

"Prime hus—" He looked as if he might choke. Alarmed, she jumped up and grabbed her glass off the cocktail table, offering it to him. He simply rolled his eyes, throwing his hands skyward. "I knew you were trouble," he said. "I knew it in my gut the moment I saw your... oh, hell!"

She grimaced and smoothed his brow with her free hand. "There, there. It isn't as bad as all that. Try to understand. I've given it a great deal of thought myself. I'd be a superior wife, a wonderful mother. All my best talents point to it. In fact, if you must know, my homemaking skills are second to none. Why, marriage is just the thing for me. It's only a matter now of finding the right man."

He shook off her hand and glared at her as though she'd sprouted horns. "Lady, you're downright scary."

She sighed. This wasn't working out at all as she'd hoped. The attraction was there, but he seemed positively paranoid about the notion of marriage. How were they to investigate the possibilities of marriage if he wouldn't even accept the idea? "Try to think rationally about this," she pleaded.

"All right, all right." He licked his lips. He looked a trifle wild about the eyes but seemed to be concentrating, then he nodded, as if having reached a decision. "Now this is it," he said. "You listen and get this through your head." He was perched on the balls of his feet, for all the world as if he'd flee if she so much as edged toward him. He wasn't going to be reasonable, and it was all her fault. She'd done it again. Resigned, Ginger folded her arms, wanting him to feel safe. Maybe once he'd gotten over the shock they could talk again.

"Go on," she prodded gently. Might as well get on with it.

"I am not going to marry you," he said slowly. "Did you get that? I am *not* going to marry you, not in your wildest dreams."

"Yes, I have it," she told him calmly. "You're absolutely not interested in marrying me." He nodded but remained a bit wary. She tried again. "You wouldn't marry me if I were the last woman on the face of the Earth." He closed his eyes, seemingly relieved. Pleased with herself, she went on. "You are not going to marry me," she stated firmly. "Unless, of course, you should find that I'm everything you want in a wife. Naturally then you'd have to reconsider."

He was looking as if he might explode again, his eyes big as half-dollars and protruding slightly. Oh, dear. When would she learn to control her tongue? But her logic seemed perfectly reasonable to her. Why would a man reject a woman who was everything he wanted? And how could he say he didn't want her until he got to know her better? He was upset. She had to be patient with him. After all, it was common knowledge that most men had to be dragged to the altar kicking and screaming, and yet, throughout the ages, men had been making women their wives. If other women could get themselves happily married, she certainly could. A little patience, a little understanding and a lot of sex appeal could work wonders. It only needed time, careful wording and a bit of demonstration—but just a bit.

"As we're getting to know one another better," she told him gently, "you can think about it. We'll just see where it goes."

He actually smiled at her. "Ginger," he said, "*it* isn't going anywhere, but *I* am. I'm going home to my nice, sane house and my nice, sane sister, and *you* are going to stay away from me! Craig Russell is off-limits to Ginger Brenan. Period. Find another victim, someone I don't know, but forget about me!"

He backed away from her, one hand held out in front of him as if he expected her to charge like a rhino. Ginger bit her lip. Then she remembered that old saying about the way to a man's heart being through his stomach. As he disappeared down the entry hall toward the front door, she called out to him.

"Craig, wait! What about the—" the sound of the slamming door made her jump "—bouillabaisse."

Carrying her wine punch back to the sofa, she sat down and brooded on the matter, wincing inwardly. That attractive man thought her frightening, and he was nice when he wasn't foaming at the mouth. He was easy to look at, too, with his rich, walnut brown hair and milk-chocolate eyes. She remembered what it had felt like to kiss him, to feel his arms close about her. She bit her lip, feeling her heart speed up. Oh, yes, she was right about *that,* very right. But she had been wrong to tell him what she had in mind.

She'd have to undo it somehow if they were going to have a chance to get to know each other, to find out if they were really right together. But how? And why did she feel this sense of urgency about it? He wasn't going anywhere. He did, after all, live right next door. Maybe she should let it rest for now, but what about his dinner? She had promised him the bouillabaisse for helping her hang the painting. She looked around, wondering what to do, and spied his jacket draped over the arm of the opposite sofa. Well, that settled it. Surely he'd want his jacket returned, and she *owed* him the bouillabaisse. She squared her shoulders. Craig Russell wasn't as off-limits as he wanted to believe, and she intended to keep it that way—somehow.

Craig stalked across the yard, stepping over or plowing through whatever was in his way. That damned lunatic *would* fill her yard with every conceivable plant, including something growing up out of a prickly base that looked like an avocado on steroids and tore at his slate gray Henry Grethel socks. Scowling, Craig stopped long enough to examine his ankle. That blasted plant had sliced right through his sock and drawn blood! Muttering curses under his breath, he stomped on, putting his foot squarely into a clump of tiny purple flowers growing in neat, symmetrical mounds along the edge of the sidewalk. With some satisfaction, he noted the blossoms were crushed. Served her right, the screwball. She wanted to get married, did she? He was "prime husband material," was he? He'd show her "prime husband material"! Grumbling, he labored up the slight incline of his own drive, past his car beneath the overhang and into the house, slamming the door behind him. Almost immediately his sister appeared out of the kitchen, her pale face drained of what little color it usually contained.

"Craig!" She threw himself at her, her thin arms trembling as they closed about his waist.

"Jo? Honey, what is it?"

She shook her head, her face pressed against his chest. "Where were you?" she asked his shirtfront. "I heard you drive up, and when you didn't come in, I looked out the kitchen window, but the car was empty!"

He closed his eyes briefly. *Thank you once again, Ginger Brenan,* he thought. Turning his sister away from him, he fixed an arm about her shoulders, disturbed as always by her slightness. She felt no bigger than a bird.

"I had to go next door for a minute," he explained. "I'm sorry you were worried."

"Is that all?" she exclaimed. "I thought you were kidnapped or something!"

Kidnapped? He had to bite the inside of his cheek to keep from laughing, and even then when he spoke, his voice trembled slightly with suppressed amusement. She'd sounded just like Maggie. Females! He ushered her gently toward the living room, talking as they went.

"It won't happen again, sweetheart. From now on, I get right out of the car and come right into the house, no matter what. I don't want you worrying about me—or anything else. All right?"

She nodded, and he seated her in the center of the closer of the two white, overstuffed couches that stood in the middle of the room. He glanced around him, frowning because it seemed that something was missing, yet all was in place. It struck him how colorless the room was then, and he thought of the soft, cool pastels with which Ginger Brenan had surrounded herself. Pushing the thought away, he sat down beside his sister.

"So what were you doing at Ginger's?" she asked.

Frowning again, he looked at her. "You've been talking to her, haven't you?"

Joan shrugged. "A few times. I like to go out and sit on the deck. Sometimes Ginger's out on the beach and she comes over. She says neighbors ought to get to know one another."

He could have told Jo that Ginger Brenan had a lot more in mind than getting to know them, but he didn't. The less said about Ginger Brenan, the better, as far as he was concerned. Joan, however, seemed hung up on the subject.

"So why'd you go over there?" she wanted to know, her light brown eyes alight with curiosity.

Craig sat back and crossed his legs, laying his arm along the back of the couch. "She needed help hanging a painting."

Joan sent him a look over her shoulder. "She asked you to hang a painting?"

Yes, in retrospect it sounded rather ludicrous to him, too, but he didn't let Jo know that. He leaned forward and flicked the end of her nose with his fingertip. "It was a very large painting, enormous, in fact, like ten feet long and as tall as you almost."

Her slight, straight eyebrows went up in tandem. "Where'd she get something that big?"

"Actually, I think she painted it herself," he muttered absently.

Joan's mouth dropped open, and she squirmed around to face him, one knee drawn up onto the couch. "Ginger's a painter? Imagine that!" Craig inwardly winced at the awe in her voice.

"Lots of people paint, Jo," he said, but the sparkle in his sister's eyes told him that she wasn't really listening.

"Oh, I think she's just fascinating!" the girl breathed. "I mean, have you ever seen anyone like her? I figure Marilyn Monroe must have been like that, you know, and I've wondered why Ginger didn't follow her footsteps and go into the movies. I bet she could. Gosh, she's pretty. And a painter! You know what else? She's really nice, too, not stuck-up or anything, and I bet you didn't know her family's got money."

"Er, I believe she mentioned it," he commented, remarking to himself that Ginger Brenan certainly liked to get that bit of information out.

"I wish I looked like her," Joan said, following this comment with a forlorn sigh.

What female didn't? he wondered, but to Jo he said, "Don't be silly! There's nothing wrong with the way you look. I think you look very sweet."

"Oh, Craig..." She groaned. "That's so lame."

"It's not lame!"

"Mary Jane Ilecky looks sweet, and trust me, nobody wants to look like her!"

"Who's Mary Jane Yucky or whatever?"

"Mary Jane *Ilecky*," Jo repeated impatiently. "She's a brain at school. You know the kind, so smart they've advanced her up several grades already. She has big blue eyes and yellow hair, and she wears it in these braids tied with these little red heart-shaped things, so she looks like this sweet little kid, you know. Only when you accidentally bump her or something, she reams you out really bad. I mean cuss words and everything." Joan shook her head. "I do have a mirror," she said, "and I know I'm not pretty or anything, but if I thought I looked like Mary Jane Ilecky, I'd just go to bed and die!"

"Well, you don't look like Mary Jane Yucky," Craig assured her, purposefully mispronouncing the surname to make Jo smile. "You look like yourself, and that's just what you're supposed to look like. Now I don't want to hear you say you're not pretty anymore. I certainly think you're pretty."

She flattened her lips in a grimace, letting him know just what she thought of his opinion. "I bet even Mary Jane Ilecky would want to look like Ginger does," she said.

"Who cares what Mary Jane wants?" Craig asked, and Joan nodded in agreement, then grew pensive, a faraway look in her eyes.

"You don't suppose I could paint, do you?" she asked dreamily. "I could be this great artist, living just to paint, and no one would even have to know what I looked like, only that I did the greatest art!"

Craig had gone cold as stone as she'd spoken, but he told himself that it was mere fantasy, just silly kid stuff. Still, what else about Ginger Brenan might Joan want to emulate, and just how much had Ginger told the girl about herself, anyway? He lifted an eyebrow in contemplation. With a woman like that, there could be an awful lot to tell, and he doubted very much that he'd want his little sister hearing it. But what was he to do? Forbid her to speak to the next-door neighbor? That didn't seem workable. Maybe he was making too much of it all. Or was he? He sent Joan off to her room to finish her homework, saying that he'd start dinner. She informed him that Maggie had brought a meat loaf, and only then did he remember the bouillabaisse Ginger had offered him. Sighing, he pinched the bridge of his nose and tried not to think how much he'd have preferred the fish stew to Maggie's dry, flavorless meat loaf.

The doorbell chimed. Grumbling, he got up and trudged to the door, telling himself Ginger wouldn't possibly show up after what had just gone on at her house. But Ginger would. She had his suit coat and a pot of the bouillabaisse in tow, a smile in place. He glowered and the smile wavered, but she gamely widened it, cocking her pretty head in the process.

"You forgot these."

He reached out and snatched his coat off her arm. "You can keep the bouillabaisse." Her face fell and regret assailed him. He steeled himself against it.

"Don't you want it?" she asked, proffering the pot.

"No."

Liquid shimmered in her eyes, but she hardened her jaw. "Well, Joannie will even if you don't."

True enough, but he hesitated anyway. Finally, Ginger struck a cryptic pose, one knee flexed, her rounded hip sliding out to the side.

"You know, Craig," she said quietly, "I could've lied to you. I could've let you think that marriage was the last thing on my mind, in which case you'd be taking not only my bouillabaisse, but anything else I cared to give you."

True again, and he felt like a fool because of it, but that wasn't any more her fault than his own. "Granted," he said, "but that doesn't mean I wouldn't have regretted it later."

She flinched, and he suddenly wanted to shake her, but she quickly recovered, tossing her head regally.

"There are things you could regret more," she told him, a forced lightness in her tone. "Like missing out on one of the world's great dishes." She lifted the pot toward him and he could smell the delicate aroma of the fish stew, already warm and just waiting to be eaten. "Please," she said. "For your help." His stomach rumbled hungrily. He threw the coat over his shoulder and snatched the pot out of her hands.

"Thanks," he said tersely.

"Thank you," she said, and backed up. He shoved the door closed with his elbow.

The aroma of the stew wafted up to entice his nose. All right, he'd eat her bouillabaisse, but then that was it. Marriage! How stupid did she think he was anyway?

He carried the stew into the kitchen and left it on the counter, quickly setting the table. He felt as if his stomach had a hole in it, gnawed there by his suddenly ravenous hunger, and he concentrated on that, putting Ginger Brenan firmly out of mind. For the moment.

Joan pulled her feet up onto the step and dusted sand off the toes of her tennis shoes, then wiped her slender hands together before tucking them beneath her elbows. Ginger smiled indulgently and folded back the wide brim of her flower-crowned straw hat.

She was very aware of Craig, who sat crackling the newspaper on the deck behind them, his displeasure at her presence sharp. He could not bear having her around, and she found his discomfort rather reassuring. He was as aware of her as he'd have been of ants in his shorts, and she intended to keep it that way, but at the moment it was Joan who needed her attention. Something about this kid got to Ginger as nothing and no one ever had. She was sitting here now, one of the world's finest private beaches at her feet, scrunched up into a knobby ball. She reminded Ginger of a frightened animal seeking protection.

"You know, Joannie," Ginger said lightly, "a little sand won't hurt you." She wiggled her own toes in the fine white sand and leaned closer, lowering her voice, but keeping it clearly audible. "It feels like steel wool in your swimsuit, though."

Joan smiled blandly, but her brown eyes sparkled. Inwardly, Ginger sighed. She had never known anyone as repressed as this child, and yet Joan occasionally showed her glimpses of a bright, happy girl. Ginger wondered why Craig couldn't see it? A man as intelligent as he was ought to have realized right away that his little sister needed someone to give her permission to live. Was this typical of children who had lost both parents within a short period of time? She made a mental note to check out the theory. Somebody had to help this girl. Craig Russell was too busy being the Road-building King of the Southeast. He had surprised her, though. She'd fully expected him to declare his sister off-limits to her, just as he'd done with himself. Apparently, however, even she was better for Joan than no friends at all, and that's just what Joannie would have had if Ginger hadn't taken an interest in her—no friends at all. It was pitiful.

Something moving at the rim of her field of vision snagged her attention and she turned toward it, feeling the step of the Russell's deck bite into her hip as she pivoted against its edge.

"Oh, look!" she exclaimed, pointing to a pair of ducks waddling toward the water. "Where did they come from?"

"I don't know." Joan's answer came in her usual soft monotone, but when Ginger glanced at her, she saw that the girl's gaze was fastened avidly on the small brown-and-black fowl.

"Watch," Ginger instructed, sensing Craig's interest now, also. "They're so awkward on land, but look at them take to the water."

Right on cue, the first duck waddled into the shallow edge of the water, retracted its carroty legs and glided easily across the surface of the still, blue lake. Ginger laughed as the second followed suit and quacked wildly as it shot out over the water with surprisingly graceful speed to catch up to its partner.

"Do you suppose they'll stay?" Joan asked, whispering as if the sound of her normal speaking voice would spook them into flight.

Ginger shrugged. "If we feed them they might."

Joan perked up a bit. "What do ducks eat?"

"Some heels of bread ought to suffice."

"Oh." The enthusiasm faded.

"We don't have any," Craig spoke up, and Ginger sent him an amused glance over her shoulder.

"Forget to go to the store?" she asked, biting back laughter when he glowered and raised the newspaper in front of his face again. "Well, that's all right," she told Joan. "Most anything will do. Crackers, maybe? Or cereal?"

Jo quickly pushed up to a standing position. "I'll go get it. Rice flakes okay?"

"Great."

Jo strode away with quick, mincing little steps, her brown, nondescript slacks flapping about her ankles. Ginger told herself for the umpteenth time that she really had to do something about that child's clothes. Joan dressed like an old woman. What was wrong with Craig, letting her do that? Didn't he know his sister's self-image was at stake? Apparently not.

Ginger got up and walked across the deck on her bare feet, aware of Craig's gaze as he made a show of folding the newspaper in quarters. "May I?" she asked, indicating the chair beside him, then dropped into it without waiting for his reply. He grimaced, pulled in a deep breath and fixed his gaze on the newspaper, seemingly engrossed in some article. She knew better. Sitting back, she crossed her legs and arranged the sides of the net cover-up she wore over her bright yellow bikini. Craig's eyes slid off the page and up her body to her face, then quickly dropped back to the paper again. She did her best to suppress the surge of triumph she felt, striving to keep it out of her voice.

"I'd like to take Joannie shopping," Ginger said, coming right to the point.

He straightened, frowning, but kept his eyes on the printed page. "That's not necessary."

"Well, yes, it is," Ginger argued. "She obviously hasn't got any decent clothes."

He dropped the paper to his lap. "I beg your pardon! I'll have you know that kid's closet is full of clothes."

"Full of disasters, you mean."

Craig shot forward in his chair, crumpling the paper hopelessly. "You have some nerve!"

"She needs help, Craig."

"Don't you think I know that?" he ground out. "But what do you want to do? Tell her she looks like Old Mother Hubbard and crush her completely?"

"Don't be absurd."

"I'm not—"

The door swung open and Joan stepped out onto the deck, a box of cereal in her hand. Craig quickly drew back, fumbling with the wadded paper.

"What's wrong?"

Craig forced a laugh. "What could be wrong? We were just discussing—"

"Self-improvement," Ginger supplied, getting to her feet.

"Oh?" Joan's slender eyebrows pulled together.

"Yes," Ginger said smoothly, "I was just saying to your brother that I'm a great believer in improving one's self."

Joan shook her head, for once failing to tamp down her emotion. "Gosh, Ginger, what could need improving about you?"

Ginger cupped Joan's chin with one hand. "I used to think everything needed improving," she admitted. "Do you know I had plastic surgery?"

Joan's eyes widened. "Really?"

Behind them, Craig sounded as if he was strangling, but Ginger stifled the impulse to glare at him.

"Uh-huh. I had a nose job." She put a finger to the tip of her nose, directing Joan's attention.

"No!"

"Oh, yes."

Suddenly Craig was at her elbow. "I don't think we really need to hear this. It is rather personal, and Joan, you know it's not polite to pry."

"Oh, for Pete's sake, Craig! It's not as if she asked. I volunteered the information."

He showed her his straight, white teeth in a parody of a smile. "Now why would you do that?"

"Because I want her to know that it didn't make much difference," she told him.

"I don't understand," Joan said. Ginger elbowed Craig out of the way.

"The cosmetic surgery didn't make much difference."

"It didn't?" Joan's mouth bunched up in confusion.

"Oh, look," Craig interjected, "the ducks are coming ashore!"

Ginger shook her head and remained focused on Joan. "Not until I improved my attitude about me. You see, Joannie, we can make all kinds of cosmetic improvements in our looks, and that's fine, but if we don't believe we're beautiful, they can't make the least difference."

"That's easy for you to say," Joan commented, looking doubtful. "You *are* beautiful."

"And you're not?" Ginger's tone indicated that she thought just the opposite.

Craig, bless him, finally caught the drift and supported her. "Ginger's right," he said. "You're a real knockout, kiddo."

But Joan wasn't buying it. Not yet, anyway. She glared accusingly at her brother. "The other day you said I looked like Mary Jane Ilecky!"

"I did not!" he defended. "I said you looked sweet, and I wasn't thinking about Mary Jane Yucky."

"Who?" Ginger laughed, but Joan was embarrassed now. She shook her head stubbornly.

"Never mind."

Craig threw up his hands. "She won't believe me!" he exclaimed to Ginger, who sent him a quelling glance and turned her attention back to Joan.

"One of these days," Ginger predicted, "you're going to look in the mirror and see just what you've always wanted to see."

Joan looked away, silent, her eyes narrowed. Beside her, Craig seemed to be holding his breath. Ginger shot him what she hoped was a comforting look and dropped an arm about the girl's shoulder. "Come on," she said, "let's feed those ducks."

At once, the tension slid out of Joan's thin body and she nodded, turning toward the steps. Ginger urged her forward with the gentle pressure of her arm. Craig sighed audibly.

"We're going to spoil those ducks so rotten, they'll never go back to where they came from," Ginger said. "And maybe one of these days we'll have a whole bunch of baby ducklings quacking all over the place."

Joan laughed aloud at the prospect, and they stepped down onto the sand, hurrying toward the place where the ducks were coming ashore. Ginger glanced back at Craig, who had followed them as far as the railing of the deck. Unless she missed her guess, that was a look of approval on his face, reluctant though it seemed. Smiling, she turned away again. They'd take that shopping trip yet and, who knows, they might even get Craig to tag along. Stranger things had happened. In fact, she was banking on them.

Chapter Four

Craig thought he heard a kind of pecking, but when he stopped pedaling and got off the stationary bike to turn down the television, only silence greeted him. So he got back on and had just worked up to the proper speed when the doorbell rang. Grumbling, he got off the bike again and snatched a towel from the bench of the weight machine, draping it about his neck as he moved toward the sound. By the time he got out of the den, down the hall, through the kitchen and into the entry, the doorbell had rung no less than three times, making five in all, and he knew exactly who he would find on the other side of that teak barrier. Only Ginger Brenan would ring a doorbell five times and still expect to be greeted with a smile. He pulled the towel from his neck and wiped his face before yanking the door handle.

"What?"

A number of objects fell onto the floor at his feet, whacking his ankles and shins. Craig yelped and jumped back.

"Don't step on them! I had to put them down to ring the doorbell. I tried knocking." Her arms full of additional canvases, Ginger gently kicked at those that had fallen, pushing them farther inside, and worked her way through the door, bumping it closed with her bottom. "Okay, now if you'll just pick those up and take them to Joannie's room so—"

"What in God's name do you think you're doing?" Craig bawled, grabbing both ends of the towel and whipping it over his head.

Ginger straightened, her ample breasts filling the little halter top of her purple minidress near to bursting, and pushed her sunglasses up onto the top of her head. She had pulled the sides of her hair up into a ponytail, teased it into a spiky poof and secured it with a multicolored pom-pom. With her sunshades perched on top of it, she looked as though she were wearing a clown mask on her head, the pom-pom making a huge nose, the poof of her hair an equally ridiculous wig. She lowered the half-dozen paintings she had managed to keep a grip on and gave Craig a pointed perusal, her eyes widening as they moved over his chest. He had forgotten that he'd removed his shirt before beginning his workout, but he'd be damned if he'd let her make him feel self-conscious when she was walking around with a clown's face on her head.

"I repeat," he said in the most reasonable tone he could manage. "What do you think you're doing?"

She pursed her lips. "That's just what I was trying to tell you when you interrupted."

"Then by all means get to it!"

She twisted her shoulders and ducked her chin in a prissy gesture of compliance. "Joannie wants me to choose a painting for her bedroom."

"*Joan* isn't here," he pointed out, emphasizing his sister's given name. He hated cutesy nicknames. Jo was much more sensible. Ginger rolled her eyes.

"I know that. She told me about the field trip." She grimaced. "Some sort of bug-collecting thing. Anyway, that's why I came over now. I want to surprise her. I tried to do it earlier, but that dragon of an aunt who guards your house wouldn't let me in.''

He grinned knowingly. "Maggie is rather forceful at times."

"Maggie is downright rude at times," Ginger said, then whined, "Come on, Craig. I promised."

He made a face, capitulating, irritated that it should come so easily. "Oh, all right."

She beamed. He glowered and strode forward, bending to gather up the fallen canvases. The bottom one had fallen faceup, and he studied it a moment. It was a pretty picture of a carousel horse done in soft, muted shades. He saw by the signature scrawled across one corner that Ginger had painted it herself, but he checked the complimentary comment he'd been about to make. He would not encourage her. Perhaps she'd made a friend of Jo, but she wasn't about to make a conquest of him. The sooner she realized that, the better off they'd all be. He only hoped Jo wasn't hurt when her "friend" lost interest in her, although he had to admit that Ginger did seem to have taken the girl to heart. In truth, he sometimes worried that his sister was merely a means to an end for Ginger, but over the past few weeks, she had done nothing to confirm that suspicion. Ginger Brenan, it seemed, was nothing if not honest. He admired her for that—but he wasn't about to let her know it!

He got the paintings in hand and led the way to Joan's room. Actually, he was secretly looking forward to getting Ginger's opinion of this particular room—professional, of course, her being a decorator as well as an artist. During the building of the house, Joan's bedroom had received more of his attention than any other, mostly because getting Jo to state her preferences was like conjuring rain. One had to have all the elements on one's side in the beginning, and he hadn't even known where to start. He'd asked Aunt Maggie for her opinion, but she'd just sniffed and started lecturing about how "some people" could waste hard-earned money on the most frivolous things. As far as she was concerned, all a body needed in a bedroom was a good mattress and a door with a lock on it, but he had wanted Jo's own personal space to be special for her, a kind of sanctuary. He'd never known if he had been successful or not. His sister just wasn't forthcoming about her feelings. It still bothered him.

He fumbled the door open and stepped aside like a gentleman to let Ginger enter first. Her gasp caught him unawares, his first thought being that someone had burglarized the place. He rushed in, arms full of clumsy canvases, only to see—nothing at all out of the ordinary. He glanced sharply at Ginger, and she crumpled in laughter, the paintings sliding out of her grasp as she turned circles.

"What?" he demanded, thoroughly flummoxed.

"Honey," Ginger drawled, "she told me the room wasn't 'her,' but this is ridiculous. For heaven's sake, Craig, she's seventeen, not seven!"

His initial reaction was anger, but a cold feeling in the pit of his stomach followed swiftly after. He put the canvases down, stacking them carefully against the wall, and turned to Ginger, his hands going to his waist.

"Jo *told* you she didn't like this room?" he asked slowly, surprised when compassion softened Ginger's face.

"She didn't have to," Ginger answered. She leaned forward on one leg and slipped an arm through his, tugging him toward the center of the room. How could she manage these intimate little gestures with such ease, he wondered, and why was he letting her get away with them? He knew the answers. Because she was generosity itself, because she was so good with Jo, because he really didn't want to hurt her feelings. But neither did he want to encourage her ridiculous marriage goals. That in mind, he extricated his arm from her grasp. Her face set rigidly, but she said nothing, merely directed his attention to the many yellow ruffles and flounces, the canopied bed piled high with pillows and teddy bears, the teddy-bear prints on the walls, the teddy-bear-and-parasol lamp occupying the white French-provincial table. The decorator working for the builder had said the room would be sunny and gay, and yet at the moment it seemed neither, merely—silly.

"I thought it would cheer her up," he said quietly, profoundly grateful when Ginger smiled, imparting understanding.

"You couldn't be expected to make the correct choices," Ginger told him. "After all, you weren't ever a teenage girl."

Sighing, he lifted both hands to his temples. "She never would say what she wanted," he grumbled. "I racked my brain over this, and she never would say one way or another."

"She doesn't want to offend you, Craig. She's afraid to say what she wants."

"That doesn't make sense! I'm her brother. I love her. I want her to be happy."

For a moment Ginger's smile warmed him, then suddenly her eyes were brimming with tears. She laughed them away, saying, "You really are a sweet man, a little lost maybe, but good at heart."

The compliment pleased him more than he was willing to admit to either of them. Defensively, he summoned his scowl and retorted, "Just choose a picture."

"They're not pictures," she came back smoothly. "They're paintings, and I think I'll choose two, if you don't mind."

"Fine," he agreed, thinking it couldn't take much time whether she chose one or two. He was wrong.

Ginger first positioned all ten paintings around the room. Then she took them one by one, held each out at arm's length and walked from spot to spot, eyeing first the surrounding area then the painting in her hands, over and over again. Next she abandoned the paintings altogether and started taking the teddy-bear prints off the walls. After that, she began moving paintings around the room again, trying one against first this wall then that, as if there was any difference in the walls, for Pete's sake. Finally Craig had had enough. He strode over and yanked a canvas out of her hands.

"Holy cow, Ginger, stop playing musical paintings and choose one!"

She got a belligerent look on her face, a positively pugnacious expression. "Two!" she retorted. "I want to choose two!"

"Then choose them!" he shouted, dumbfounded when she fixed him with the smuggest smirk he'd ever seen.

"And you wonder why Joannie wouldn't state a preference," she said.

He closed his eyes and did a slow count to ten before replying. "*Joan* doesn't make me lose my patience."

"She told me you never yell," Ginger conceded. "But she says you talk through your teeth at her."

He gaped. "I do not!"

"I wasn't criticizing," she came back. "Better to talk through your teeth than roar."

"I don't roar, either!"

She folded her arms, her smug look back. "Don't you?"

He took a deep breath, strangled the urge to yell, turned and walked out of the room. Muttering under his breath, he stalked back to the den and climbed upon the stationary bike. Pedaling furiously, he sweated out his anger, but a few minutes later Ginger walked in and flopped down on the couch, putting him on edge again. He stopped, leaned over the handlebars a moment, then got down.

"What now?"

She frowned up at him. "Craig, we've got to do something about that room," she said pleadingly.

He rolled his eyes, but after a moment he'd mastered the need to lash out at her. She was trying to help, he reminded himself. For Jo's sake, he could be civil at least. "What did you have in mind?" he managed.

Ginger sprang up hopefully, bouncing back down to sit on one ankle. "Paint the walls white and leave the woodwork yellow, then put something cushy and comfortable on the bed—no ruffles—and get rid of the canopy. Instead, we could hang sheers at the sides and tie them back. We'll do the same thing at the windows. The teddy bears, by the way, have to go, especially that lamp. I'll find something to replace it. We'll cut the ruffles off the throw pillows and keep them, but we need to add some stronger colors, green, I think, maybe orange. Then we ought to add a chair of some sort, or maybe a hassock, something she can sit on instead of the bed. The French provincial is a problem, but I can work around it. After that, all we need is a couple of paintings and as many framed posters as she wants. I'll take her to buy the posters. She's too bottled up with you to recognize her own preferences. What do you think? Say yes. Please."

He was nuts to let her take over like this, but just once he'd like to do something right with Joan, and God knew he'd tried everything else he could think of to make a real home for the girl. Moreover, he sensed that Ginger's judgment was right in this. Before he knew what was happening, his irritation was beginning to subside; Ginger's enthusiasm proved catching.

"Oh, all right," he said, grumbling only a little.

"Yes!" Ginger leapt up and launched herself at him, throwing her arms about his neck despite his clamminess. He prepared to rebuke her, but just as suddenly as she'd done it, she undid it, dropping her arms and backing away. "I'll leave the paintings here for now. Let me tell her, okay?"

"Fine," he muttered, still off balance. He hadn't forgotten how she'd felt in his arms that day, but he was damned well going to. "I'll, uh, send her over when she gets home."

"Great!" Ginger hunched her shoulders in a gesture of pure glee. "This is such fun! And you know what? I'm good at it, too, not just the decorating, either." She fixed him with a frank look. "I always knew I'd be good with kids."

Craig shook his head, torn between that and shaking her. He was almost relieved to feel his irritation returning. "Go home, Ginger," he warned her, "before I change my mind."

She made a show of disciplining her smile, then let it slip free again as she moved toward the doorway. "Thanks, Craig," she said as she swung through the opening. "Thanks a lot!" That last she shouted from the hall.

He found himself grinning, then caught himself and walked back to the bike. He'd be damned if he'd let her wear him down. Fixing up Jo's room was one thing, getting next to him was something else. His life was already too crowded as it was. If he had an ounce of sense, he'd get rid of her for good, but Jo didn't have any other friends around the neighborhood yet, and he had to admit that Ginger had a way of bringing the kid out of her shell. If anybody could get an opinion out of Joan, Ginger could. Maybe it was her eccentricity that Jo found so disarming. He really didn't know what it was. He only knew that Jo liked her—and that he had to stay away from her.

It seemed damned unfair. He only wanted a little peace for himself and to see Jo happy again. Why couldn't he have moved next door to some harmless little old lady who would take his sister under her wing and treat her like a daughter? No, he had to move in next to a husband hunter loaded to the teeth with every imaginable weapon. Well, she was just going to have to get it through her head that he was not fair game. There could be no argument about the fact that she was a woman of vast sex appeal. He couldn't help thinking how she'd filled out that little purple knit thing she'd been wearing, and it boggled the mind to think she ever could've felt cosmetic surgery was necessary. Now *that* was a waste of money. Nevertheless, he'd have felt better about the whole thing if she hadn't just announced that she had marriage on her mind and he was a likely prospect. On the other hand, he had to admire her honesty. But he didn't want to admire her. That was treading on dangerous ground. It just wasn't fair, and there wasn't a thing he could do about it but keep his distance. And so he would. As best he could. Blast.

He could've pedaled to Miami and back that afternoon by the time he'd worked the frustration out of his system. Well, one thing about it, Ginger Brenan was going to keep him in good shape—and help fix Jo's room, too. He supposed it was all he could ask. It was certainly all he dared to.

Ginger flopped onto the bed, her arms flung out to the sides, and laughed like the kid she felt herself to be at the moment. On her knees, Joan continued to bounce up and down, giggling hysterically. It had been a long time, Ginger reflected, since she'd jumped on a bed. She wondered if

Joan ever had before. Rolling to her side, she brought a hand up to support her head and rode out the waves of motion as Joan continued to bounce with rapidly decreasing enthusiasm. Gradually, both the giggles and the bounces ceased. Sighing, Joan collapsed face first onto the mattress, her legs still bent at the knees. Ginger reached out a hand to smooth the girl's hair, then thought better of it. They were friends, pals, and Joan was seventeen. Ginger knew without having to be told that she'd best stifle this mothering instinct for Joan's sake. Joan needed to grow up, not linger in babyhood all her life.

Joan flopped onto her back and lifted her head to stare at the painting of daffodils on the far wall. "I just love it," she said.

"The room?"

"Yeah, that, too." She turned onto her side and mimicked Ginger's pose. "Do you suppose I could paint?"

"We could find out. I'd be glad to give you the benefit of my experience."

"You would?"

"Of course. I'll speak to Craig about it today, if you want."

"Speak to Craig about what?"

Ginger turned her gaze toward the sound of his voice and found him standing in the doorway of Joan's room, hands in his pockets. He'd shed his suit coat and put down his briefcase. His jaws and chin were shaded with a bristly growth that seemed to be more than a mere five-o'clock shadow, and he looked utterly exhausted. Ginger scrambled into a sitting position on the bed, bare legs crossed Indian-style. He truly was a handsome man with those dark eyes and finely honed features and that full head of glossy brown hair. Looking at him, she felt an odd sadness, a sense of loss. It occurred to her that they could make beautiful children together and then that it was a pretty silly thing to be thinking. She laughed at herself, and to her surprise, a smile broke the gloom of his face.

"Do I look that bad?" he asked, stepping into the room and spreading his arms.

She shook her head. "No, you look that good." His smile vanished. Inwardly she sighed. She had to do something about her mouth before it got her into real trouble.

Craig walked around the room, eyeing the posters and paintings they had put up, having finished the wall the previous afternoon. He stopped in front of a poster of a group of wildly made-up rock musicians, and Ginger thought for a moment that he might object to it, but then he moved on. After he had made the rounds, he walked to the center of the room and turned back to the bed. "Do you like it?" he asked Joan, and she bobbed her head up and down. He smiled again. "Good." He looked at Ginger then. "Thank you."

She felt warmed to her core. "My pleasure."

Nodding, he turned back to the poster. "I didn't know you liked this group, Jo."

"I don't," she admitted. "But the poster's great!"

He shot her a pleased smile. "Yeah, it is." He pivoted, hands sliding into his pockets again, and he flashed a look at Ginger. "Now what was it you wanted to talk to me about?"

"Joan would like to try her hand at painting," she said, surprised by the huskiness of her own voice.

"Ah." He seemed to be considering. After a moment, he looked at Joan. "I am parched. Honey, could you get me a soft drink, please?"

"Sure." Joan's voice was laced with disappointment, but she got up off the bed and left the room.

Ginger glared. Obviously he had some objection to her giving Joan a few painting lessons, no matter what it meant to the kid. "There are other teachers, of course," she said the moment Joan was out of earshot. "But Joan likes me. She trusts me."

He waved a hand, dismissing her concern. "Oh, I know. I wouldn't dream of getting anyone else. It's just . . . well, what happens if she doesn't have any talent?"

Ginger had to shrug. "Well, then she won't paint very well."

"That's what I mean," he pointed out patiently. "She'll be crushed if you tell her she can't paint. Do you think she can take that? I mean, is it wise to set her up for that kind of failure?"

Ginger understood now, and a part of her sympathized with his concern, but everyone had to learn to deal with failure. She certainly had, and maybe that more than anything made her the person to teach Joan. She unfolded her legs and stretched out on her side again, her head propped in her hand. She smiled at him.

"Listen," she said. "I've mastered failure the hard way. You know what I mean. I'm the gal who's tried her hand at everything from advertising to teaching. And that's just the beginning! You want to talk about failed relationships? Honey, I wrote the book on failed relationships. I've been through them all—the gold diggers, the macho men, the playboys. Lord, I knew this poet once. He was the sensitive type—until you told him no. Then he was the brutal type. I wound up punching his lights out. Couldn't get a date after that for a month. Everybody called me Boom-Boom for a while." He was laughing at her. "Don't laugh! I cried for a week." She spluttered, thinking about it. "Gad, what a dope I was!"

They laughed together in a companionable way that made her feel good, safe. She sat up again, her legs stretched out before her, upper-body weight braced by her arms. "The point is, Craig, I can't guarantee she'll succeed, but I can help her through it if she fails."

He nodded, still smiling. "Okay," he said softly. "We'll try it your way."

She knew it was as close to a vote of confidence as she was likely to get. "Thanks. It's all right then if she comes over one or two afternoons a week?"

"Sure. I'll pay you, of course, and pay for any supplies."

The good feeling vanished. "Don't be stupid. I don't take money for doing something I love with people I like."

His expression suddenly was guarded. "All right. But I ought to at least buy her a canvas or something, shouldn't I?"

So he should. Ginger swung her legs to the side and got up off the bed. "I'll let you know when we get to that point," she said dryly, and he nodded.

Joan showed up with the soda just then, and Ginger felt her smile coming back. She walked over and put an arm around Joan's shoulders. "Tomorrow," she said, "we'll try our hand at a bit of sketching. How does that sound?" Joan beamed. Her gaze went immediately to her brother.

"Really?"

He chuckled and reached out for his soft drink. "Sure. Why not?"

Joan hugged them both, Craig first, then Ginger. Once more Ginger felt that surge of maternal instinct, and once more she suppressed it. One day she wouldn't have to, though. One day she'd be a mother with a house full of kids and a husband who'd come home looking as tired and bedraggled as Craig did now. She'd kiss him and tease him and make him forget everything but home and her, and he'd love her as she loved him. She looked at Craig over the top of Joan's head, wondering why he couldn't see that he needed someone to love him as only a wife could. And it could be her. She felt it every time she looked at him, every time she thought about kissing him, every time she daydreamed about what it would be like to be loved by him.

She wondered if she was nuts and decided that she definitely was. After all, it wasn't written in stone anywhere that she belonged with Craig Russell. In all honesty, she had been infatuated before, and what she felt now was very much like that. What saddened her was that she wasn't likely to get the opportunity to find out if what she felt for Craig Russell was the real thing or not. She might never know whether it was her instincts or her hormones drawing her to him—or possibly both. It would have to be both to be love. But as things were now, it might as well be neither.

* * *

Art was not Joan's forte. Ginger knew it right away, but she tamped down her own disappointment, concentrated on making it fun and let Joan figure it out in her own time. The discovery proved not to be traumatic at all. It occurred to Ginger that Joan had only wanted a good excuse to spend time with her, but she wasn't sure if Joan knew it herself, and they did have fun, something of which Joan seemed to have pitifully little. It was enough for Ginger to hear the child actually giggle. That happened for the first time when Ginger accidentally scratched her nose with blue paint on her finger. The second time it was cerise in her eyebrow, and Joan laughed right out. By the time Joan had given up trying to paint, Ginger had taken to smudging her whole face to get a rise out of the kid. The day she sent Joan home with her own face painted, even Craig Russell knew the painting lessons were a bust. He must have noticed, too, that the exercise hadn't sent Joan to her bed to pull the covers up over her head. It hurt Ginger that he didn't at least comment on that fact. He could have given her just a bit of credit for handling the situation well, but he remained distant and silent. She realized finally that she had to do something about it.

Her opportunity was not long in coming. They were neighbors, after all. They shared a beach. She still took her morning swims. It was early April and warm enough to play in the shallow water for prolonged periods of time. Florida was at its very best as far as she was concerned. The humidity was at its lowest. The scent of citrus fruit hung in the morning air, making the sunshine feel sparkling clean. She had every reason in the world to linger at the edge of the water. One day she began early enough and lingered long enough that she was there when Craig came out on the deck for his morning cup of coffee.

When she rose up out of the water in a white bikini, her hair streaming down her back, he lowered his cup and leaned forward in his chair before he could catch himself. Thrilled to the soles of her feet, Ginger walked majestically across the sand and up the steps. As she drew closer, it became obvious that he was gritting his teeth with the effort to act nonchalant. She tried not to smile as she stood before him.

"May I sit down? I'd like to talk to you." Good manners never hurt when one was about to plead a case. He went stiff as a board, but he had the good sense not to act startled and nodded. She sat down and crossed her legs. "It appears that you are not going to loosen up," she began, regretting her choice of words the instant they were out of her mouth.

Craig glared at her over the top of his cup, looking incongruously neat in his crisp white dress shirt, dark slacks and carefully knotted flower-print tie below a glare that was startlingly savage. For a moment she was too stunned to think. Then he looked away with a contemptuous slide of his eyes.

"What are we talking about now, Ginger, my sister or your marriage plans?"

The sarcasm hurt, surprisingly so. She swallowed hard and put it aside.

"I only meant that I'd hoped we could get to know one another," she said meekly. "We are neighbors, after all, and Joan likes me."

He raised an eyebrow. "Yes," he said, "Joan likes you, and yes, we are neighbors. As far as I'm concerned, it begins and ends there. You can't possibly fail to understand why after that stunt you pulled with that monster painting!"

"Stunt?" Anger overcame pain. "That's not fair!"

"Well, what would you call it?" he shot back, leaving her stuttering.

"Ah, a—a—a . . ." It came to her suddenly. "An experiment!"

The look on his face was incredulous. "And just what the hell do you think you proved?"

She opened her eyes very wide. As if he didn't know. She brought her hands together at her waist, the retort already rolling off her tongue. "Well, first of all," she quipped, "you kiss well."

He almost choked, spluttering coffee all over his pant legs. He jumped up, balancing the cup in one hand, swiping at his pants with the other. She jumped up to try to help him, but he effectively barred her attempts with an uplifted arm.

"Ginger," he said as soon as the coughing subsided, "this has got to stop. I am not interested in getting married. In fact, I'm not interested in an affair. The only things I'm interested in are my sister, my business and my home, and the only way you figure into that is as a friend of my sister's. And while we're on the subject, let me tell you this— If I ever find out that you're using her to get to me, I'll forbid—"

"Whoa!" Ginger straightened, incensed. "Now that is too much! I only told you I'm interested in marriage because I'm attracted to you—and you're attracted to me, whether you want to admit it or not! I was being honest with you. That's how I am, so you can darn well believe me when I say that I like your little sister as much as she likes me. In fact, it goes beyond that. She needs me!"

"For what?" he erupted. "Painting lessons?"

"Try friendship!" she retorted. "Or don't you know the meaning of the word?"

He didn't seem to have anything to say to that, so he just glared at her, but the battle stance was hard to maintain, and Ginger found herself softening. The surprise was that he seemed to soften, too. After a while, she took a deep breath, glad the argument was over.

"I'm sorry," she muttered. "I didn't mean to shout."

He nodded, laying a finger beside his nose. "Me, too." He sighed. "You're good for Jo," he admitted carefully. "On the other hand..."

Ginger leapt in before he could finish the thought. "Couldn't we just relax with one another?" she asked. "I mean, couldn't we just get to know one another?"

Craig opened his mouth, a doubtful look on his face, but again Ginger beat him to the punch.

"You never know what might happen. We could wind up friends, too."

Craig opened his mouth again, closed it again, considered. Finally, reluctantly, he said, "I suppose we could."

Then again, she thought, unable to resist taking it one step farther, *we could wind up more than friends*.

Craig seemed to read her mind. "Just don't get it in your head that there's more to it!"

Shocked at his acuity, she took refuge in umbrage. "I'm not stupid, Craig."

He fixed her with a level stare. "Neither am I."

And so he wasn't. She looked away. Was a chance too much to ask, then? Glumly, she pressed him. "I just don't see why we have to be at drawn daggers all the time. We're neighbors, after all. Just because you're a man and I'm a woman—"

"Who, after kissing me, has declared her desire to marry!"

"All right, don't keep reminding me!" Why hadn't she realized that was a bad idea? Obviously she couldn't have screwed up any worse. Ginger felt her chin tremble and she clamped her jaw to stop it.

He muttered something under his breath, then lapsed into silence. After several moments, he said softly, "I don't mean to hurt your feelings. It's just that I don't want you to misunderstand. I don't want to get married, Ginger, not to anyone."

"Fine," she said, forcing a brightness she did not feel. "You don't want to get married, and you don't really want to be friends."

"I didn't say that. I don't want to get married. I *do* want to be friends."

She shot him a skeptical glance, but for once his expression was open, accepting, even apologetic. Hope rose in her. Suddenly it was important that she protect it. She nodded, smiled and stuck out her hand. "Great. Friends it is, then." He grabbed her hand, jerked it down and released it in what was the quickest possible of all handshakes. Obviously he couldn't bear to touch her, but why? Because he found it displeasing? Or because he found it more pleasurable than

he wanted to admit? She didn't know then, as she turned
and ran back to the water, but she wasn't going to stop until she found out.

Chapter Five

Craig opened the door, knowing beforehand whom he would find leaning on the bell. Ginger flashed him a smile. Dressed incongruously in skimpy pink shorts worn over a black maillot swimsuit, terry-cloth scuffs, a frilly white apron and oversize oven mitts, she held a baking sheet steaming with freshly baked croissants. The aroma did amazing things to his stomach; he suddenly felt as if he hadn't eaten in a week. He ignored what the sight of her did to the rest of his body and opened the door wide, moving aside to let her enter.

"Good morning," she said brightly as she stepped into the house. She kept talking as she walked down the hallway and turned into the kitchen. "I hope you haven't had your breakfast. I need an honest opinion. Where's Joannie?" She shook off one mitt, tossed it onto the table and set the baking sheet on it. "Get the butter, please. Or do you use margarine? Flavorwise some of them are just as good, and there's the cholesterol problem, too. Where are the plates? Is the coffee fresh? Better bring the strawberry preserves, too. Joannie's wild about it.'' She removed the other mitt and turned to look at him.

Craig was still working on the honest opinion she'd mentioned at the beginning; he decided to give her one. ''You're nuts.'' He smiled to let her know he was kidding—sort of.

She stuck out her tongue at him. ''But I'm an excellent cook, if I do say so myself. Now come here and taste these. I want to know what you think.''

He walked over to the table and pinched off the end of one fragrant, soft, flaky croissant, popping it into his mouth, where it practically melted. ''Mmm, delicious.''

''What about the butter?'' she asked, then waved a hand. ''Never mind, I'll get it.'' She padded over to the refrigerator and stuck her head inside, emerging seconds later with a tub of margarine, an empty strawberry-preserves jar and a small pitcher of orange juice. Craig had managed to wolf down the pinched croissant and was starting on another. Ginger set the jar in the sink before carrying the margarine and juice to the table, then went back to prowl through his cabinets for plates and glasses. As she looked through his cabinets, she called out to Joan. ''Joannie? Honey, come and eat! Joan? Breakfast!''

Joan appeared, carrying her shoes, an anxious look on her face. ''Hi, Ginger.''

''Sit down, darling, and have a croissant,'' Ginger said, slinging plates onto the table. Joan obediently sat, placing her shoes on the floor, and Ginger dropped a kiss on the top of her head. ''Sorry, there are no strawberry preserves,'' she said, pouring juice. ''I'll send over some more later.'' She plopped a croissant onto Joan's plate and another onto Craig's before taking a chair and helping herself. ''So,'' she said, her attention focused wholly on Craig now, ''what do you think?''

He swallowed and lifted his shoulders. ''They're great.''

''But are they as good as the last ones you ate?''

''Better.''

She looked at Joan, who agreed. ''They're good.''

Ginger slapped the tabletop with the tips of her fingers and sat back. ''I knew it! It cuts the chilling time in half!''

Craig hadn't the slightest idea what she was talking about and Ginger didn't enlighten him. Instead, she delicately shredded her own croissant and began to consume it, obviously quite pleased with herself. A moment later she popped up to get coffee, napkins and a knife for the margarine no one was using. She was puttering around at the sink, and he was leaning back in his chair, pleasantly sated, while Joan nibbled, when he realized what a chummy domestic scene Ginger had created. And he had let her, his stomach completely overruling his head. He felt a flash of anger with himself. This, of course, was what she meant by "getting to know one another." They'd just had breakfast together! And now she was washing his dishes. He leaned forward in his chair, rested his forearm on the edge of the table and shook his head. Schlemiel. He was a schlemiel. But this was the last time. For ten cents he'd tell her to go home and leave him alone, but before he could say a word, she turned from the sink, blinded him with that brilliant smile and padded across the floor in her bedroom slippers.

She touched his wrist, shooting electric currents up his arm, and twisted around to get a look at his watch, which brought her full, firm breast to within inches of his face. Her scent suddenly assailed him, a combination of flowers, fresh water and baked croissants. His mouth watered. The hand in his lap drifted upward. She stepped back, as placid as the untouched surface of the lake on a still morning.

"I'd better get out of here," she said. "You're going to be late."

"Late?" He glanced at his watch. "Holy cow!" Craig launched to his feet, the chair scraping across the tiles. "Jo, grab your books!"

"I'll get them," Ginger said, moving fast toward the back of the house, "while you put your shoes on, Jo."

He stood like a lunk, his mouth open, watching her take charge of their lives, while Joan chomped croissant and slipped into her shoes. Ginger was back in a flash, books in hand. Joan popped up, took the books, hugged Ginger and rushed out into the entry hall. Stupefied, Craig watched as Ginger snatched up the now-empty baking sheet and oven mitts and followed. What was happening to him? How had she gotten to be so comfortable in his home, so close to his sister, so damned much a part of things? She stuck her head back in.

"Craig, move it," she ordered gently.

It struck him, finally, that he didn't have time for rumination. Murmuring, he spun out of the kitchen, his hand going into his pocket for the car keys. She was holding the door open now. He could see Jo standing beside the car. He brushed past her, the door slamming at his back. He was sitting in the car, the engine running, Ginger flip-flopping across the yard in her house shoes, when he realized he'd forgotten his briefcase and suit coat. He smacked himself in the forehead with the heel of his hand, then got out of the car, cursing savagely, and let himself back into the house.

He apologized to his stricken, confused sister all the way to the school. He didn't know what was wrong with him this morning. He was out of it, grouchy, overworked. He didn't approve of rough language, etcetera, etcetera. Joan told him rather tremulously that it was all right. Everyone had a bad morning now and then. At least, she said, brightening up, he'd had Ginger's yummy croissants for breakfast.

"And wasn't it sweet of her to bring them over?" she added cheerily. "I just love Ginger."

Before she got out of the car, Joan stretched across the front seat and kissed him on the cheek. He couldn't remember her doing that before, certainly not since she'd come to live with him, and he realized then that some part of him had been waiting a long time for that casual little kiss. As he watched her walk away, he thought of how Ginger had dropped that kiss on the crown of Joan's head earlier, as if it was the most natural thing in the world, and now suddenly Jo was kissing him in the same affectionate, unconscious way. Finally, the kid was loosening up, and he knew it was due to Ginger's influence, not his own. Suddenly, he felt worse than a schlemiel. Maybe if he'd put his arms around the kid from time to time, the next-door neighbor wouldn't have been the one to inspire a little affection in her. And maybe he ought to give Ginger the benefit of the doubt.

Ginger wasn't so bad really. She was certainly generous, showing up with welcome gifts and food and paintings. Then, too, Ginger had helped him straighten out Jo's room. There could be little question that the girl was pleased with it now. Also to her credit, Ginger had handled the matter of the art lessons with great aplomb. She'd definitely surprised him with that, and so had Jo. Plus there was no arguing that the woman was a good cook. And she looked good, too good for his peace of mind. He had to admit that all in all, eccentricities aside, Ginger was a likable, helpful sort of person. He thought he could have been very fond of her if only she hadn't let him know she was looking for a husband.

On the other hand, with her sexy looks, generosity and general neighborliness, she could have trapped him like a rat, maybe even gotten him into bed, then started pressing for marriage. Nevertheless, the fact remained that she was hunting for a husband, and the only thing in this whole mess he really knew for sure was that he *didn't* want to get married. He had enough on his plate already, thank you very much. Maybe eventually Ginger would see that and turn her attention elsewhere. Meanwhile, Jo would still have a friend to whom she somehow managed to relate, and that would be that.

Craig felt better. Until he realized he'd driven several blocks past his office building in fast-moving traffic that was going to carry him right up onto the toll road if he didn't do something quick. He crowded over into the left lane, made an illegal U-turn and headed back the way he'd come. Playing friend to Ginger Brenan, he decided, was going to be one of the most difficult things he'd ever done.

Ginger was thrilled.

"It bloomed!" she said, not at all put off by the scowl, the puzzlement and the look of amusement that crossed Craig's face in rapid succession.

"All right." Craig lifted his sunglasses to get a better look, then lowered them again, not moving from the chaise. "Now what is it?"

"An orchid, silly. My first one!"

"Ah." Laughter vibrated his voice, but Ginger felt the indulgence there, too, and it warmed her.

"I want to give it to Joannie," she declared, and his head pivoted far to the right, his attention fixed upon her, but his eyes unreadable behind the black lenses.

"You don't have to do that."

She smiled. "I know. I want to. Something this special should go to someone special."

He returned her smile. She wondered what he was thinking, wished he would remove his glasses again, and yet felt a certain contentment. The sunset was particularly brilliant this evening, bathing the world in a rosy, silken glow. Perhaps it accounted for both her contentment and his lazy manner. She had never seen him so relaxed. He lay there in faded navy shorts, a sleeveless T-shirt of pale yellow and stained canvas deck shoes, just soaking up the light and vegetating. He needed to shave. The stubble on his jaws, chin and upper throat had a surprising amount of reddish gold mixed in with the brown, and her palm itched to touch it, to feel the stiff, tiny hairs scratch against her skin. His smile turned dreamy, and he crossed his ankles, threading his fingers together over the taut, ridged flat of his stomach.

"Go on in," he said. "Jo's in her room."

Ginger didn't want to go in. She wanted to stay there and just look at him, feel the contentment stretch and grow inside of her, but presently he exhaled deeply, and then his chest began to rise and fall in slow, easy rhythm. He had fallen asleep and all at once she felt like an intruder. Carefully, she opened the door and slipped into the living room, carrying her precious orchid in its shell-shaped pot. She wasn't even to the center of the room when she knew what she was going to do. Something about this room had bothered her since the first time she'd seen it, and even though this was Craig's house she felt compelled to fix whatever was wrong.

She looked around her at the soft, heavy couches and chairs, the big, blocky tables, the glass pedestal lamps with inverted shades. Everything was of a neutral color, even the vases and figurines that were scattered about. It was all cool and comfy but bland and strangely impersonal, not at all like Craig Russell himself. As Ginger took measure of the room's contents, small ideas came to her, how to bring focus to a corner, heighten the effect of the colors, spotlight an interesting piece and, most of all, bring warmth and personality to this place. She felt a thrill of excitement, and at the same time she wondered what Craig would say if she did what she was thinking of doing. She dared not ask him beforehand after the way he'd reacted initially to her criticism of Joan's room, and she didn't want to have to explain every little change in detail, either. But doing it this way could well put an end to the uneasy truce she'd managed to negotiate with him. She bit her lip, fighting two equally strong urges, until she realized she could have an ally in this, a powerful ally.

Craig loved his sister. He'd go along with anything that truly pleased her. Ginger's excitement built as she hurried to Joan's room to describe just what she wanted to do.

"Craig."

His sister's voice came to him from a great distance, and at once he tried to think where she might be. Then again, where was he?

He sat up and looked around him. He was on his very own deck. The sun was long gone. Darkness was swiftly gathering. Already the surface of the lake was a dark glass. Soon it would reflect the stars to the heavens. He put a hand to his head, trying to visualize the sunset. It had promised to be a breathtaking display, but somehow he had missed it. Then he remembered. Ginger. He smiled despite himself. She'd brought over some absurd lily plant or some such thing, and while he hadn't seen any harm in it, he hadn't wanted to give her room to turn it into more. So he'd pretended to sleep. Apparently he'd pretended so well he'd even convinced himself, and thereby had missed the sunset, not that he minded too much. He felt rested and, well, at peace.

A giggle made him turn his head to find his sister standing in the living-room doorway. He lifted a fist to rub a knuckle against an itchy eye.

"Hey, sprite. Guess I was napping."

"You were napping," she said, "but we weren't."

We? That could only mean she and Ginger. What, he wondered, was that woman up to now? Whatever it was, he hoped it involved food, because his stomach felt as empty as the sky overhead. He got languorously to his feet, stretching and yawning to get oxygen into his system. He shook his head to clear it, feeling strong and fit, strong enough to face whatever lay in store. He felt, in fact, almost eager, and why not? Life was certainly never boring with Ginger Brenan around.

He turned to follow Jo into the living room, oblivious of the picture framed by the immense window overlooking the deck. He was all the way into the room and closing the door behind him before he noticed that something was different. Something? Everything! His jaw dropped. What in heaven's name had happened to his living room? As if he didn't know! Furiously, he sought and spotted Ginger. The hopeful smile on her face wavered and faded, and she dropped her head and began to twist her hands together. The anger went out of him, his heart contracting as she put on a brave new face and lifted her chin. Damn her. He spun away, unwilling to relinquish his sense of outrage, to feel tenderness.

"Craig?" It was Jo, timid, easily influenced, easily frightened Jo. "Don't you like it? We thought you'd like it."

Like it? At the moment he couldn't even see it, but the tremor in Joan's voice told him that she anticipated an ugly scene, and that took precedence. He would not subject his sister to more upset. That in mind, he took several deep breaths and got a hold on himself. He was not going to shout, at least not yet, not in front of Jo. For Jo's sake, he would make himself look at what they—Ginger—had done.

Then he would shout as soon as he got his sister out of the way.

Stiffly, he stepped back and forced himself to really see what had been done. He wanted the whole picture. He took it all in and saw that it was . . . softer. The overall effect was unmistakably softer. And green. Plants were scattered everywhere, several of them in large pots, and a few were actually flowering, which accounted for the sweet smell. Those had to have come from Ginger's house. He looked around for further additions but found none. Everything else was his, just arranged differently. In fact, now that he really looked at it, the room seemed more, well, complete. It was, in fact, the sort of look he'd been striving for to begin with: clean, cool, comfortable and homey, tastefully so.

His gaze was drawn to the corner where window and wall met. One of the two tall, narrow tables that he had placed at the backs of the big, wheat-colored sofas had been pushed up into that corner. A cut-glass bowl and a set of matching coasters had been grouped at one end. Two leather-bound books stood at the other, and in the center sat the plant Ginger had brought for Jo, the something special for someone special. What was it she had called it? A violet? No. An orchid. Her very first one.

"Craig?" Jo again. "Is it all right? Do you like it?"

To his amazement, he did, but some perverse part of him did not want Ginger Brenan to know it.

"Uh, it was j-just a shock," he said.

"But do you like it?" Jo persisted.

Before he could say anything more, Ginger intervened gently.

"No harm done. We can put it all back."

"No!" he said quickly, too quickly. "Er, that is, don't bother. It's . . . all right."

Something in his voice must have communicated that it was better than merely all right, for Jo laughed and rushed to hug him. "We wanted to surprise you!"

He gazed over his sister's head to get a look at the mastermind. "You certainly did that."

"It was all Ginger's idea," Jo went on, as if he didn't know that. "Aren't we lucky to live next door to Ginger?"

Once more Ginger Brenan surprised him. A lovely blush actually rose on her cheeks. She tried to ignore it, head high, gaze moving leisurely about the room, but she wasn't fooling anyone.

Craig gave up the final shreds of his anger, clearing his throat. "Yes," he said. "We're lucky to live next door to Ginger."

The woman's relief was almost palpable. She swallowed, and her mouth curled into a tremulous smile. He shook his head. She had expected his anger, not his acceptance, and yet she had gone right ahead and done it. What was it that compelled this woman to rearrange other people's lives? And why'd she have to be so darned good at it? He would be less than honest with himself if he didn't admit that he had benefited from her meddling. He was even big enough to admit it to her. Resolutely, he moved his little sister aside and reached out an arm, offering his hand. It was Ginger's turn to be surprised. Her pretty mouth dropped open, but she quickly placed her hand in his.

"Looks good," he said casually. "Thanks."

For a moment he thought she was going to cry, but then that saucy grin flickered, and her chin came up a notch. Suddenly she was very pleased with herself, rather smugly so. He almost groaned, but laughed instead, deliberately choosing to look on the bright side. Who knew? He could get his whole house done over before she finally gave up, and in the meantime, his sister would be happy.

He took his hand back from Ginger, tightened his arm about his sister's shoulders and surveyed the room once more. Living next door to Ginger Brenan wasn't all bad. So why did that conclusion make him want to pull up the welcome mat and bolt the door? He could appreciate the woman, even like her, without wanting to marry her, couldn't he?

Something wasn't right. The colors were exactly what she wanted, beiges and whites with various touches of orange shades from peach to terra-cotta, and a smattering of soft green. The subject matter was unlike anything else she'd ever done, and yet she thought she had captured the whimsical view she wanted of an old and crumbling brick wall with the mimosa tree beyond. Both seemed to possess a mysterious, silent history. She remembered seeing something very like it around Tallahassee when she'd driven up to visit the family of a college friend. It had lain in her memory all this time, only recently having risen to the surface, and she felt her rendition of it was quite good. Still, something was wrong and she didn't know what it could be. She needed an objective opinion.

She didn't even bother to remove the stained chambray shirt she wore as a painter's smock over cutoff jeans and the flowered bra top of an old bathing suit, nor did she remember the oiled brush stuck in the thick base of her ponytail. She simply put down her stained palette, dropped her loaded brush into a jar of linseed oil and walked out of the house, across the yard and up the drive to Craig's front door. He answered the bell with a half-eaten sandwich in one hand and a paper napkin in the other. She grabbed the one with the napkin and turned for home.

"What now?" he groaned around a full mouth.

"I need you to come over," she pleaded. "I'm stuck and I can't figure out what's missing."

They had reached the edge of the drive, and there he dug in his heels. She turned, fixing him with a pleading stare. She was desperate. She had to have an objective opinion, and he was the only one she could call on at such short notice.

"Is it too much," he said dryly, "to expect you to make sense? How can you be stuck and here, too? Or are you missing whatever you were stuck on to begin with?" It was the hint of a smile that told her he truly was not so much put out as confused. Was this progress? she wondered. She folded her arms, offering explanation.

"I'm painting."

"Walls or canvas?" He took a big bite of the sandwich.

"Canvas," she said, knowing he was only teasing her. She could tell by the way he smiled as he chewed. But this was important, for a lot of reasons. "Something is wrong, but I can't figure out what it is! I was hoping that an objective opinion, a different eye, could help me understand what it needs."

He shook his head, swallowing, and the teasing dance of his smile was stilled. "Ginger, I'm no art critic. I don't have the kind of eye you need."

"I don't want an art critic's opinion," she insisted. "I want an observer's. It needs something to catch the casual viewer's eye, something... Oh, I don't know! Just come and look. Please?"

To her surprise and immense relief, he nodded. "Lead on. I'll do my best." This *was* improvement. Thrilled to the soles of her bare feet, she snagged his hand again and tugged him forward, feeling the balled-up napkin between their palms. "Just don't expect miracles," he warned her, popping the last of the sandwich into his mouth.

She didn't tell him that miracles occurred every day, that all a person had to do was stop and notice, that she counted it a miracle he wasn't fighting her on this. She didn't tell him that he had to be the one to help her because she'd painted with him in mind. For some reason, he had made her think of that old tree and the older wall with their mysteries and secrets and beauty. He was the only one who could help her get it right.

"How's the cookbook coming?" he asked as she led him into the house. The question took her by surprise.

"What?"

He chuckled. "The cookbook."

"Oh!" She laughed, knowing how flighty she must seem to him. There was a cookbook to be compiled and written, but she was spending her days dabbing paint on a canvas. She would enlighten him. "The publisher is having some of my more-recent recipes tested before we go on."

"Doesn't trust you, huh?"

She compressed her lips into a mincing, humorless smile. "We're attempting to translate some rather vague instructions from an old French manuscript and update them at the same time. That means interpreting not only ingredients, amounts and directions, but intentions, as well. We want to get as close to the original creation as possible, but simplify with modern ingredients and technique. Not an easy task.''

"Obviously, especially as you wouldn't want to poison anyone.''

"Not just anyone, no,'' she came back archly.

He laughed, then made a bow, crossing his free arm across his middle. "I'm impressed.'' As he straightened again, she tugged him sharply forward, leading him across the living room to a spot near the first pair of French doors, where the light slanted in to fall strongly upon her easel. Its back was to them, so she pulled him around in front of it, already concentrating on her study of the canvas.

He stood for a moment without saying a word, and only when he squeezed her hand did she realize she still had hold of him. She let go and folded her arms, suddenly too distracted to think. He stepped back, shaking his head wonderingly.

"It's marvelous.''

Desperate, she exploded. "It's not right!''

He looked at the canvas more intently, his hand coming up to his chin. For a long while, his eyes moved back and forth, up and down. Then suddenly he snapped his fingers.

"It should be blooming,'' he said. "Those little pink, feathery blossoms.''

The tree. Pink blossoms. Tiny, feathery strokes of pink and white among the leaves, the perfect contrast for the yellowish oranges, just enough to grab the eye. Frantically, Ginger snatched up her palette and rummaged in her shoe box of paints. She chose a flamingo pink and added the barest touch of violet, tossing tubes and caps back into the box unmated. Mixing furiously with a small spatula, she smeared the new color against the array of oranges on her board. Too bold. She added a smattering of paper white next to the pink, mixing in only what she needed to achieve the proper hue. Satisfied, she pawed through the brushes grouped by bristle shape and size in the holders clipped to the easel. The tiny one needed was not there. She looked in the linseed-oil cup, plucking dirty brushes out one by one. It was then that she felt the tug of her hair and reached upward, her hand colliding with another in midair. Craig smiled down at her and extended the brush he had pulled from her ponytail.

"Could this be what you're looking for?"

She glanced at the tip and flashed him a smile. "It is! Thank you."

He delivered it into her hand, inclined his head and stepped back, an air of patience about him. Was he going to stand there and watch? Apparently he was. Well, why not? He had a larger hand in this than he even knew. She dismissed him and fixed her mind on the task at hand. She studied the leaves of the tree for a good while, deciding where to start and how many blooms to paint. As soon as she had the picture she wanted firmly in mind, she began.

The strokes were so delicate at first that an unpracticed eye could hardly have seen them, but it had always been her way to begin small and build, in that way layering the paint and creating her picture with texture as much as color. She worked diligently, and after a while, mindlessly, her hand responding by rote to the picture before her mind's eye. When she was done with the pink, it seemed a shade too strong, a bit too much, but she wasn't worried. Far from it. She was inordinately pleased, knowing as she cleaned her brush that the feather strokes of white she was about to add would soften the pink and create the correct illusion. Aware now of Craig's presence as she had not been before, she added the delicate finishing touches to her mimosa blossoms. She had never done better, she decided, dropping the brush into the linseed oil and cleaning her fingers with a bit of cloth that hung from a hinge of the easel. She turned to Craig.

"Well?"

He cleared his throat, and she realized suddenly that he had been moved in some way by what she'd done. Her heart skipped a beat and a lightness swept over her.

"I was right," he said huskily, his eyes seeking hers. Her breath caught, and she thought, *So was I. About you.* He blinked and looked away, focusing again on the painting. "This is very good," he murmured. "Better than the ones in Joan's room, maybe even better than that...." As he spoke, he turned toward the huge painting he had helped her to hang that day they had kissed. "I'm not qualified to critique, of course."

"No, it's true," she said. "I thought for a while that I'd never again do anything as good as the seascape, but I know that isn't so now."

He sent her a smile, eyes twinkling. "Maybe you went on to cookbook writing a little too soon."

She laughed, shaking her head. "Not quite soon enough," she said. "Oh, I know I have talent for this, but I'm just not commercial. I have to paint for a specific purpose, you know, a certain place, a special person."

He turned back to the easel. "And for what special person did you paint this?"

She didn't answer. She couldn't. The word was lodged against a lump in her throat. He pivoted sharply, pinioning her with a gaze so astute, it startled her. She didn't have to tell him. He knew. The only question was how he was going to react.

"You little idiot," he said gently, stepping close. She searched her mind for a snappy comeback, something to break the tension, and found none.

"Well, it would look perfect on the southeast wall of your living room," she said lightly. The colors of that brick wall were the same colors of the room she had rearranged only a few days ago, all except the pink, the necessary contrast. It seemed somehow telling that Craig had been the one to see what was needed. Were they connecting finally? She swallowed, feeling her heart wham against her ribs, and narrowed her gaze to his face.

"Why did you do this?" he asked softly, and she lifted a shoulder in a shrug.

"I love to paint, but like I said, I need a certain kind of inspiration, so when I get it..." She let it go at that, expecting that he would, too, but he seemed unwilling, so much so that when she started to turn away, his hand came up to cup her cheek. Her heart turned over.

"Ginger, I can't let you go on doing these incredibly generous things for us."

She blinked at him. "Why not, if I want to? What's wrong with doing something nice for a...friend...without expecting anything in return?"

He stared into her eyes for a long moment. "Nothing," he said finally, his gaze dropping to her mouth.

Oh, do it, she thought, willing him to kiss her. *Do it. Please. Now. We've come so far already. We both want it.*

He bent his head. His mouth was there, mere inches from hers. She parted her lips, breath bated, the lightness rising and brightening inside her. His hands fell onto her shoulders, hot, strong. She waited, paralyzed, entranced, yearning.

Suddenly, he lifted his hands. His head came up, and he stepped back. His face looked raw with regret. Disappointment flooded her, followed swiftly by compassion. He had stepped over the line and was obviously castigating himself.

"It's all right, Craig," she said quickly, but he merely shook his head, turned and, without another word, walked out of her house.

She closed her eyes. They had come far, just not as far as she had hoped, and not far enough, not nearly far enough.

Chapter Six

Craig stared at the painting on his wall, an after-dinner cup of coffee in his hand. He'd tried broiling a piece of fish this evening, the result being mostly edible. A packaged noodles-with-sauce dish and canned green beans had rounded out the meal. It had been a pretty good effort, if he did say so himself, and with every bite he was thinking of Ginger's fabulous bouillabaisse, flaky croissants and sweet preserves. That woman had a way of making herself felt even when she wasn't busy rearranging his life for him. She had a talent for it. Not her only one, he had to admit, staring at the painting. No, indeed. She was a woman of many talents. She painted. She cooked. She decorated. She looked like a million bucks when she walked. She was a certifiable loon with marriage on the mind, a predatory, dangerous, sexy piece of female, and while he had undoubtedly benefited from much of her effort on his and Joan's behalf, he still didn't know if he was doing the best thing by allowing her involvement in their lives.

If he was smart, he told himself, he wouldn't worry about it. Ginger was an adult, after all. She'd been honest with him, and he'd been honest with her. She was looking for a husband. He wasn't interested. Now which of them was the idiot? Him, for letting her hang around? Or her, for knocking herself out to impress him? And what about Jo? She liked Ginger. In fact, it appeared that Ginger was Joan's only friend. But was that healthy for a teenager? Which was worse, an inappropriate, older only friend or no friend at all? He didn't know what to think anymore. Ginger was right about one thing, though—that painting was perfect for his living room. The room itself was perfect, and he knew he had Ginger to thank for both. He just didn't know whether he was glad about it or not. He couldn't help thinking that he'd almost kissed her again. Knowing what he knew, he'd almost kissed her. But only *almost*.

He wandered, cup in hand, to the window overlooking the lake and turned his attention to the gathering night. Lights were on in the house on the opposite side of the lake, silhouetting the little cabana that stood on the edge of that section of private beach. He supposed there was a hot tub inside, and he thought idly of getting one for his own use. A good hot soak in the evenings could be an excellent tension reliever. It might even be an antidote for this restlessness he was feeling lately. He'd talk to Jo about it, see if she evinced any interest. With that resolved, he turned slightly, letting his gaze sweep around the shoreline of the miniature lake. He drew up short of his own property line, catching the black, angular lines of what looked surprisingly like a small tent pitched beyond the hedge separating his yard from Ginger's.

What was that woman up to now? he wondered. Or were his eyes playing tricks on him? He stared into the deepening darkness, hampered by the reflection of light in the window through which he peered. Was that a spark? Somewhat alarmed now, he moved to the door, opened it and stepped out onto the deck. As he watched, a tiny flame flickered to life and grew into a real fire. Almost at once the sound of a guitar being played came to him, and seconds later a clear, female voice lifted in accompaniment.

"There was an old woman who swallowed a fly.
I don't know why she swallowed the fly.
Maybe she'll die.
There was an old woman who swallowed a spider
that wiggled and jiggled and tickled inside her.
She swallowed the spider to catch the fly.
I don't know why she swallowed the fly.
Maybe she'll die."

Craig grinned to himself. What would she think of next? The growing fire had reached maturity, and he could see by its light that it was ringed with smooth stones. Ginger sat beyond it, her bare legs folded, the guitar in hand. The firelight turned her hair and skin to gold, and there was a lot of both to see. She wore nothing more than a skimpy bikini, and her hair fell loose about her head and shoulders and down her back. Just looking at her made his mouth water. Without realizing it, he moved toward the edge of the deck.

"There was an old woman who swallowed a bird.
Whoever heard of swallowing a bird?
She swallowed the bird to catch the spider
that wiggled and jiggled and tickled inside her.
She swallowed the spider to catch the fly.
I don't know why she swallowed the fly.
Maybe she'll die."

He paused. Was he going down there? Should he? What if she was not alone? Maybe he ought to check out the situation for Jo's sake. No telling what their next-door neighbor might be up to right there in plain sight. He went down the steps and walked across the sand, listening to that clear, high voice.

"There was an old woman who swallowed a cat.
Just think of that, she swallowed a cat.
She swallowed the cat to catch the bird.
She swallowed the bird to catch the spider
that wiggled and jiggled and tickled inside her.
She swallowed the spider to catch the fly—"

"I don't know why she swallowed that damned thing, either," Craig said, stepping into the ring of light. Ginger put down the guitar, laughing.

"Hello, Craig. Pull up a towel and have a seat." She handed him a folded rectangle of faded blue, which he shook out and spread on the sand beside her, sinking down onto it.

"Hello, yourself. What in heaven's name are you doing out here?"

"Camping."

His lips quirked. "In your own backyard?"

"Sure. Why not? I've always wanted to go camping. Why not here and now? I have everything I need—a good spot to pitch a tent, a beautiful lake, adequate facilities near to hand, a tent, a blanket, a fire and a guitar, not to mention all the ingredients for those melted-chocolate and marshmallow thingies." She picked up the guitar again and strummed the strings lightly. "What's your favorite song? Maybe I know it."

He laughed, noting how the firelight was reflected in her golden eyes. "I don't have a favorite song."

She caught her breath, leaning forward and grasping his wrist. "Oh, that's sad. Everyone ought to have favorite things."

"Really?" He was amused but keenly aware of the heat of her touch. Her hand felt as if she'd been holding it too close to the fire. In comparison, the night air suddenly seemed chill. She released him, moving her hand to the strings of her guitar.

"Of course. What could be better than having a favorite snack when you're really hungry, or rediscovering a favorite book when you're feeling lazy, or seeing a favorite person when you're lonely?''

''Or hearing a favorite song when you're in the mood for music?'' he asked, carrying the thought to its logical conclusion.

She flashed him a smile. ''Exactly. How about this one?'' She began to play a vaguely familiar tune. When she started to sing, he recognized it immediately. '''Somewhere over the rainbow...'''

Smiling, he leaned on one elbow and listened, mentally adding a good singing voice to her list of attributes. Judy Garland would have been pleased.

She moved on to other tunes, gliding in and out of them effortlessly, her sweet voice lifting and falling and lifting again.

She seemed to have an endless repertoire, and he discovered a hidden fondness for each and every song. When she at last gave it up and demanded to know his choice, he could only tell her that he liked them all. She moaned in frustration and fell back onto the sand, her guitar falling to one side. Craig laughed as she pounded her forehead with the flat of her fist. She struggled up onto her elbows and glared at him, but a smile tugged at her pretty mouth, and soon she was laughing, too.

''Let's eat,'' she said suddenly, sitting up and dusting herself off.

He watched with interest as she rummaged around inside a well-used brown paper bag, producing skewers, marshmallows, graham crackers and pieces of a broken chocolate candy bar. She pushed marshmallows onto the sharp ends of the skewers and stuck the rounded ends into the sand at an angle so the marshmallows hung over the fire, then plucked off the bubbling marshmallows one by one with blocks of graham crackers and chocolate, mashing them flat. They were cooking faster than she could rescue them, and she started stacking the messy bars, popping one into her mouth every so often and pushing several at him. But he couldn't quite figure out how to get the things into his own mouth without stringing sticky stuff all over himself.

"Oh, here, let me," she said, plucking one from his hand and shoving it between his lips, fingers and all.

The sweet, crunchy, gooey mess filled his mouth, tasting of chocolate and cinnamon and faintly of another flavor he couldn't quite name. But most of all, he tasted Ginger. Recognition flooded him as he remembered the honey and gold, spice and sunshine, musky female flavor of her. He shuddered, feeling the hot rush of his blood as she slowly extracted her fingers from his mouth and almost absently licked them clean of the sticky sweetness, her rose pink tongue curling around each in turn. Stricken with sudden desire, he turned the mass in his mouth with his tongue and started to chew, uncertain whether or not Ginger was aware of what her intimate gesture had done to him and striving to retain at least a semblance of his previous relaxed demeanor. Seemingly unaffected herself, Ginger popped one more of the gooey bars into her own mouth, then picked up another and carried it toward him. Unthinkingly, he grasped her wrist, preventing a second sensual invasion, and instantly her tawny eyes lifted to meet his.

She knew. Damn her, she knew what she did to him, had known all along. Well, she could just deliver, then. He tightened his grip, drawing her toward him, and her gaze fell to his mouth. The taste of her—how he craved the taste of her, the pressure of her lips, the feel of her small pink tongue gliding over his. Just the thought of it made him throb with need. A tug and she would come into his arms, damned near naked already, thrust those full breasts against him, wrap her slender legs about him. But it wouldn't stop with a kiss. He would make love to her, right here and right now. And then what? She couldn't make him marry her, and neither could she cry foul. They were two consenting adults, two healthy, passionate consenting adults on a beach beside a campfire next to a lake ringed with houses full of people, one of them his sister.

He released her, snatched the confection from her fingers, and stuffed it into his mouth, chewing furiously. Disappointment flickered in her eyes, but she said nothing, merely licked her fingers and reached for her guitar, picking out a soft tune that meant nothing to him but escape. He was not going to kiss her. That he had again been tempted was nothing more than a fluke. She had created an atmosphere, and it was that to which he had responded. He would not let her believe otherwise. He leaned heavily on his elbow, pretending indifference, reaching for a way to let her know that he could not be so easily manipulated as she seemed to think.

"So," he said, inwardly wincing at the abrupt sound of his voice, "why didn't you just go off camping somewhere with a friend?"

Ginger shrugged, her fingers picking effortlessly at the strings of her instrument. "Easier to do it this way. Besides, I like my own company, and I believe in being my own friend."

"Oh?"

"Mmm-hmm. As I told Joannie recently, we would all be healthier if we learned to be our own best friends." She stopped playing suddenly and pinioned him with her gaze. "You're welcome to join me, of course, if you like sleeping on sand."

An open invitation—to what? Craig was no longer as certain as he had been. He shook his head, making himself smile.

"I have a nice soft bed inside, thank you, and anyway, Jo would be nervous staying in the house alone at night."

"Yes, I know," she said, flattening her hand over the guitar strings. "Your sister is awfully uptight. She doesn't even like to stay in the house alone in the afternoons."

This was news. He pushed up into a sitting position. "Did Jo tell you that?"

Ginger nodded solemnly. "It's pretty much a pattern now. She comes to my place almost every afternoon."

"I didn't know," Craig admitted, dismayed. Why hadn't Joan said something? Why go to Ginger instead of him? "I don't want her to take advantage of you—" he began, but Ginger cut him off.

"Don't be ridiculous. I'm fond of her. She's always welcome, and she knows it."

"I appreciate that, but there's just no reason for it."

Ginger stiffened, hugging the guitar to her. "I enjoy her company and hearing about her day. She's a sweet girl, really, and I know she'd be well liked if only she liked herself a little better."

That might be true, he mused, but it didn't explain why Jo couldn't bear to be alone in her own home. It was safe here. The entire neighborhood was protected with a brick wall. The only way in and out was guarded by an attendant whose salary was paid by mandatory contributions of the homeowners. Everyone moving through that gate was noted. No one was allowed in without reason. Visitors seeking a specific address had to have the resident's permission to pass the gate. Homes on the market were shown strictly by appointment. There was no reason for Jo's fear, none whatsoever. He had taken every precaution. Why couldn't Jo see that she was safe with him? He would speak to her about this. He had to. Ginger was not responsible for her. Moreover, it was time that Jo took a little responsibility for herself.

He wondered if he ought to make his feelings about this known to Ginger, but instantly decided against it. He wouldn't want her to think he wasn't grateful for everything she'd done for Joan. He wouldn't want to hurt her. He genuinely appreciated Ginger's affection for his sister and didn't doubt its veracity. Neither could he fault Ginger's recently stated philosophy, but Jo was *his* sister. Besides, all of Ginger's theories were not as harmless as her be-your-own-best-friend business. Witness her "experiment" the day of the hanging of the monster-size seascape. He reminded himself once more that Ginger Brenan was not a woman with whom he could dally, in spite of what had almost happened here—or perhaps because of it. If he seemed to be having an incredibly difficult time keeping his distance, that was all the more reason to do so; otherwise, he was likely to find himself standing at an altar, wondering how he came to be there.

Ginger was fingering the guitar again, picking out a complex Spanish ballad with the ease of natural expertise.

Did she do everything well? he wondered irritably. Why was it that the woman's one obvious fault was this absurd determination to hunt down and trap herself a husband? She couldn't have been a petty thief or a claustrophobic or a nail biter, something a man could live with in a sexy, golden-haired next-door neighbor. No, she had to be a marriage commando packing every weapon known to man, from a well-stocked kitchen to a well-stocked bikini. One thing, though, she sure could play that guitar.

He liked guitar music. He had, in the past, entertained notions of learning to play himself. She certainly did make it look easy, fingers dancing over the strings with nary a misstep. He leaned down on his elbow again and closed his eyes, letting the music flow over him like water tinkling over a rocky streambed. It seemed to come all of a piece, the continuous fabric of song. When the last note shimmered over him and faded into silence, he sighed and opened his eyes, surprised to find her leaning down and staring at him, tawny eyes sparkling.

"What?" he demanded a tad defensively.

She laughed. "Nothing." But her eyes twinkled knowingly.

She knew very well how much he had enjoyed that last piece, how much, in fact, he enjoyed her. But if he was wise, he reminded himself, he wouldn't enjoy her or anything about her too much, not her music, not her painting, not her decorating skills, not her cooking, not her smile, not her voice, not her kicky little getups and certainly not her looks. To that end, he hauled himself to his feet.

"I brought home a briefcase full of work," he explained. "Guess I'd better get to it."

"All work and no play makes Craig a dull boy," she quipped, gazing up at him.

"Uh-huh, but a successful one," he came back.

"Do you like what you do?" she asked.

The question rather startled him. He had to think, but then he knew. "Yes," he said. "Very much."

She smiled, looking as pleased as if he'd complimented her.

"Good," she said, then went back to her guitar. "See you."

"Yeah," he mumbled. "See you."

She started humming and plucking those strings again. Strangely bemused, he left her. Why would she care whether or not he liked what he did for a living? he wondered. Maybe one of her requirements for a husband was that he enjoy his work. And maybe she was just a caring person, period. And maybe he'd better get his head on straight and stop worrying about what Ginger Brenan did, said or thought. The only female who concerned him was his sister, and he decided suddenly that getting some things straight with her was more important than reviewing last week's field reports.

He climbed the steps to the deck and went back inside through the living room. Jo was lying on her bed, listening to music through earphones, a glum, bored expression on her face. Craig went into the room and tapped her on the ankle. The kid nearly jumped out of her skin, yanking her legs up so that she lay curled on her side in a tight ball. Seeing that it was him, she immediately relaxed and uncurled again. It wasn't precisely a relief for him as all the animation drained from her face. He felt a flash of concern mixed with irritation. Wouldn't she ever be happy again? He knew it was tough losing both parents by the age of thirteen. He knew it had even retarded her maturation. She just wasn't like other girls, and ninety percent of the time he didn't know how to help her be like other girls, but somehow, someday she just had to be. And now was as good a time as any to start. He sat down on the edge of her bed, smiled benignly and pulled the earphones from her head.

"Jo, honey, something's been called to my attention, and I want to talk to you about it."

"All right."

"Ginger says that in the afternoons you go over to her house and stay, and I was just wondering why you do that."

Joan lifted one shoulder and let it drop again, eyes downcast. "I like to go over to Ginger's."

"I understand that, Jo, but Ginger has things to do. She works out of her home, you know. We shouldn't be imposing on her. She's done quite enough for us already."

"But Ginger doesn't mind me coming over."

"That's not the point. This is your home, this is where you ought to be spending your time. Besides, you should be doing homework in the afternoons instead of visiting."

"But that's one of the reasons I go over there," the girl declared. "So Ginger can help me with my homework."

Craig felt sure that was nothing more than an excuse. "Now, Jo," he said, "you know perfectly well that you don't need Ginger's assistance to get your homework done."

"But I do!" Joan cried, suddenly panicked. "Oh, Craig, you have to let Ginger keep helping me with calculus. I was failing until she started explaining things to me. I—I don't know why I can't get it in class like everybody else does, b-but Ginger knows just how to put it so I understand. And literature! She's got most of Shakespeare committed to memory, and reading Chaucer is like reading nursery rhymes for her! She gets it first time every time. Everything's just so clear when she explains it. Oh, Craig, please let Ginger keep helping me. I don't know what I'll do if you don't!"

For a moment he was speechless, purely flabbergasted. Jo couldn't be talking about the same sometimes spacey but unquestionably talented, quirky, eccentric female sitting cross-legged out there on the sand in front of a pup tent this very moment. Could she? He shook his head, hoping to clear it of this absurd idea. It didn't go away. The direct approach was required. He leaned close to Jo, his gaze narrowing in on her face, the better to judge her expression as she provided him answers to the obvious questions.

"Are you telling me that Ginger Brenan is some sort of whiz at calculus?" he asked.

Jo's head bobbed affirmatively. "My calc teacher says she's a genius, and Mrs. Hebron, in English lit, wants her to come and speak to the rest of the class when we start *King Lear.*"

"Genius?" Craig echoed. "Ginger Brenan?"

Jo faced him impassively. "It's pretty obvious she's smart. Look at all the stuff she can do. Do you know she scored so high on her college entrance exams that colleges contacted *her?*''

It seemed there was a lot about Ginger Brenan that Craig didn't know. For instance, so Joan informed him, Ginger was valedictorian of both her high school and college classes. *Valedictorian?* Craig thought. *Our Ginger? Gorgeous, sexy, husband-hunting Ginger?* He didn't know what to think, let alone what to say. After a while he realized he was sitting there with his mouth open, so he closed it and got up, managing to mumble something about discussing the matter further another time.

That night he dreamed about Ginger Brenan. He walked into his own kitchen and found her there, stirring a pot with one hand, painting a masterpiece with the other, playing the guitar with her toes and lecturing an avid Jo on mathematical theory, while wearing a mortarboard and a short, tight graduation gown opened down the front to display her impressive cleavage. She saw him and smiled provocatively. The next instant they were standing arm in arm before a sloping bank of flowers. Organ music was playing, and Ginger wore a white bikini, high heels and a headdress with a long, billowing veil. Someone said, ''She baked the wedding cake herself.'' Another voice added, ''And looks good enough to jump out of it,'' while a third jeered, ''Old Craig finally came up against a woman smart enough to outmaneuver him!'' And finally, ''I now pronounce you husband and valedictorian.''

Craig came awake with a start, realized where he was and growled into the darkness, then punched his pillow before settling down onto it again. He would not think of Ginger Brenan. He absolutely would not think of her. She could not impact his life unless he let her. She could be a female Einstein, and she still couldn't make him marry her. So why was he wasting energy like this?

He closed his eyes and blew out a deep breath, consciously relaxing. It was a little trick he used to clear his mind when things got hectic at the office and as always, it worked. His mind was blank, void, as gradually he slipped toward sleep. All that existed in the world was this comfortable bed and the clarity of his mind. Then gradually even the bed disappeared and he was floating, at peace, adrift in a silence as beautiful and lilting as any music. He gave himself up to it, letting it roll over and around him, until the silence became sound, notes, melody, the fluid, trilling music of a Spanish guitar played by slender, feminine fingers belonging to a tawny, voluptuous woman wearing only a bikini and sitting cross-legged on the sand before a golden fire. He reclined beside her, propped up on one elbow, utterly enthralled. She leaned toward him, smiling. He knew what it would feel like to kiss her, what would happen if he lifted a hand to touch her, and that he shouldn't do so, but the music was positively compelling, though she had ceased even to play it. He lifted that hand—

He woke reluctantly and, eyes closed, reached out to smack the alarm clock that buzzed on the bedside table. Sunlight reached right through his eyelids to announce the advent of day. He had to get up and go to work, but never had he wanted less to do it. He pulled a pillow over his head and tried to thrust himself back into the welcome state of slumber, reaching for some indefinable sense of comfort. He strained toward the place he had been before consciousness had claimed him, searching for some shred of what must have been an unusually erotic dream, if the condition of his body was any clue. Dreams did not normally affect him so strongly, and he found it odd that he should wake with both a throbbing groin and a sense of overwhelming well-being.

Lying there, he knew within moments that he wasn't going back to sleep. His brain was functioning much too rationally now to allow it. He had to get up, but it wouldn't hurt to dawdle long enough to remember the dream. Stretching, he rolled onto his back and folded the pillow beneath his neck. It had been night in his dream. There had been stars, but somehow he was looking down on them, or rather, on their reflection. He had it now. He had been looking at the reflection of the stars in the surface of the lake, and there had been music, guitar music. But that had been no dream. It had happened.

He remembered sitting beside Ginger on the beach, remembered the way her hands had moved over the strings of her guitar, remembered eating from her fingers, remembered how she'd leaned toward him, her gaze on his mouth, remembered that he'd lifted his hand and slid it into her hair, pulling her down to—

He sat bolt upright in bed, the memories coming back to him with stunning clarity. He hadn't, he *couldn't,* have really made love to her on the beach last night. Could he? For a moment he wasn't sure, then he knew and expelled a breath in relief.

What he had dreamed was part reality and part fiction supplied by his treacherous mind in his sleep. It was what might have happened if he hadn't had sense enough to resist the attraction he felt for that walking bundle of apparently uninhibited sexuality that was his next-door neighbor. He sighed, putting thumb and third finger of one hand to his temples and squeezing gently. Was there no escaping that woman? Must she share either his bed or his dreams? If so, then better his dreams, he told himself. And yet he could not help feeling a bit of resentment that she had invaded his life in this manner. It was true that she had brought some improvements with her. He and Joan had benefited from Ginger's many varied talents, but was it worth the price of unfulfilled desires and treacherous dreams? Was Ginger Brenan bringing more harm than good to their lives? He suddenly had no energy even to consider the answer to that question, and it was past time to get dressed and begin taking care of the day's business.

Sluggishly, he flipped back the covers and swung his legs to the floor, vaguely aware of his relief at the knowledge that he had other things with which to occupy himself, other needs to consume his time. With the automatic ease born of long practice, he mentally switched gears, fixing his mind on the never-ending, day-to-day details of running a large, successful business. He left Ginger Brenan there with the final unwelcome images of his troublesome dreams. But they would all be there waiting for him at the end of the day and in every unguarded moment until then.

Chapter Seven

It had been a rough week, and Craig groaned aloud when he spied his aunt's distinctive 1985 Chevy sedan parked in front of his house. The car was distinctive only because, despite its age, it looked as though it had just left the showroom floor and because the seats and carpets were covered in heavy protective plastic. Maggie believed that anything to be walked or sat upon should be covered in plastic. She then expended vast amounts of energy trying to keep the plastic clean, apparently unaware that she had not saved herself an instant of trouble, never mind the discomfort of sitting and walking on plastic sheeting.

Craig guided his Jaguar past the Chevy and parked it, then fetched his jacket and briefcase, leaving only the yellow hard hat on the back seat. He could not help glancing in the direction of Ginger's house before he turned and walked toward his own. Try as he might, he could not seem to get that woman out of his head. He opened the front door to the sound of his sister's sobbing.

"What the hell . . . ?"

He broke off at the doorway to the kitchen. Maggie stood with folded arms, glaring down at her seated niece. She wore an unflattering shirtwaist dress made of a dark plaid fabric overlaid with paisley, its narrow belt straining about her thick middle. Her handbag hung on her arm. Short, white gloves covered her hands. A small navy blue pillbox hat with a whisper of crushed veil and a rigidly starched feather was perched squarely atop her overly large head. Beneath it, her dull gray hair curled tightly against her white scalp and over her ears. She looked rather like a fat poodle in a dress and sensible shoes. Jo, on the other hand, simply looked miserable and bereft. Craig took a slow, calming breath, realizing that anger would serve no useful purpose here.

"Hello, Maggie," he said tightly. "Jo, are you all right?"

Her reply was a soft, mewling wail that tore at his heart. He closed his eyes against the rising tide of his rage, then opened them again and walked into the room to lay a comforting hand upon his sister's shoulder. As usual, her frailty disturbed him. He remembered her as a tiny, cooing infant, dainty beyond belief, her eyes looking too big for her face, her mouth wavering with uncertainty. Whenever a door had slammed, her tiny limbs had jerked, her face had crumpled and she'd erupted into screams. Now, in response to his touch, she turned up her tear-stained face and stilled her quivering chin.

"I'm s-so embarrassed," she whispered, before lowering her face to her hands again.

"I should think so!" Maggie declared, stiffening with outrage. "If you were a proper guardian, Craig Russell, I wouldn't have to witness such shocking goings-on, and your sister wouldn't be sitting there eaten up with shame! Your poor mother must be spinning in her grave. To think that I should walk into your house and find this child cavorting about with that . . . that stripper!"

Craig rolled his eyes, laughing soundlessly. Why, it was absurd! Where on God's earth would Jo meet up with a stripper? And even if she had, was he supposed to believe she'd bring the creature home and take lessons in the craft?

"Mags," he said, shaking his head, "are you sure you haven't taken too many of those blood-pressure pills?"

That got him a "Hmph!" and a regal toss of the poodle's head. "You always were a disrespectful young whelp," Maggie complained. "But one would think you'd have developed some good sense by now! Just what were you thinking of, Wayne Craig," she demanded, using his full given name, "moving in here next to that Bohemian?"

Understanding dawned. Ginger. Ginger had been here when Maggie had arrived. But what could she have done to get herself labeled a Bohemian stripper? And why was Jo sobbing in embarrassment? He decided he'd better get Jo's version of the story while it was still recognizable as such. Going down on his haunches next to her chair, he fished out his handkerchief and pressed it into her hand.

"All right now, honey, let's hear what happened. What were you and Ginger doing when Aunt Maggie arrived?"

Jo sniffed and swiped at her nose. "We were just sunbathing and kind of talking, you know?"

"Is that what you call it?" Maggie interjected. "Talking? In my day, we called it soliciting!"

"Maggie, that's enough!" Craig ordered sternly.

"Enough!" the older woman gasped. "I tell you what's enough! It's more than enough to walk in and catch your niece exposing herself on the beach with some half-naked trollop!"

Jo wept bitterly at that, and Craig pinched his nose. He could see that he wasn't going to get any straight answers from anybody just now. Obviously Maggie thought she'd walked in on some highly questionable activities, but Craig couldn't believe Jo would be a part of anything truly untoward. He had less trouble imagining Ginger Brenan in that role, but he doubted that even she would put Joan in a compromising position. At least, he didn't want to think so. Sighing, he turned his attention back to his sister.

"So you and Ginger were sunbathing on the beach when Maggie came in," he summed up softly. "Then what?"

"She . . . she threw her out!" Jo wailed. "Aunt Maggie c-called Ginger names and th-threw her out of the house!

Ginger didn't want to leave, but *she* threatened to call the police! And she tr-tried to send me to my room, but I wouldn't go!'' That last was delivered in a near-belligerent tone that surprised him. Jo had actually resisted. His fragile little sister had actually stood up to old Aunt Maggot. He felt a small surge of pride on Jo's behalf.

''Good for you,'' he said, clasping her hand. ''But now why don't you leave us alone so I can talk to Aunt Maggie.'' He had to force his tongue around the correct syllable to keep from using the old secret moniker he'd assigned his disagreeable aunt during his childhood. He'd never liked the woman, but she was his mother's sister, family, and there was too little family left him now. Nevertheless, he wouldn't have Maggie upsetting Jo like this. This was his house, his and Joan's. They would say who was welcome and who was not.

He rose with his sister, seeing her off with a little push of his arm. When she had shuffled down the hall and disappeared into her bedroom, he turned on Maggie.

''You have some nerve!'' he declared hotly. ''What were you thinking, coming in here like that?''

''You're implying that I shouldn't have let myself into the house?'' she asked, drawing herself up to full indignation. ''Well, I'll have you know I rang the bell, and when she didn't answer, I got worried. After all, I took that child into my own home after her mother died, God rest her, and me a poor widow, all alone but for the two of you!''

That was true enough, but it would have been much easier to be properly grateful if she didn't bring it up and wield it like a cudgel at every opportunity. He fought down the urge to tell her so and took another tack.

''You're always welcome here, Maggie,'' he said with some effort, ''but this is *my* house, and I have final say on who comes here and what goes on. Remember that in the future.''

''Well!'' Maggie had pulled up straight and was leaning slightly backward now. Any further indignation and she was going to be turning a flip. ''Are you telling me,'' she demanded, eyes narrowing, "that you approve of that woman?"

Approve of Ginger? Craig sputtered a bit but finally got as close to the truth as he could. "Ah, some . . . that is, usually . . . Well, yes, where Jo's concerned."

Maggie gasped. "I'm stunned!" she declared, fanning her face with a gloved hand. "Then again, I'm not. She's just the sort of fleshy tart you men like to have around, never you mind that she's a terrible influence on that child in there!"

"She is not!" Craig protested, stung more than he'd like to have admitted. How dare Maggie question either his judgment or his intentions? He'd turned his life upside down in order to make a proper home for his sister. He'd foregone more temptations since Jo had joined him than in the whole of his life, Ginger among them. He felt insulted, and truly justified in doing so. "Ginger Brenan is a good neighbor," he insisted. "Maybe she's a little eccentric, but she's hardly a bad influence on the hunt for impressionable teenagers to lead astray."

"Oh, isn't she?" Maggie countered. "Then I'd like to know just what she was doing out there on that beach today?"

"I don't know!" he roared. "But I'd bet it wasn't anything nearly as heinous as you want to think!"

"As if I want to think anything of the sort! I'm only interested in what's best for my niece."

"Then leave her alone, Maggie!"

"Leave her at the mercy of that tramp next-door, you mean."

"I mean, mind your own business, Maggie! Jo is *my* concern. And for your information, Ginger Brenan has been a lot of help with Jo. The woman is not, I repeat, *not,* a tramp. She's Joan's friend, and now, thanks to you, I have to go next door and apologize!"

"Apologize!" Maggie grabbed her throat as if the very idea of making an apology to Ginger Brenan was somehow life threatening. For just an instant Craig hoped she would choke on the thought, but then he merely wanted her out of

his sight. Without another word, he turned and strode out
of the house, yanking the front door shut behind him with
both hands. He would have liked to have slammed it, but the
blasted thing was so massive and the hinges upon which it
swung so finely balanced that actually slamming it once it
was opened any great distance was next to impossible. He
settled for stomping down the drive and into the thick grass
of Ginger's yard, over the low hedge and various other im-
pediments, to Ginger's front door.

She answered the bell in an apron and darned little else
that he could see. A cordless telephone receiver was jammed
between her ear and her shoulder, her head cocked to hold
it. She had pulled her hair up into a ponytail at the crown
and wielded a long wooden spoon in one hand.

"Oui, oui, savoyarde," she was saying. She waved Craig
inside. *"Pardonne-moi, s'il te plaît."* She covered the bottom of the receiver with her hand and spoke directly to Craig
for the first time. "France," she said simply, motioning for
him to follow her as she walked back into her kitchen, her
bikinied bottom swaying provocatively with every step. He
ignored the sight and moved along. The instant he entered
the room, the delicious aroma of grilled onions and
browned butter filled his nostrils.

Ginger walked to the stove, hefted a heavy cast-iron skillet and dumped the contents into a stew pot sitting on a lit
burner, all the while chattering in French into the telephone
caught in the crook of her shoulder. She transferred the
skillet to a trivet beside the sink, then stirred the stew pot
with the wooden spoon. Again, she put her hand over the
bottom of the receiver and turned to Craig.

"How's Joannie?"

He shrugged his shoulders. "Upset, but she'll be all right.
Listen, about Aunt Maggie—"

She cut him off with an uplifted hand. *"Formidable!
Donne-moi une minute pour trouver un stylo.* Craig, could
you take this down? There's a pencil and paper beside the
computer there."

"Uh, all right," he said, searching for the pencil and paper and finding it, "but I really just wanted to talk to you about Aunt Maggie."

"Oh, *that.*" She made a face, then promptly started translating what was obviously a recipe. "A medium onion, one clove crushed garlic, basil and the green part of a leek, chopped and sautéed in butter. *Bien sûr, j'utilise de la margarine.* Got that?"

He wasn't certain that last was for him, but he nodded anyway. She went on without pause.

"Four chicken breasts, just enough water to cover, bay leaf, two cups chopped carrot, one cup white wine... *As-tu des suggestions particulières ici?* Uh-huh, flame the cognac. *Un moment, s'il te plaît.* How are you doing, Craig?"

"Ah, one cup white wine," he read. "Listen, Ginger, I only came over to apologize for Maggie's behavior."

"Don't worry about it. All that concerns me is Joannie. I hope she likes this. It's a special recipe for chicken soup. I've been meaning to try it for some time, and I thought, why not now? So I rang up my friend, Marcelle."

"In France?" Craig asked, amazed. She seemed surprised by his amazement and lifted a shoulder in a shrug.

"Well, yes."

"You called all the way to France for a recipe for chicken soup for Joan! Ginger, you shouldn't do that. I mean, it's very nice of you. Hell, it's wonderful of you. But Jo wouldn't care if you opened a can, for pity's sake."

"A can!" she exclaimed. "Bite your tongue, Craig Russell."

"But Ginger—"

"Besides, I told you, I've been meaning to try it for a long time." She suddenly went back to the phone. "*Qu'est-ce que tu as dit?* Write this down, please. Simmer twenty minutes, add one cup cut up—*Quelle sorte de courge?*—zucchini." She waved a hand dismissively. "Five minutes. Ignite the cognac. Pour over. Put on the lid." She rattled on in French again, then began snapping her fingers as if to get Craig's attention. "Sour cream, salt and pepper." He started writing again. "This is the important part," she went on. "One tablespoon flour, one-half cup grated Parmesan, one-half teaspoon dried mustard. *C'est tout?* Did you get everything?''

Again, Craig could only assume that the final part, as it was spoken in English, was meant for him.

"I think so," he replied, hoping it was true. She went off in French again.

"Je suis très ravie! Merci bien. Je sera sûre à remercier ta grandmère si nous l'employons dans le livre. Merci encore. Au revoir." She turned off the phone and laid it on the countertop. "Sounds scrumptious, doesn't it? I hope it will make her feel better, poor darling. She was so upset. You're a dear to help me." Ginger flashed Craig a smile that he felt all the way to the soles of his feet. He cleared his throat.

"I just hope you can read my writing."

She laughed. "Oh, don't worry about that. I've got most of it in my head anyway. Now about that Aunt Maggie of yours..."

He winced. "I can't tell you how sorry I am about that. Maggie thinks she's the final bulwark against evil in the world, and she sees it in everything, but I can't for the life of me figure out what she thinks is so awful about you and Jo sunning yourselves."

It was Ginger's turn to wince. "Well, to be honest, it was a little more than that," she said carefully, going to the refrigerator for vegetables.

Craig folded his arms and waited, a sense of dread coming over him. "Go on."

Ginger began washing carrots and chopping them into pieces, talking as she worked, her movements just jerky enough to signal her nervousness. "It was all very innocent. We were sitting out there on the beach, you know, and Joannie was all wrapped up in those dark, stuffy clothes of hers. Honestly, Craig, she dresses like a middle-aged frump. Anyway, I just wanted to loosen her up a bit. I got her to pull her blouse out of her waistband and tie it up. Then we rolled up the legs of her pants, and I talked her out of those awful knee-high stockings and those clodhoppers she wears everywhere. Then, finally, I made her let her hair down. She protested everything, you know, saying she'd look like a limp dishrag no matter what she did, but once I was through, she seemed to feel better.''

"And that's when Maggie walked out and lambasted you?" he prodded helpfully. Again, Ginger shook her head, scraping chopped carrots from her cutting board into the soup pot. "Not precisely."

"Then when, precisely?" he pressed, impatient to know the worst of it.

Thoughtfully, she measured a cup of white wine brought down from the cabinet and poured it into the pot. "Well, then we just sat there," she said offhandedly. "Until those gorgeous Petrie boys came along."

Craig felt a sense of shock, and then the ignition of his temper. "The *gorgeous* Petrie boys?" he said, doing a slow burn. "I don't believe I know them."

Ginger shrugged apologetically. "They're a couple of young men, brothers, who live across the lake," Ginger told him. "It's that house where they have the big ski boat at the dock and the little cabana on the beach. And anyway, Marc and Heath—that's them—like to take the boat out in the afternoons, kind of strut their stuff and, well, you know how guys that age are." She laughed uncertainly.

Craig sent her a quelling look. "And what age is that?"

She gulped and began rinsing zucchini. "Well, let's see...Marc's maybe nineteen, and Heath's, oh, early- to mid-twenties."

"Hmm, and how *are* guys that age?"

She lifted a shoulder. "Oh, you know how it is. They'd rather flirt than breathe."

"And they stopped to flirt," Craig supplied, an edge to his voice that he hadn't intended.

"That's right, and naturally I introduced them to Joan."

"Oh, naturally."

"I think she was surprised that they liked her."

"Her?" he repeated, thinking, *Not you?*

Ginger dropped the zucchini into the sink and turned on him, rotating a hip against the counter. "Of course her," she said testily. "You know, that's part of Joan's problem. If her own brother can't think of her as attractive, how can she be expected to see herself that way?''

The truth of that hit Craig like a sledgehammer. He was instantly contrite. "I—I didn't mean it like that. That is, I..." He broke off, realizing what he'd been about to say, that he'd been thinking of her, Ginger, not the little sister who so desperately needed all the confidence she could get. It wasn't as if he hadn't thought of these things himself, and why should he care if the nineteen- and twenty-something-year-old gorgeous Petrie brothers flirted with Ginger anyway? He ran a hand through his hair. It was shaking slightly. He shoved it down onto the top of the bar. "It's just that, ah, Jo isn't very good with guys."

"No, she isn't," Ginger agreed. "But the boys didn't seem to notice that, and I don't know for sure, but I think my being there gave her confidence, because she actually opened up after a bit and talked to them."

Craig lifted his eyebrows. Joan had actually managed small talk with a couple of guys? His irritation was fast giving way to amazement. Then he thought of Ginger doing so easily, so naturally what Jo was having to *learn* to do, and his irritation was back. "Then Maggie showed up?" he asked, wanting this conversation over with.

Ginger shook her head. "No, actually, Maggie didn't show up until a few minutes later. After the guys had sat and talked to us for some time, they invited us on a boat ride. Craig, you should have seen Joannie. She turned the most panic-filled eyes on me, but I could see she wanted to go, so I just accepted for both of us. I don't know if she was more grateful than terrified or the other way around, but I just about had her in that boat when Maggie stormed out!"

"Oh, God," Craig moaned, visualizing the row that must have ensued, Maggie demanding Joan get away from those nasty boys, Ginger demanding just who Maggie thought she was, Joan so embarrassed she burst into tears on the spot, the gorgeous Petries roaring off in their boat, thinking the whole crew was mad. No wonder Joan had been sobbing when he'd come in, and to think she had still managed to defy Maggie! He was prouder than ever of the little goose and feeling a good deal of relief, the source of which he did *not* want to explore. "I'm so sorry that happened," he said.

"So am I," Ginger replied.

"Not that I'm at all sure I want the Petries sniffing around yo—my sister."

Ginger flipped a hand dismissively. "They're really harmless."

Right, he thought. "Well, I don't think Jo's quite up to the Petries yet, but you certainly didn't deserve Maggie's harangue."

"That's not what bothers me," Ginger said. "It's what she's done to Joan. That girl needs all the support she can get, Craig, not tearing down. She needs confidence, not criticism. Otherwise she's never going to learn to make friends."

Once again, she was right on target. Craig pushed a hand through his hair. "I know what you mean. I've tried to help her along by introducing her to a few young people, but it never seemed to work out. My partner's got a couple of kids, a little girl and a teenage son, Paul, Jr. Jo's seen them a dozen times, and they're still like strangers. Now this."

Ginger sighed elaborately. "It just isn't fair, poor girl. It's already complicated enough as it is. Look, a girl wants to be admired by and attractive to the opposite sex. That's only natural. But it's scary when all most men seem interested in is sex. Of course, it isn't helpful to generalize, and there are a lot of really nice fellows out there. I mean, *you* aren't interested *only* in sex, are you?"

His mouth fell open. "What?"

"I said—"

He knew what she'd said, he just couldn't quite believe she'd said it. "No!" he interrupted. "I mean, of course not."

"Good," Ginger said, turning back to the sink. "Not that sex isn't important."

"Oh, it *is*." He heard himself agreeing, and winced.

"But there's more to love than that, isn't there?" Ginger went on.

He had the feeling he'd stepped off into deep water when he'd only meant to go wading. "Ah, I..."

Ginger went on pointedly. "Real love," she said, "means a home and family and a whole life together, doesn't it?"

"Er..."

"Well, doesn't it?" She spun suddenly and smiled at him, blatantly provocative.

How had this conversation gotten so turned around? He took a deep breath. "Sometimes," he said carefully.

She nodded as if he'd agreed without the least reservation. "That's why I've decided to get married," she said, walking forward. She stopped in the very center of the room and put a hand to her hip, as if to emphasize her point. "For love," she concluded. "I've decided to get married for love."

He didn't know what to say to that. What did she expect him to say? And why were they talking about love—and sex? God, he wished she wouldn't look at him like that!

The simmering chicken soup had steamed the room, the aroma enticing, but it wasn't the smell of the soup that made his mouth suddenly water. It was what he could see of her behind that absurdly frilly pinafore apron—and what he couldn't see but could imagine all too well. She turned away again, displaying her neat, plump bottom at least partially encased in a blue, bandanna-print bikini. Below it were her shapely legs. Above it, the strings of her white apron were tied lightly at her waist, emphasizing her voluptuous curves. Then came the tiny band of her bikini bra, followed by the ruffled neckpiece of her apron. For some reason, the addition of her apron over her bikini made the outfit all the more fetching. He shook his head as if hoping to dislodge the picture and realized she was speaking.

"...Joan will one day, too, you know, and we have to prepare her for that, teach her to respect herself and to relate to men so she'll know when the right one comes along."

We? He blinked, having a hard time following. "Come again?"

She shot him a look over her shoulder. "I said, Joan will want to get married someday, too, and we have to prepare her for it."

Joan, married? His face must have clearly registered what he thought of that possibility, because Ginger set her mouth in a stern line.

"Well, she will."

Craig had the grace not to laugh, but he couldn't quite squelch a certain smile. His resistance suddenly hardened. "I think you may be projecting your own desires onto my little sister."

Ginger gave him a toss of the head. "Balderdash. Mind you, I'm not saying that every woman needs or even wants a man. Some women just aren't cut out to be wives. They're meant to be executives or scientists or great artists, completely consumed by their careers. Then again, many average women's lives are so satisfying that love is just the icing on the cake, but for me—and I think for Joan—love is the cake itself."

She sounded as if she expected an argument, and he was certainly willing to give her one. "But what about your talent?" he asked. "You paint. You decorate. I'm told you're a genius at calculus."

She shrugged and picked up a spoon to stir the soup. "I can cook, too," she said bluntly, trading the wooden spoon for a smaller metal one, "but all that's just the icing on *my* cake." She scooped up some of the steaming broth and carried it toward him, gently blowing on it. "Taste this."

It was a deliberately provocative gesture. He looked at her, then opened his mouth. She stuck the bowl of the spoon inside and tilted it. The broth was flavorful and almost sweet. "Mmm. Very good."

She didn't seem pleased. "It isn't quite finished yet."

"It does prove my point, though," he said. "You're a woman of great talent. Joan says you've even committed the full works of Shakespeare to memory!"

She frowned. "Hardly the full works," she said, leaning forward slightly.

Suddenly he realized how very close they were. If he just straightened, shifting his weight fully to his feet, they would almost touch. He did so, very carefully, noting how her head tilted back as she followed his ascent, so that her mouth was tilted up, her lips slightly parted. He could see the edges of her white teeth and the gentle swell of her rose pink tongue. Why the hell couldn't he just kiss her? *Because,* he told himself, *she wants you to.* The absurdity of it struck him. He wanted to kiss a woman who wanted to *be* kissed, but he didn't dare do it because kissing wasn't all she wanted. *You don't want only sex, do you?* asked a voice inside his head. *You don't want to get married, do you?* chided another. How much room was there in between? he wondered. She leaned into him then, the soft fullness of her breasts making contact with his chest. Electricity jolted him and he jerked back. Ginger frowned, her shoulders dropped and she turned away. *None,* he thought. *No room at all where Ginger Brenan is concerned.*

"Uh, I have to..." *Run like hell,* he thought, but he managed to say, "Go."

She lifted her head and put on a smile, sending it at him over her shoulder. "I'll bring over the soup as soon as it's finished."

He was already moving toward the door. "Great. Thanks."

"Don't mention it."

He stopped in the doorway, anxious to leave and reluctant at the same time. The desire to kiss her was still with him. Memories that were nothing but dreams filled him with a nostalgic yearning to which he had no right whatever, but then he didn't want such rights. Did he? That the answer didn't leap immediately to mind shook him, and she noticed, damn her.

"Craig? Is something wrong?"

He balled his hands into fists. "No, I was just..." Sudden inspiration put words into his mouth. "I don't, ah, want you to worry about Maggie. She's unpleasant while she's around, but she never stays long."

Ginger's smile was weak, even sad. "That's good to know."

"And I'm sorry about what happened," he went on. "She had no right."

Ginger shook her head. "Forget it. Just concentrate on Joan right now."

"All right."

Craig hesitated a moment longer, resisting the urge to reach out to her, then said goodbye and walked out. Did she have to be so blasted disappointed? What did she expect after announcing that she was looking for a husband and considering him a likely candidate? Did she think she was so damned luscious she could make him forget? Well, she wasn't. Just luscious enough to be driving him crazy, luscious enough to have him dreaming about her.

He put a hand to his head as he walked across her yard and up his own drive. Why couldn't she be just what Maggie said she was? It was easy to reject a tramp as a wife, even while enjoying her favors, but a woman like Ginger . . . She wasn't just luscious, she was talented in a number of ways, caring, generous, domestic in a uniquely offbeat manner, good with kids, if Joan was a proper example. She would be, frankly, a wife of whom any man could be proud, provided the man wanted a wife, which left *him* out. And for good reason.

Mentally he ticked off all the reasons. Top of the list, Jo had to come first with him right now. Second, he was much too wrapped up in business to be a decent husband. He had to be; so many people depended on him for their livelihoods, not to mention Paul, his partner. Third, he was too old for a first marriage. At thirty-six he was much too set in his ways to adjust to the intimacy of marriage.

On the other hand, maybe it didn't have anything to do with age. Maybe it was something fundamental about him. Deep down, he'd always felt that there was something unnatural about marriage as it was practiced in the twentieth century. Men just weren't the docile creatures marriage demanded them to be. How could an animal as basically selfish as the human male be expected to sense, protect and maintain the delicate feelings of a spouse? Maybe some men could do it and do it happily, but he had always suspected that he was not one of them. And yet, there was no denying the basic attraction between the sexes. The act of a vengeful god? he wondered. Or merely nature's way of propagating the species? And that was another reason why he should not get married. If he couldn't be responsible for the emotional well-being of another adult, how on earth could he be responsible for that of an infant?

No, the whole ideal of marriage seemed unrealistic to him, and he suspected a great deal of the male population agreed with him. Certainly he'd met—and enjoyed—his share of attractive, sexy, talented, sweet women without finding marriage necessary. Moreover, he had reason to believe those women had enjoyed him, as well. That seemed proof positive that marriage was necessary for the rearing of children and little, if anything, else, but most especially not for the sexes to get together and do what truly came naturally. Now if only Ginger could be made to see that, his problems might be solved. Or would they? *You don't want only sex, do you?*

It seemed he had come full circle, and suddenly he was exhausted. Pushing away these troublesome thoughts, he let himself into the house and went to his sister's bedroom. She was alone, sitting in the room's only comfortable chair before the window overlooking the lake. Maggie, mercifully, had disappeared for the moment. He knocked on the wall to let Joan know he was around. She turned a slightly blotched face to him, but he was relieved to note that her eyes were dry.

"Maggie said you went next door."

He nodded. "I thought I'd better talk to Ginger about what happened."

His sister's anxiety over the episode was demonstrated in the manner in which she grasped the upholstered arms of the chair and leaned slightly forward, every muscle seeming to go tense. "What did she say?" Jo asked. "Is she all right? She doesn't hate me, does she?"

He smiled in reassurance and walked across the room to lay a hand upon the top of her head. "Of course not. In fact, she's making us a special supper. She called France for a recipe for chicken soup because she thought it might make you feel better."

Jo's eyes got round and big. "All the way to France?"

"All the way to France," he echoed. Her smile, though tentative and weak, warmed him thoroughly.

"Thanks, Craig," she whispered.

He went down on his haunches and put his arms around her. She laid her head on his shoulder. This, he thought, as her smile widened appreciatively, was something he was glad he started doing more often. Sometimes, he mused, the smallest things seemed to make the biggest differences. Like hugs—and chicken soup. Whatever their personal conflicts, he wished suddenly that he and Ginger Brenan could work in concert on one matter. As Ginger had said, his sister needed all the support she could get. He just couldn't help wondering if the rest of it wasn't going to get in the way at some point. The attraction was too strong between him and Ginger. Even if she could be shaken free of this idiotic notion of marriage, he couldn't just carry on an affair right under his sister's nose. No, he had to keep his distance from Ginger Brenan somehow. It was the only way.

Chapter Eight

Craig opened the door and Ginger swept in, arms laden with a red lacquer tray upon which sat matching service pieces and a crock filled with incredibly fragrant chicken soup. She had donned white, knee-length spandex leggings and an oversize T-shirt of shocking pink. On her feet were skimpy wedge sandals sprouting pink flowers on the toes. Her hair, held back from her clean face by a white flowered headband, cascaded past her shoulders in a sleek golden fall of which she was inordinately proud. Relieved to have seen Maggie's car pull away from the curb a few minutes earlier, Ginger had plucked up her courage and decided to assault Craig's seeming indifference head-on. She had even added earrings to her ensemble, big white daisies with pink centers. She hoped Craig wouldn't mind too much her inviting herself to join them for dinner, but they could all use a festive evening after the incident that afternoon, and Joan had to know that Ginger hadn't let that old dragon upset her. She considered it imperative that she appear unruffled and happy after that awful scene. How else was Joan to see that she must not let the Maggies of the world get to her?

As for Craig, he mustn't get the idea that she was abandoning their so-called friendship. It was her only real link to him. She didn't think of Joan in that context. She would have befriended Joan even if Craig wasn't her brother, though any man who would have taken on a teenage sister under similar circumstances was worth consideration. Aside from that, however, Craig was only wildly attractive, and she didn't think the attraction was all one-sided, either, even if he hadn't kissed her just now—unless, that was, something had changed since the evening of the campout. The attraction between them that night had been electric, alive, like lightning that crackled and danced around them, and sooner or later that lightning was going to strike—unless Craig had lost interest. She bit her lip, then forced away the doubts with a smile. It was just a matter of time, and tonight was as good a time as any.

"How's Joannie?" she asked, carrying her burden toward the kitchen.

"All right, I think, though she says she'll die if she has to face the Petrie brothers again."

Ginger grimaced, depositing her load on the countertop. "I don't think she'll have to worry about that for now. By the way they whipsawed across the lake earlier, I'd say Marc and Heath aren't too keen on renewing the acquaintance just yet. It's a real pity, too. Those boys liked her, Marc especially." She sighed and lifted her shoulders in a what-can-you-do shrug, then turned to the more-immediate matter of dinner. "Where do you want to eat, in the kitchen or the dining room?"

Craig was loitering around the door as if reluctant to get too near her. A good sign, she hoped. He shrugged now and edged closer.

"The kitchen will do, but you've done enough. Don't bother yourself about serving. We can manage fine."

Obviously, he didn't mean for her to stay. Well, maybe he'd change his mind, and if he didn't, she could always retreat gracefully. She'd just set the table, see Joan and let the evening take its course. She made herself smile and started setting the red lacquered plates and bowls on the table, along with black napkins and a small basket of warm whole-wheat rolls. "I don't mind," she said. "I rather like doing this sort of thing. But you can help if you want."

"A-all right. I'll get some glasses and, er, utensils."

She nodded, then went in search of salt- and pepper shakers. She had them both in hand and was on her way back to the table when the unmistakable sound of the front door opening halted her in her tracks. The sound of heavy footsteps followed. Ginger looked to Craig, whose face was set stiffly. Then Maggie entered, a small paper bag riding in the fold of one arm. Ginger's spirits took a nosedive.

Maggie's glower was no less disapproving than it had been before, and every bit as haughty. Ginger felt her hackles rise defensively but put on a serene face, striving for calm.

"I—I didn't realize you still had company," Ginger said quietly to Craig. He was frowning at Maggie.

"Well, umm, Maggie probably won't be staying long," he said pointedly. "She doesn't like to be on the street at night. Do you, Maggie?"

"I do what's necessary, Craig," the woman came back sharply. "You know that better than anyone."

"Yes, but we wouldn't want to keep you when there's no need."

"I see great need," Maggie came back, drawing herself up. "And it seems to me that for your sister's sake, if not your own—"

"And it seems to me," Craig interrupted, his voice low but steely, "I've made it very clear that since Jo is *my* responsibility now, your comments are unwelcome. I'll thank you to keep them to yourself."

Maggie turned six shades of purple and drew herself all the tighter, her nose aimed at the ceiling. "I suppose that means *I* am unwelcome, as well!"

Ginger hoped with all her heart that Craig would tell the old biddy she was correct for once, but he didn't. Instead he softened noticeably.

"Of course you're welcome, Maggie. We're family, after all."

Somewhat mollified, the old girl slid over to the table, sniffing at the setting. "Somebody sure wasted a lot of time here," she said baldly. "Like I said before, if it's chicken soup you're wanting, you can get it out of a can." With that, she drew proof from the sack in her hand and plunked it down on the tabletop.

Ginger recoiled in horror. The very idea that anything out of a can could compare with her own culinary masterpiece was absurd, but Maggie honestly seemed to believe such was the case. Ginger thought briefly of arguing the point but decided against it. Nothing could be gained from arguing with the likes of Maggie. It was Craig who could best cow his aunt. So Ginger said nothing, looking to Craig for defense. He sent her a guilty look that skittered away to nowhere. Her heart sank.

Maggie squared her heavy shoulders smugly. "Well, if there's to be four of us for dinner, I can heat the canned stuff for myself. Or," she continued shrewdly, "we could just add it to the other."

Ginger's hand flew to her chest. Surely Craig would speak now. Surely he would not allow Maggie to adulterate the special dish she'd prepared with such love and concern. But Craig said nothing. Neither would he meet her gaze. She knew then that he would not put Maggie in her place, simply because the old crow made such an excellent buffer between the two of them. Obviously, this was Craig's way of keeping her at a safe distance—or he just didn't like her. Ginger felt a thickening in her throat, the beginning of tears. She managed to be gracious, nevertheless, knowing that to be anything less would justify Maggie's opinion of her.

"Please," she said to Maggie, hating the way her voice trembled, "don't concern yourself. I'm not going to stay. I'm . . . not very hungry anyway. I'll go and let the three of you enjoy your dinner."

Craig looked away from her and it felt like a physical blow. He really didn't care. Maggie, on the other hand, seemed smugly pleased. She lifted an eyebrow imperiously and looked down her nose at the floor.

"Very sensible of you," she muttered.

Sensible, Ginger thought, *but it's a little late for that now.* She put her head down to shield the hurt and resentment she knew must be spilling over onto her face and started toward the entry, only to be halted by Joan's soft voice.

"Don't go."

Ginger froze, despairing that the girl should appear now. Quickly she rearranged her expression and turned back, a smile at the ready.

"Joan, darling," she said, moving across the room to put her arms about the slight shoulders. "How are you feeling?"

"All right."

"Oh, good. I'm so glad."

"Will you stay?" Joan asked, not to be put off.

Ginger shook her head, reinforcing her smile. "No, darling, I really shouldn't. You need to eat your dinner and...I—I have so much to do." She hugged the girl to her, hoping she lied better than she sensed she did. "But don't worry," she went on brightly. "I'll look in on you tomorrow, and in the meantime if you should need me... But, of course, you won't. Craig is here." She could not bring herself to add Maggie's name to his.

Joan nodded resignedly, and Ginger kissed her on the cheek before hurrying once more toward the entry. She paused in the doorway, her gaze going involuntarily to Craig. He shifted uncomfortably and she looked away, wishing with all her heart that she hadn't barged in where she wasn't wanted. Well, not completely. Joan wanted her. That was something. It was, in fact, quite a lot. With a last smile for Joan, she left them, escaping just as the tears started to fall down her cheeks.

Maggie's narrowed eyes stayed trained on the empty doorway for several moments, as if she expected Ginger to sneak back in the instant she let down her guard. At last, satisfied the woman would not return, Maggie dragged out a chair and sat down at the table.

"Well?" she said, that single word a demand that the others join her.

Craig itched to throw her out of his house and tell her not to come back, but since he'd allowed her abominable behavior toward Ginger, he didn't feel that he had the right to take offense at her high-handedness now. But it was for the best, or so he told himself. Glumly, he pulled out a chair for Joan and then another for himself. Maggie served, and in silence they first tasted, then ate the delicious soup. Somehow, though, Craig could not enjoy the dish. His palate recognized and appreciated the quality of the stuff he poured over it, but somehow the enjoyment did not translate to his brain. In point of fact, he felt downright miserable, and it angered him that Ginger could affect him so. He was right to put distance between them. It would be best for everyone.

"Best," Craig muttered, aware he'd spoken aloud only when he sensed the sudden stillness around him. He glanced up, catching both Maggie and Joan with their spoons poised in the air. He felt his face flush. "Mmm, good soup," he said with false enthusiasm.

Maggie's spoon resumed its ascent, but Joan's descended to the bowl once more.

"Ginger's a good cook," the girl said pointedly. "Isn't she, Craig?" He nodded. No doubt about it. The girl went on. "She's such a good cook that she even writes cookbooks for a living, doesn't she?"

He nodded again, then sent her a look that he hoped would silence her, but Jo seemed determined to ignore his displeasure for once. A truly dogged expression came over her face, and she folded her arms on the tabletop, slanting an almost malicious glance at Maggie.

"She's a good decorator, too," Jo announced. "She decorated my room, didn't she, Craig?"

He put down his spoon and wiped his fingertips on the napkin in his lap, wondering what the scamp was up to. If he hadn't known her better, he'd have thought she was trying to start an argument! As it was, he could only wonder. "She decorated your room," he said slowly, "and the living room, as well."

Jo smiled at him. "And that's not all," she went on, directing herself to Maggie. "She even painted that picture in there, the one with the brick wall and the tree. She painted it just for us, didn't she, Craig?"

"She did," he answered softly, astounded at Jo's spirited defense of her friend. What was happening here? Where was the timid little sister he had always known? Had Ginger Brenan wrought this dubious miracle, turned timidity into combativeness? It occurred to him that he might be finding fault where none existed, but he rejected that notion.

"Well, she's nearly a genius," Joan declared. "She's even taught school, and she's got a green thumb, a natural-born gardener. Oh, and she plays the guitar, sings, too."

"The point?" Craig asked testily, seeing that the conversation was getting to Maggie, too.

"The point," Jo said, "is that Ginger's wonderful. She's not at all like Maggie says."

Maggie's spoon clattered against her plate. As usual she went right for the jugular—Craig's, to be specific.

"How can you let her defend, even admire that . . . that . . . *woman?*" she demanded. "I don't care if she cooks like Julia Child and paints like Rembrandt, she's a calculating hussy, and anybody with any moral foundation whatsoever can tell it!"

"She is not!" Jo was shouting, their words overlapping, so that Maggie, too, raised her voice at the end just to be heard.

"All right, calm down, both of you!" Craig shouted, gratified somewhat when Jo at least lapsed into sullen silence. Maggie, however, was another matter.

"Wayne Craig Russell," the imperious woman stated flatly, "if you're any kind of a brother at all, you'll ban that woman from this house and forbid her to even speak to this child!"

"Oh, for Pete's sake, Maggie," Craig said, but the flow of his aunt's words didn't even slow.

"I just hope it's not too late," she opined. "The damage could well be done already."

"Holy cow," Craig began, but suddenly Jo leapt to her feet, her chair scraping back from the table.

"I won't stop seeing Ginger!" she yelled. "She's my friend."

"Ridiculous," Maggie said with a sniff.

"Don't you understand?" Jo cried. "Ginger makes me feel good about myself. It's so easy to be with her! She's so much fun! And she listens to me. She *really* listens. She *likes* me!" Joan declared, as if surprised that it was so. "She likes both of us, Craig *and* me. She's more than just a neighbor, she's..." Words finally seemed to fail her. Casting desperate looks at both Maggie and Craig, she balled her hands into fists, her face contorted into a visible plea. "I *need* Ginger," she whispered, collapsing once more onto her chair.

Craig was shaken, more disturbed by that last statement than anything else he'd heard all evening. Was he wrong to have allowed Ginger such leeway with his sister? Was there harm in this dependence? The proof seemed to be sitting there in front of him.

"Well...?" Maggie said, arching one eyebrow.

He didn't know quite what to say. "Look, Maggie," he began, "Jo needs a little companionship. She's shy. She doesn't make friends easily, and Ginger's been, well, thoughtful. She's gone out of her way to make us feel welcome. She's..."

"Thoughtful?" Maggie supplied. "Thoughtful enough to convince your sister that she's indispensable." Her eyes narrowed shrewdly. "Thoughtfulness?" she asked. "Or manipulation?"

Craig opened his mouth, but nothing came out. How could he refute Maggie when he'd wondered the same thing himself? Even if she didn't mean to use Jo to get to him, not even Ginger herself could deny that spending time with Jo was a surefire way to at least encounter him and more. Witness what had happened today, for starters.

Craig's thoughts must have shown on his face, for Maggie smiled knowingly. "It's obvious," she said, "that you're the real target of Ginger Brenan's attention. She's infatuated with you." She paused long enough to slant a shrewd look at Jo before going on. "And she's undoubtedly using your sister to get close to you."

Joan's face twisted and crumpled into tears. "That's not true!" she exclaimed. "Is it, Craig?"

What was he to say? He could defend Ginger to Jo, but that would only serve to maintain the status quo, and he wasn't so sure now that this would be best for Joan, not to mention himself. But not defending Ginger was sure to hurt Jo. How could he let *that* happen? Why hadn't he foreseen this? It was bound to come to this sooner or later, unless Ginger changed her mind about him as a potential candidate for marriage, and how likely was that, given Ginger Brenan's personality? Not very, unless he missed his guess. But that still didn't tell him what to say.

Without words, he clamped his jaw grimly and lifted his gaze to his sister's pale, anguished face. It was enough. Her eyes flickered, then she gasped, her hands going to her cheeks. Regret washed over him. The lie sprang into his mouth, anything to comfort her. But Joan abruptly launched out of her chair and fled down the hallway to her room, the slamming of the door cutting off the sounds of her sobs. It was like a blow to the heart for Craig, and yet in some part of his mind that small voice was saying that it was probably for the best, all things considered.

Maggie, predictably, was pleased and being very smug about it. She calmly resumed eating her soup. Craig's anger spilled over.

"It doesn't bother you one bit to see that kid torn up, does it?" he accused bitterly. Maggie looked shocked.

"It's not *my* fault Joan's upset. If anyone should be upset, it's that woman next-door. She's the one to blame for this, and if you've any sense at all, you'll keep her away from that child before she does her real harm."

Oh, he wanted to blame Ginger. If only Ginger had not declared herself so openly, he and Jo would at least have the illusion of her friendship. But no, that would make her like other women. Normal females played hard to get. Not Ginger. Oh, no, not that one. But he couldn't really condemn her for her honesty, and he did believe she cared for the girl. Nevertheless, some of the attention she showered on Joan just didn't make sense. Ginger was much too young to feel motherly toward Joan and much too old to feel like her contemporary, and a good deal of what she did for Jo brought her into contact with him. The implications were inescapable, and considering how she affected him physically and Jo emotionally, maybe it would be best if he kept Ginger away from both of them.

"All right, Maggie," he said, "you've made your point. I'm chastened, and Jo is properly disillusioned. You can now withdraw your long nose from my business and take it home."

"Honestly, Craig!" his aunt admonished. "I should think you'd be glad to benefit from my long experience."

"Your long experience at what, Maggie? Hurting people?"

She stiffened and dropped her spoon. "Wayne Craig Russell," she said, "if you weren't my own sister's boy, I'd march out that door and never come back. As it is, I'm simply going to leave you to think about your rudeness and ingratitude." With that, she got up, snatched her purse and stomped away. An instant later, she was back. "Forgot my can of soup," she announced. Then, paper bag in hand, she repeated her exit.

Craig might have laughed. As if he wanted canned chicken soup, as if he did not have in front of him right now the finest homemade soup ever to grace a bowl, the French version, of course, not another bite of which he could possibly touch. He lifted his hands to his face briefly, then got up and walked away, cursing women everywhere, but one in particular, one very attractive, very unique, very exasperating, very dangerous woman.

* * *

She would not be turned away, Ginger told herself, breathing deeply. She would be pleasant but firm, concerned but insistent, and after she got her foot in the door, she would make an opportunity to speak candidly with Craig. Why was he doing this to her? Why suddenly was she persona non grata? Even Joan was ignoring her, and that hurt most of all. But today she was going to get to the bottom of it, pleasantly, firmly, with much concern and more insistence—if she just didn't lose her courage. She lifted her chin and shook out her hair, feeling it swing between her shoulder blades. Quickly she shifted the weight of the basket of flowers in her arms, then reached out a slim forefinger and punched the doorbell several times in rapid order. After some moments, she heard the door handle being manipulated. She put on her brightest smile, getting it in place just as the door swung back.

"Craig."

"Ginger."

"I, umm, brought you some fresh flowers."

"So I see."

"I thought you might set some on the kitchen table and in the dining room, the living room, of course, and maybe even in Joan's—"

"Jo isn't here," he cut in flatly. "She's spending the day with a friend from school."

A friend from school? This was news; to her knowledge, Joan had no friends—except her. She cocked her head.

"That's good. That's wonderful! But I'm sorry I'll miss seeing her—again. Oh, well, as long as she's happy."

Craig nodded and reached for the basket. "Well, thanks," he said. "These are really nice. I'll take your suggestion and spread them around."

Ginger smiled and jumped into the fray boldly. "I'd better help you with that. I haven't met a man yet who could manage a decent flower arrangement."

"Well, you have now," Craig parried confidently. "Besides, I wouldn't dream of inconveniencing you."

"Oh, it's no inconvenience," she assured him, but he was shaking his head adamantly.

"No way. You've done quite enough. I insist you go right on and tend to your own business."

"But—"

"And have a good day," he said pleasantly, backing out of the doorway. "Oh, and I'll return your basket."

"All right," she said slowly. "Thank you."

"Thank *you.*"

He closed the door. She stood there for a few seconds, dealing with her disappointment, yearning to be with him. *Face it,* she told herself, *he doesn't want you around.* But what about Joannie? She knew Joan liked her, wanted her around, even *needed* her, and Craig had to know it, too, if he was honest with himself. And if he wasn't, well, she'd just have to see that he was. When he returned the basket, she would be most charming. She'd invite him in, making it clear that she wanted to discuss Joan. How could he deny her that? She had a right to know what the problem was, didn't she? Things had been going so well with her and Joannie. The girl had actually been loosening up. What had happened? Was it the Petrie boys? Something Maggie had said? Had she herself done something of which she wasn't even aware? Ginger bit her lip and clenched her fists. If so, then she had to make it right. Joan deserved better, *needed* better. Slowly, she turned and walked back to her own house.

The next morning, she found the flower basket on her doorstep. Dismayed, Ginger brought the basket inside and cried over it. Wasn't she allowed even to know what had happened to their friendship? Okay, it was no mystery where Craig was concerned. Once again she'd come on too strong and blown it. But what about Joan? They really were friends. Weren't they? She tried to resign herself to simply not knowing what had gone wrong, but somehow she just couldn't leave it alone. So it was with relief that bordered on relish that she found a flat tire on her car early one morning a few days later.

Craig wouldn't turn his back on a plea for help, would he? She was about to find out. Hurrying inside, she dialed the Russells' telephone number. Craig answered and, when she explained the problem, agreed to come right over. He came out the door wearing jeans and pulling a T-shirt over his head, the muscles of his chest bunching and gliding beneath his tanned skin. Ginger had quickly changed into a denim miniskirt and a simple cropped top made of white eyelet with a bright yellow bandeau beneath. She wore yellow canvas slip-ons over bare feet and left her hair down, a yellow barrette holding it back from her face on one side. If Craig even noticed, he gave no sign, but she refused to be discouraged.

While he made quick work of changing the flat tire, she kept up a steady stream of chatter. He answered her questions with as few words as possible. Joan was "fine." He was "busy." Business was "okay." He loaded the flat into her trunk and suggested she drop it off to be repaired as soon as possible. She'd be without a spare until she did. She insinuated that she didn't know where to take it, but he didn't offer to take care of it for her. Instead, he gave her the name and address of a service station he'd used for just such repairs. She thanked him and invited him inside for a cup of coffee, but he was already walking back toward his house.

"No time," he called. "Got a busy day."

"Please," she called after him. "I need to talk to you about—"

"Sorry." He waved and kept walking. Once he was back inside his own house, Ginger kicked the replacement tire in frustration. She bit back the yowl of pain that accompanied this silly act and limped around the remainder of the day. She grew a dark blue bruise on the top of her big toe and a mood to match, but what else could she do?

Over the next week, she watched and wondered, but kept her distance. Most afternoons Joan didn't even come home until Craig did, but about the middle of the second week, they began slipping back into the old routine. Joan came home alone on the school bus and trudged up the drive like some defeated automaton. It took all of Ginger's will-power not to run to her and throw her arms about the girl, but she sensed that this would be the wrong thing to do. Instead, she managed to be outside on the front lawn and kept her limited conversation light and bright.

"How pretty you look today," she'd say, and Joan would put her head down and mumble something about her hair or clothes before escaping into the house.

If Ginger invited her over, the girl would say she had too much homework. It was invariably homework with which she needed no help. Once Ginger asked her to come over and try a new recipe she was testing, but Joan declined, saying she had snacked on the way home on the bus and was just too stuffed to eat another bite. When Ginger wanted to swim, Joan wanted a nap. She no longer cared for guitar music or long walks or feeding the ducks. The girl had no interest in shopping or painting or anything else. It was very much as if she had no interest in living—and no interest in Ginger. More than once the situation moved Ginger to tears, but she was careful not to let the girl know. It wasn't the kid's fault, after all. Somehow Ginger was certain that Craig was behind this new aloofness, and she wasn't about to let him get away with it, provided he would give her a chance to speak to him.

Angry now, she began a campaign. Any excuse she could dream up was reason enough to contact the Russells. A frayed telephone cord that she had been meaning to replace for months came in handy. She described the problem for Craig, but he insisted that there was no point in actually taking a look at it. He knew what to do. The next day she found the proper replacement cord hanging on her door-knob, with written instructions about hooking it up to the phone. An idiot could have done it. When she went over to reimburse him for the purchase of the new cord, he calmly named the price and took her money, then sent her away, saying he had brought work home. Defeated, she had no choice except to go, but there would be other opportunities. She was going to make them.

She used everything she could think of. She carted over paintings for "objective opinions," saying she was thinking about trying another show. She got the first critique on the doorstep. He liked it, but not as much as the seascape or the one hanging in his living room. It lacked the "intent" of the others, not that he was an expert by any means. All he could tell her was what he liked personally. She was pleased, even though she didn't get inside the house, but then he crushed her, excusing himself by saying that he had a date and he had to go or he'd be late. She went home and threw things, but before long, she had convinced herself it didn't matter. They were neighbors. If nothing else, they could—should—be friends. She would go right on as if nothing had happened, taking advantage of the opportunities presented her, and soon he would see that she could add something to his and Joan's lives.

Before long she caught him on the deck one morning. She hauled out a four-year-old effort with which she had never been pleased and trotted over with it.

He took a long look at it, shook his head and made his pronouncement. "I don't care for it," he said bluntly. "It's almost amateurish compared to the others. I wouldn't include this one. Of course, I'm no—"

"Expert," she said. "Yes, I know, but you have a good eye, and I value your opinion."

He smiled. "Glad to be of service. Now if you'll excuse me..."

"You have to go to work," she said. "I understand. Thank you."

For a moment his smile took on a wistful quality and she held her breath, hoping he would ask her to stay for a few more minutes anyway. But then the moment passed. Briskly, he bid her goodbye, picked up his paper and went inside. She tamped down her sense of despair, took her painting and went home.

That very afternoon she baked up a batch of bread and took a loaf over to the Russells'. It was Joan who answered the door this time. Craig, it seemed, was in the shower. The girl was completely flustered. She took the still-warm loaf, but only after Ginger insisted. Ginger didn't want to press her, but Joan lingered for a moment, seemingly trying to decide if she should say what was on her mind or not. Ginger hugged her, unable to resist the urge this time, and hurried away, but not before she saw the tears glistening in the girl's eyes. Any doubts she might have had were banished. Joan needed her. Craig was obviously another matter, but Joan desperately needed a friend and companion, and come hell or high water, Ginger meant to see that she had one.

Chapter Nine

Never before had Ginger been at such a loss. Day after day she watched Joan watch her with longing eyes, only to turn away and flee the instant Ginger made the slightest overture. She was sick at heart and angry with everyone, including herself. What had she done to cause that haunted, regretful look on Joan's delicate face? How could she have been so insensitive to hurt that girl and not even know how it had happened? Was it something she had said to the Petries? To Craig? To Maggie? She went over and over it in her head and could settle on nothing that would make Joan shy away from her at this point in the relationship.

Craig seemed the only avenue open to her. At least, she could approach him, but that was as far as she could get. The moment she broached the subject of Joan or anything else remotely personal, he deftly extricated himself from contact and left her standing with her mouth open in midword.

It was the most frustrating experience she had ever endured, and for the first time in a long time, she could not

even sleep nights, and she wandered around days grumpy
and confused. She lived with a deep, abiding, defeating
sense of rejection, and telling herself that it was foolish to
feel that way helped not at all. It was no wonder, then, that
things began to slip. She wasn't working, wasn't painting,
wasn't accomplishing anything. The majority of her time
she spent lying on the beach in a kind of lethargy. Then one
afternoon she drifted off into an uneasy sleep, waking hours
later with a nasty sunburn.

She cried, sitting before her mirror with her back turned,
neck craned to look over her shoulder. The fall of her hair
had shielded the back of her neck from the punishing rays,
but the slightest stretching of the skin below was agonizing.
She could not even lift her arms without suffering greatly.
She had to have help, and she was in no mood to fence about
it.

She called her brother, Will, who attended a nearby college, but was not surprised when he failed to answer the
phone. After all, he was a very busy twenty-year-old with
erratic hours and a whirlwind social life. She didn't even
leave a message on his machine. She needed someone to help
her find relief right away. Other names came to mind and
were as quickly dismissed. She had friends, a great number
of them, but most had families that required their attention, or else they were single and on the fast track both in
their careers and social lives. Quite a number of them were
unattached men whose attentions, for one reason or another, she did not wish to encourage with so intimate an exercise as tending her scorched skin. In fact, she wished to
encourage only one man in such a fashion, and when he
lived so close to hand, it seemed ludicrous in the extreme not
to go to him. Suffused with fresh anger, in pain and filled
with longing, she determined her course.

Doggedly, grimly, she got up off the stool before her
dressing table, snatched the aerosol can of medication from
the corner of the marble tabletop and marched from the
room, shoulders and spine stiff. It was that hour when the
sun had dropped below the horizon and the light gradually
waned into the soft darkness that preceded the heavy black

of true night. It was then that lights blinked on and people moved out onto their lawns and decks to bask in the Florida climate at its most gentle. Unless she missed her guess, Craig would be no exception. She went out the back door, across the deck, down onto the white sand and around the end of the hedge that served as a privacy fence between the two properties. There he sat, a glass in his hand, staring out over the deep blue mirror of the lake's surface.

"Craig Russell!" she called out, giving him no opportunity to flee and pretend that he hadn't noticed her. She caught the scowl that momentarily twisted his face, but dismissed it, the pain it caused overshadowed by the sheer physical agony of merely walking, an agony that increased markedly when she lifted and bent her legs to negotiate the steps of his deck.

"Ginger," he said at her approach, "what on earth is wrong with you?"

"I fell asleep on the beach," she told him petulantly, then thrust the aerosol can at him, turned her back, swept her hair over her shoulder, and commanded him to, "Spray!"

He came to his feet. "Good grief! Is that a sunburn or did you actually set yourself on fire?"

"I told you I fell asleep on the beach. My whole backside is cooked, but this stuff is supposed to help, only I can't reach around there to put it on. If I could, I wouldn't be bothering you, but don't worry, it won't take long. Now just point the damned can and spray."

"You should have used sunscreen," he told her after a pause, and she heard the cap of the can pop as he pulled it away.

"I did," she said through her teeth, bracing for the first blast.

"That must have been some nap then," he came back. "Here we go."

The icy spray against her heated skin made her jerk and erupt in gooseflesh, but she gritted her teeth and stood her ground. He paused from time to time to shake the can and reposition, then resumed until she was covered with the oily, freezing, soothing spray from shoulders to heels. For several seconds she merely stood and reveled in the lessening of pain, then slowly she became aware of a problem in the center of her back. The band of her bikini bra felt as though it was tearing her skin to shreds. She realized suddenly that any effort on her part to free it would be devastating, even in light of the temporary relief she was feeling at the moment. She bit her lip, knowing she had to ask and in no mood to deal with a refusal.

"Listen," she said, wishing that she could see his face. "Don't take it personally, but if you could just unhook my top, I'd appreciate it." She waited impatiently, forearms folding up to hold the bra against her chest so it wouldn't fall off when he freed the hook. The straps bit into the tops of her arms, the backs of which were burnt, but that pressure, too, would be eased when he did what she asked—*if* he did what she asked. "Come on, Craig," she said testily. "It hurts like the dickens."

Nothing.

Suddenly she knew he wasn't going to do it, and just the idea that he couldn't bring himself to touch her even to help was more than she could bear. To her own chagrin, she burst into tears, but she'd be hanged if she'd stand there in front of him and sob out her humiliation. As quickly as she could manage, she got out of there, forgetting the medication in her painful haste. She didn't realize Craig was following her until, just as she'd reached her own deck, his hand fell on her shoulder. Crying out, she dipped and spun away.

"Don't touch me! You can't bear it, and neither can I! I'd rather this blasted thing cut me to shreds than have you...oh!" She spun away again, fresh tears washing from her eyes, and hurried awkwardly up onto the deck, across it and into the house.

She didn't stop until she was in her bedroom, where she hung her head and quietly cried, hurting inside and out. The faint squeak of hinges alerted her when he entered the house. Then came the sounds of slow footsteps on marble. Quickly, she grabbed a handful of tissues and dabbed at her eyes and nose. She was still doing so when he stepped through the opened doors of her bedroom, the thick carpet

abruptly silencing his movements. She stood before the
dressing table, her back to him, and felt the heat of his body
through her sensitized skin as he stepped close.

He reached past her and set the spray can of medicine on
the corner of the table. "Here," he said, "let me help you
with this." He began to work the hook free. His touch was
gentle, but still she flinched, having all she could do to hold
still and get her arms back up to her chest while he loosened the band of her bikini bra.

"Thank you," she muttered, but bitterness drove her to
add, "I know how appalling you find contact with me." To
her own surprise, she began sobbing again.

A sigh, and then a hand stroked her hair, once. He said
softly, "That's not true."

No? How badly she wanted to believe him! But how could
she? She swallowed back the sobs and turned to face him.
"Then what is it? What have I done? Why have you locked
me out?"

He grimaced, clearly regretting that the subject had been
broached. "Ginger . . . it's so complicated. . . ."

"I need to understand! Joan's so special to me. I thought
we were friends. I even thought you and I were becoming
friends! What's so awful about me now that you can't even
bring yourself to touch me?"

He stared at her as she bowed her head and swiped at the
tears, and when she lifted her gaze to his again, she saw ca-
pitulation there and something else, something that made
her go still inside and out. He brought his hands to his hips,
head shaking. "Can't bring myself to touch you?" he said.
Then he stepped close and reached out with both hands to
cup her face. "Little fool," he whispered. "It's because I
can't stop myself!" And for proof, he brought his mouth
down on hers.

At first she was too stunned, too utterly stymied, to respond, but after the initial, bruising contact, his lips softened, the kiss deepened, and unexpected pleasure banished
both pain and sorrow. She could scarcely believe this was
happening. Instinctively, she lowered her arms and slipped
them around him, amazed to find him real and solid and

warm. Then she jumped as the bathing-suit top fell at their feet. With a low groan, he pressed closer, one hand moving to skim the side of her breast, the other sliding to the back of her head as his mouth plied hers and bemusement gave way to joy. Sensation was suddenly heightened. Heat radiated from his hands, and the fabric of his shirt felt almost unbearably soft and smooth next to her skin, so that when he moved against her, twisting slightly, the delicate friction hardened her nipples and made them throb. He then slid his mouth over her chin and down her neck, drawing away so his hands could fully cup her breasts.

Her head fell back, and the skin on her shoulders pulled angrily, but she ignored it as his mouth, hot, moist and electrifying, burned a path to one hardened nipple and took possession. She gasped. Pleasure rocketed through the core of her body, erupting at the vertex of her thighs, wet and slick, like molten wax. Her hands found their way over the arch of his back and shoulders to burrow into his hair. Not even the sharpening of sensation in her damaged skin could diminish the pulsing wave of rapture. Then without warning, raw, wild need knifed upward through her and her knees began to buckle. It was then that his arms came around her. She cried out, pain surpassing everything else. Abruptly, he released her, straightening.

"I hurt you! God, I'm sorry. I never..." The words died in his mouth as slowly he looked her up and down. She stood nearly naked before him, one arm folded across her chest. His dark eyes flashed first with hunger and then... Panic?

Her mouth fell open. He was scared of her! He was afraid of his own desire, *terrified* of falling in love with a woman who had unequivocally stated a desire to marry. The fool! As if the coming together of man and woman in earnest commitment was not the most natural compulsion in human nature. Were all men such emotional cowards?

He bent to snatch up her bathing-suit top and thrust it at her. "You needed a reason," he said. "There's the reason I keep you at arm's length! Now cover yourself and don't come near me again! I don't want to hurt you, Ginger, but that's what will happen if we go on playing these games.''

"What games?" she began.

"Damn it!" he erupted. "Don't you get it? I'm ready to drag you into that bed, sunburn and all, right now, and let you figure out later that I'm just not the marrying kind!"

"Every man's the marrying kind," she retorted, "when he finds the right woman."

"Don't flatter yourself!" he shouted angrily.

"I don't!"

"Then you'll stay away!"

"If you really wanted me to," she argued. "But you don't! You proved it just now."

"It serves your purpose to believe that!" he accused, but she wouldn't buy it, couldn't, not with the memory of his passionate-tender touch still warming her.

She looked him straight in the eye, and said it as gently as she could. "You kissed me this time."

For a moment he looked as if he could have strangled her, and then he looked purely miserable. She wanted to reach out to him, but she didn't. Some things a man had to come to on his own, and this was one of them. He passed a hand over his face, and his gaze skittered over her.

"I guess it's up to me," he said, "to protect us both."

Her chin began to tremble. "If what's been happening the past couple of weeks is your idea of protection," she said, "then please spare me."

He opened his mouth to speak again, then closed it. A beseeching expression came over him, but she looked away. Finally he turned to go. "Take care of that sunburn," he told her softly.

"Take care of that heart," she answered in kind, listening to the sound of his footsteps as they carried him away.

The sunburn healed, but the rift between Ginger and her neighbors showed no sign of closing. If Craig had kept her at a polite distance before, he had now abandoned even the pretense of good manners. When she rang the doorbell, he simply didn't answer it. When she telephoned, he stated firmly that he couldn't talk and hung up, and the one time she attempted to speak to him on the beach, he turned around and jogged away. Since then, if he so much as sensed her coming in his direction, he beat a fast retreat. Had he known her better, he'd have realized that such behavior, following on the heels of that unexpected kiss, merely strengthened her resolve, strengthened it, in fact, to the point that she made and executed a plan.

It was a tricky plan at best. As she watched the sides of the white paper bag move seemingly of their own accord, she told herself that she was nuts to do this, but what else could she do? She'd racked her brain for days and come up with nothing better. Grimly, she lifted her chin. It would be worth it. If she could just get him to stay in the room long enough to hear her out, it would be worth it. She had only to wait until she was certain Craig had come out onto the deck behind his house. She didn't want to think what she would do if he didn't come out. Often, these days, he did not. She glanced at the doors opened onto her own deck, then closed her eyes, silently willing him to appear outside. After some time, she gave up on metaphysics, closed the door to her bedroom and went to make herself a cup of herbal tea.

Cup in hand, she opened the bedroom door to check the sack on the bed. For a moment she held her breath. The sack was not moving. Had it gotten out? A very real panic rose in her chest. Abruptly, the sack on the bed crumpled a bit, then puffed out on one side, its top trembling slightly. Ginger let out a sigh of relief. What would she do, she wondered, if Craig didn't go outside tonight? Could she sleep with that thing in the house? She swallowed a mouthful of tea and walked backward toward the opened doors of the deck, keeping watch on the sack. She stepped out onto the deck, took a deep breath and stood very still, listening, but she didn't hear a thing that might indicate anyone was occupying the deck next door. Sighing, she pulled a deck chair in front of the opened door and sat down where she could see the sack on her bed. She sipped her tea and waited—and waited.

It was dark when she heard the first sound of movement next-door. She sat up abruptly, alert for even the smallest noise. When she heard what sounded like the clink of ice cubes in a glass, she was certain. Heart racing, she got up slowly and tiptoed indoors. She set her cup down on the coffee table and walked toward the bedroom door.

The sack was crackling with movement now, something to do with the cool night air, she imagined. She bit her lip. *I must be out of my mind.* But what else could she do? Nothing short of an emergency would get Craig Russell over here now, and she couldn't very well set the house afire or hold a gun on herself. She had to do this, for Joan's sake if no one else's. One thing was for certain, if she did nothing, nothing would change.

That in mind, she crossed to the head of the bed, pulled the pillow from beneath the bedspread and flipped back the covers. Very carefully, she reached for the sack. The instant her hand drew near, all movement stopped. Her teeth ground down on her bottom lip, but she was unaware of it. Her total consciousness was concentrated on that sack, which she grasped and lifted, grimacing at its unnatural weight. Steeling herself, she positioned the sack, then turned it bottom up. A greenish black snake plopped onto the center of her bed, flopped about and slithered toward the edge—and her. She screamed quite without thinking, and the snake angled away, disappearing under the bedcovers. She screamed again, afraid it would plop onto the floor at any moment, and stumbled away from the bed.

Only when she'd achieved a safe distance did she realize she had the sack from the pet store in her hand. Quickly, eyes on the bed, she stuffed the sack into the trash can. The bedcovers rippled and the hair stood up on the nape of her neck. She ran for the living room, screaming at the top of her lungs. What was taking so long? Oh, God, what if it got away before anyone came? The last thing she needed was a snake loose in the house. An eternity seemed to pass before she heard footsteps pounding across her deck, but even then she couldn't take her eyes off that bed. Suddenly the snake wiggled out from under the bedcovers and dangled above the floor. She heard herself screaming again. Then rough hands seized her, shook her. Her head snapped back, and suddenly she was staring up into the troubled face of Craig Russell. She crumpled against him in relief, but he pushed her back, holding her at arm's length.

"What's wrong? What is it?"

She recovered enough to point a trembling finger in the direction of the bedroom. "O-on the bed. It's o-on the bed."

He gave her a questioning look, but left her at once to investigate. A sense of victory and well-being welled up inside her, but trepidation quickly pushed it aside. It wasn't enough to get him here. She also had to make him listen. Remembering her lines, she followed him at a safe distance.

"I-it must have come in through the opened doors. I, umm, like the breeze, you know. Anyway, I threw back the bedcovers and . . . there it was."

"It?" he said. Just then the bedcovers rippled. In one fluid movement, he stepped closer, seized the edge of the covers and flipped them back. Suddenly exposed to the light, the snake wriggled wildly. "Damn!"

Ginger slipped into the room and gently closed the door. He glanced around to look at her, and she pressed her back to the smooth panel of wood, hands behind her. She gulped. "I—I don't want it to get out."

He nodded grimly and turned his attention back to the snake, which had momentarily ceased all movement. "What I want to know," he muttered, easing forward, "is how the hell it got in here."

"I told you," she said. "It must have come through the opened doors."

He lifted an eyebrow skeptically. "Maybe, but that doesn't explain how it got up on this bed."

She hadn't thought of that, only of letting the snake out someplace, where it could be easily recaptured and, even more importantly, getting Craig alone in a room he couldn't easily get out of again. To that end, she had locked and blocked beforehand the double doors that led out into the entry, and as Craig's hand slowly moved toward the recumbent snake on the bed, she locked the door behind her.

Suddenly both hand and snake moved. Then Craig was holding the squirming reptile above the bed. Ginger moaned, disgusted at the very idea of touching that thing, but Craig ignored her and, with his free hand, trapped the head. The movement of the long, slender body began to slow.

"I need something to put it in," Craig said, casting about for a suitable container. She knew the instant his gaze fell on the trash can that she had made a terrible mistake. Immediately she began trying to unlock the door behind her back.

"I-I'll get something from the kitchen!"

But even as she spoke, he leaned toward the can, reaching out with one hand as he held the snake away from him with the other. "This will do. There's only a few tissues and a . . . sack in it."

Ginger gulped, knowing what he saw.

He sent her a narrow glance, repeating the words printed on the sack. "Good Friends Pet Store?"

She smiled weakly and shook her head, as if confused about his meaning. He didn't buy it for an instant. He held the snake up and took a good look at it. "Nonpoisonous, I imagine."

She lifted her shoulders in a halfhearted attempt to deny any knowledge of such things, but the glower he raked her with told her it was a waste of effort.

"Oh, all right," she said, suddenly deflated. "I bought the damned snake and dumped it in the bed."

"And then screamed your bloody head off," he added caustically.

She nodded, once. "But it's not all my fault, you know. You forced my hand."

He gaped. "Lady, you have some nerve!" With a pop, he whipped the sack open, dropped the snake into it and rolled down the top. "Your bed partner," he said, depositing the sack on the bed once more. "And I must say you deserve one another. Now get out of my way."

"No."

He shook his head. "Ginger, this nonsense has got to stop!"

"I just want to talk to you. . . ."

"We have nothing to say to one another."

"About Joan," she pleaded.

Abruptly he turned on his heel and walked to the double doors that opened onto the entry hall. He jiggled them, found them locked and turned.

"Craig, listen! I'm worried about Joan! If you don't want anything to do with me, fine, but Joan needs me, I know it."

He walked toward her, and by the look in his eyes, she knew she dared not resist him. She stepped aside. He fumbled with the lock, ripped open the door and strode out. She ran after him.

"For God's sake, Craig!" she cried. "Joan has no friends, no social outlet, nothing!" She followed him across the living room and out onto the deck. "She gets off the school bus every day like a zombie. Can't you see how defeated she is? Just a short while ago, she was starting to bloom, to blossom. Now she's wilted again, faded. It isn't natural. It isn't right!"

"Don't talk to me about right and wrong!" he shouted, pounding down the steps.

Ginger stumbled down after him, grabbing on to the rail to steady herself. "Just because you're afraid of falling in love with me is no reason to deprive Joan of her only friend!" she yelled.

That halted him. For a long, tense moment, she waited. Suddenly he whirled, a murderous look on his face, but she wouldn't let that intimidate her. If he wanted a fight, he was going to get one. She folded her arms and let him take the first jab.

"Look," he said, stepping closer. "You may be right about my sister, but you're way off the mark with me, and you might as well get that through your head right now."

She put her nose in the air. "How so?"

He lifted a hand, shook a finger at her. "I'm not in danger of falling in love with anyone, and certainly not you."

"Why not me?"

He scowled. "You know perfectly well why not."

"Because you know I want to get married."

"That's part of it," he admitted.

"Then it's not me you're afraid of, it's the idea of getting married."

"I'm not afraid of anything!"

"But you perceive yourself in danger," she pointed out.

"I do not! I just don't want to get married!"

"And that's why you're afraid of falling in love with me." She cocked her head to one side, silently challenging him to refute that conclusion.

He muttered several colorful curses and stepped closer still. "I'm *not* falling in love with you," he said flatly. "There's a world of difference between what I feel for you and love."

She felt herself pale. "L-lust, you mean."

He gave her a hard look. "Yes, that's what I mean. Wanting to take someone to bed and falling in love with her are two different things!"

Perilously close to tears, Ginger lifted her chin a notch and recited her argument by rote. "Sometimes," she said, voice trembling. "For some men, but not for you."

He gave her an incredulous look. "You don't know that!"

"Yes, I do!" she insisted. "You told me so."

He gaped at her. "When?"

"That day I made the soup," she reminded him. "I asked if you were only interested in sex, and you said no."

He stared at her, mouth agape, and she could tell that he was going over in his head what they'd said that day. He clenched his jaw. "What I meant is that I stay away from women who *only* interest me sexually."

"And that's why you're staying away from me?" she asked in a small voice.

His expression hardened. "That's right."

She felt it like a blow, but some part of her just couldn't accept his assertion. "Then why come running at my first little ol' yell?"

His eyes got very big, as if they might explode out of their sockets. "I forgot for the moment how screwy you are!"

She gasped. "Screwy?"

"And devious."

"I resent that! I've been nothing but honest with you!"

"You've pulled more stunts than your average circus!"

"Name one!" she demanded, leaning forward as her own ire grew.

"One?" he scoffed. "I'll name a dozen! There was the welcome basket."

"What's wrong with that?"

"Then you had to have help hanging a painting."

"I couldn't hang that thing by myself!"

"And God only knows how much food you've hauled over to my house!"

"Of all the ungrateful—"

"You redecorated Joan's room."

"She loves that room!"

"Then you take it upon yourself to rearrange my living room!"

"You said yourself it was an improvement!"

"And all those bikinis!" he roared. "You must have something in your closet besides bikinis and hot pants!"

Ginger gasped. "What's wrong with the way I dress? We live on a lake, in case you haven't noticed! I don't know about you, but *I* moved here because of the private beach! I like to swim, and I swim a lot. It keeps me fit, and as long as I'm in good shape, I don't see a thing in the world wrong with being seen in a bathing suit!"

"You're in good shape, all right," he retorted. "You're in *excellent* shape, and you make damned sure everyone knows it!"

"Oh, I see. Just because I'm attractive, I'm supposed to wear a gunnysack everywhere!"

"Attractive!" He laughed mirthlessly. "That's the understatement of the year!"

Ginger blinked at him. Had she heard him right? "You think I'm more than merely attractive?"

"Oh, don't play dumb with me! You know you're beautiful, and you use your looks like a weapon. You've been beating me over the head with them ever since I moved in here! That figure, that face, that...hair." He stopped and his mouth quirked up on one end. Ginger was smiling, absolutely delighted. He lifted his hands to his face and pressed the heels of his palms against his eyes, but the smile was still working its way across his mouth. He sighed, dropping his hands. "I walked right into that one, didn't I?"

She ignored the question, her mind on other things. "Do you really think I'm beautiful?"

He straightened and fixed her with a firm stare. "Yes, I do, and that's the whole problem."

"How is it a problem?" she asked eagerly.

He pushed his hand through his hair, obviously searching for words. "Look, Ginger, I don't want anyone to get hurt. What I mean is, I just can't get involved with you, no matter how tempting the idea is. I don't want anything to happen between us that either of us would regret later."

"I wouldn't regret it," she told him confidently. The look he sent her said clearly that he didn't share her belief.

"Maybe not," he said. "But I would."

"You don't know that for sure," she began, but he held up a stalling hand.

"There is another consideration. I have a certain responsibility to my sister. I gave up...that sort of thing when she came to live with me, and I'm not about to start up again with the next-door neighbor. What kind of example is that?"

"But, Craig," Ginger argued, "Joan has to learn about love from someone, and it ought to be someone she trusts."

"There you go again!" he said, throwing up his hands. "I'm not talking about love. That's what you've got to get through your hard head!"

Ginger rolled her eyes. Were they going to argue semantics all night? "Let's not get into this again," she said. "Could we just talk about Joan?"

"What about her?"

"She's miserable, that's what, and I think I can help her."

"Do you?" he asked. "Do you really? Or is she just another way for you to drive me nuts?"

Ginger didn't know whether to laugh or smack him. She did neither, just looked him square in the eye. "Joan is one thing, and you are another," she told him evenly. "And right now I'm much more concerned about her than I am about you."

Craig looked away, then back again. He sighed and seemed to capitulate. "So am I."

Ginger closed her eyes. Thank God! She opened them again. "Then what are we going to do for her?" she asked slowly.

He shook his head. "I don't know what I can do, and I don't know if she'll *let* you do anything for her or not."

Ginger felt a certain dismay. "Why wouldn't she?" she asked warily.

He lifted a hand to his temple and with some effort managed a nonchalant pose. "Joan heard Maggie say that you were using her to get to me."

Ginger's mouth fell open with righteous indignation. "That pompous, overbearing old witch!"

"It wasn't all Maggie's fault," he admitted gruffly. "I could have told Jo otherwise. She'd have believed me."

Now Ginger was truly aghast. "Oh, Craig, you didn't.... But you couldn't have thought... I told you, Joan is my friend!" She stamped a foot.

"Well, what did you expect?" he said. "Every time I turned around, there you were! I felt as though I was being attacked from all sides! And I'm just human, you know. My hormones work. But so does my head, and it tells me you're trouble with a capital *T!* And then there's Maggie and that mess with the Petrie brothers." He paused long enough to get a breath through his mouth and push it out through his nostrils. "I just thought it might be best for everyone concerned if you weren't around so much," he said. "And that includes you as well as Joan."

"You let her think I was using her!" Ginger accused. "How is *that* supposed to be best? She must have been hurt, confused at the very least."

Craig closed his eyes and lowered his head, confirming her assessment. "I didn't know how it would affect her," he said. "I should have, but I didn't."

"Well, now you do," she said coldly. "And you have to do something about it—if it's not too late."

He nodded. "I know. I—I'll tell her I was wrong, that we've talked and straightened out everything, and . . . that you're very hurt we've been ignoring you."

"You do that," Ginger said bitterly.

He looked up. "Ginger, I'm sorry. I didn't mean to . . . I was just trying to protect . . . everyone."

Ginger felt herself softening. He probably believed that, the dope, but the only person he was protecting was himself, and that could only mean that she had worked her way farther into his heart than she had known. Besides, she had pulled a *few* stunts to get his attention—and one big one. She hoped that slimy thing was still in its bag. As it was, she'd have to change the bed linens or there would be no sleeping in that bed for her. She shuddered.

"What?" he asked. She shook her head.

"Nothing." It sounded sharper than she intended, and she couldn't leave it that way, despite what he'd done. "That is, I'm sorry, too. About the snake, I mean."

He looked at her and actually grinned. "I guess I should be grateful it wasn't poisonous."

She felt the pull of that patented Craig Russell charm and she smiled. "I know it was silly, but I couldn't think of any other way to get you over here."

"All right," he said. "So we're even now. I used Maggie. You used a snake."

"Right. We both used snakes," she quipped.

He laughed, too, but quickly sobered. "So it's over," he said, making it almost a question. She nodded. "It's over, and the game ended in a tie. Now we're reviving this *acquaintance*—and that's all it is—for Joan's sake."

"For Joan's sake," Ginger repeated, but Craig wasn't finished.

"That means that from now on we're both going to behave ourselves," he said. "You're Joan's friend, but as far as you and I are concerned, we're neighbors, period."

"If you say so."

"I mean it. I expect you to behave responsibly. No more sexy outfits or batting eyelashes, at least not around me."

"I resent that! I do *not* bat my eyelashes."

"Right."

"I don't! And for your information, some people think I'd be sexy in burlap!"

"No doubt, but that's not the point. All I'm saying is, you pull any more funny stuff and I yank up the drawbridge and fill the moat."

She frowned, but crossed her heart and stuck out her hand. "Want me to spit in it?"

"No!" He hesitated, but slowly his own hand came out and grasped hers. Warmth spread up her arm. Immediately, his grip slackened, but she didn't let go.

"Craig," she said softly, but the warning in his eyes forestalled the plea she'd been about to make. Instead, she said simply, "Thanks."

His gaze met hers and his hand quickened. "For what?"

She grinned, wanting very much to lighten the mood. "Catching the snake."

He shook his head and pulled his hand away, but he was smiling. "Don't remind me. Ye gods, she lays traps with snakes! I hope I'm not making a mistake."

"You're not," she rushed to assure him.

"Just the same, I'll think twice the next time I hear a bloodcurdling scream."

"Aw," she said teasingly, "you're too much of a gentleman to think twice when a lady screams."

"Don't count on it," he warned. "I'll tell Jo you're expecting her tomorrow afternoon."

"Great!" He turned and started down the beach with a guarded wave, but she called after him, a sudden thought seizing her. "Craig, what about the snake?"

He laughed grimly and trudged on. "Turn it loose."

"Couldn't you do it?" she pleaded hopefully, pulling up on tiptoe. He stopped and turned, his hands going to his hips. She could tell from his expression that she wasn't going to get anything more from him.

He confirmed it. "I could," he said. "But I won't. You got it in the house. You can get it out again." He turned and trudged on.

She supposed she could dump the darn thing in the front yard. She shivered and hugged herself. It was rather chilly that night with the breeze coming off the lake, but that wasn't what made her shiver. Still, she had Joannie back, and she was going to redouble her efforts where her young friend was concerned. As for Craig, she was just relieved that they were again on speaking terms. *And for now, that's enough,* she told herself, watching him walk away. *For now.*

Chapter Ten

Craig stuck his head through the doorway, his eyebrows going up when he heard the giggle and saw the young woman that his sister had become. She was sprawled face-down upon her bed, telephone receiver captured between shoulder and ear, one foot bobbing in time with the music playing on the radio. She wore sweatpants that lay softly against her gentle curves and a tank top over a push-up bra. With her upper-body weight supported on her elbows, she displayed a healthy cleavage Craig would never have suspected possible. What had become of his baby sister?

She smiled and waved him into the room, saying into the telephone, "I've got to go now, Patrick. My brother's home. But you can call me later. 'Bye." She hung up and rolled over, bouncing off the bed.

"Patrick again," Craig said, trying to keep his tone neutral. "Is this Patrick someone I ought to meet?"

Joan laughed and shook her head. The sophisticated new blunt cut made her hair swing gracefully just above her shoulders, but what truly amazed Craig was the way it shined. Ginger had explained something about conditioning and highlights. He didn't understand it, but it made a huge difference in his sister, almost as much as the makeup. He wasn't certain he approved of that, though it was subtle, to be sure. It just made her look so *mature*.

"Patrick's only a friend," she said. "He's younger than I am, but he's about to get a car, and that'll be neat. I've never had a friend with a car before...well, except for Ginger, but that's different, isn't it?"

Craig didn't answer. He was too busy thinking about his little sister going off in a car with some guy whose hormones were popping like firecrackers. Was she ready for that? He watched her, studying her like a bug under a microscope. Unconcerned, Joan strolled over to her desk and picked up the guitar Ginger had recently given her. Leaning against the desk, she placed one foot on the seat of the chair, balanced the guitar on her knee and began to strum, humming softly. Craig marveled at the ease with which she picked out the tune, especially as the radio was still churning out a crazy beat in the background. She was blossoming, ripening into full, vibrant womanhood—which meant the pickers were probably lining up right around the next corner, just waiting for an opportunity to deflower *his* baby sister.

Craig wondered if Ginger hadn't gone a bit too far in these past weeks. Much as he hated to, he was going to have to talk to Ginger, be sure she knew what she was doing. True, Joan was happier now than he had ever seen her, but she was also ripe pickings for some smooth-talking, sex-crazed teenage libertine, and as her guardian and older brother, it was Craig's job to protect her. Who knew better, after all, what was on the minds of all those guys out there? Yes, he would definitely talk to Ginger—and then Ginger would talk to Jo, and he could relax a bit, knowing his sister was adequately forewarned. It didn't have to get sticky. He'd be polite, keep the conversation on Jo and simply spell out his concerns. What could be simpler? He was actually beginning to breathe a little easier already when Jo suddenly put down the guitar and started gyrating to the radio's music.

"I love this song!" she declared, wiggling her bottom and thrusting out her arms.

Song? Craig thought. It sounded like static with a beat to him and no different than anything else he'd heard since he'd come in here. He stuck his hands in his pockets and pretended not to watch as Jo went through her steps. Where had she learned *that?* Had Ginger taught her this, too? He really did need to have a talk with Miss Gingevine Brenan. The decision reaffirmed, he made some excuse and started for the door, but Joan stopped him, running up to grasp his arm.

"Craig, wait!" she said, panting from her recent exertion. "I was going to tell you. It's the neatest thing. Ginger's giving me a party!"

"A party?" he repeated dully, red flags going up all over the place. "What kind of party?"

Joan laughed, hopping up and down in time with the music. "A party party, silly. A fun party. A *huge* party. Honestly, Craig, I'm so excited! We're going to fix all the food ourselves, Ginger and me—she's teaching me to cook, you know—and I'm inviting a few of the kids from school, and Ginger's inviting some of her friends, *and* Ginger's brother is coming with a *bunch* of his buddies. He's in college, you know, *and* he's in a fraternity, the same one as Paul, Jr." She stopped bouncing and clenched her fists, pumping her elbows.

Craig was appalled. His sister at a party with a *bunch* of fraternity wild men? He knew what those freaks were capable of doing. He'd been to college. He'd even been to his share of fraternity parties. And Ginger had definitely gone too far this time, *much* too far.

His face must have said so, for Joan went very still, her gaze clearly questioning. "What's wrong?"

"Wrong?" Craig said, his voice sounding rather strangled even to his own ears. "Why, what could be wrong? My little sister—who's still very wet behind the ears, by the way—is partying down with a bunch of fraternity wild men.

What could be wrong with that? Well, we'll just see about this. I'm going over to Ginger's."

He strode out of the room and only a minute later was pounding so hard on the frame of Ginger's back door that the glass rattled ominously. He could see her in the kitchen at the computer. She peered over her shoulder, smiled and got up to come into the living room and open the door. Craig gave her his sternest glower, but her smile only widened.

"Hi," she said, pulling the door open. "To what do I owe the honor?"

"It's about my sister!" he snapped, brushing past her into the living room. "At least I *think* that's my sister over there."

Ginger laughed, either ignoring or missing his distress, and closed the door. "She's something, isn't she?"

"She's something, all right. She's...she's..."

"A teenager," Ginger supplied, heading back to the kitchen. He couldn't very well argue with that, but he had plenty of other things on his mind. He went after her.

"I'm worried about Jo," he said. "She's not acting like herself. She's talking on the phone to boys!"

Ginger tossed him an amused look, went to the oven and reached inside to poke something with a fork. "That's what teenage girls do, Craig," she told him easily. "It's perfectly normal."

"Yeah, well, I'll tell you what else is normal," he said, punctuating his words with a jab of his finger. "It's perfectly normal for guys to take advantage of innocent young girls. All they think about is sex, and you're throwing her to them like a lamb to a bunch of wolves! What on earth are you thinking of?"

"What on earth are you talking about?" she came back.

"This so-called party you've cooked up!" he shouted. Ginger's mouth fell open. "Or should we just call it an orgy? That's what it's turning into with these *fraternity* creeps!"

"Fraternity?" Ginger echoed, and then, to his utter consternation, she dismissed his concern with a laugh and a flip of her hand. "Is *that* what's got you so upset? Don't worry about it. I have everything well in hand. They're only going to flirt a little, pay a bit of court. Will arranged it for me."

"Will?"

"My brother."

"And how old is Will?"

"Twenty. Why?"

"Twenty!" Craig cried. "Twenty! Jo's only seventeen!"

Ginger scoffed at that. "Almost eighteen, Craig. Besides, Will and his friends are going to boost her ego a bit, that's all." Ginger turned thoughtful, her tawny eyes narrowing. "I asked him to bring that Paul person—you know, your partner's son. Turns out he and Will are in the same fraternity."

Craig couldn't believe it. "Now you've got Paul, Jr., in this? Holy cow, that's all I need!"

She put her hands to her hips and struck a cryptic pose. "I don't know what's wrong with you," she said. "I thought you'd be pleased. We talked about this a while ago. Joannie needs to meet some nice young men, so I'm giving a party to kind of get her started."

It sounded so innocent, a party to get her started. They did that for debutantes, to get them onto the marriage market. His Jo, launched? The idea made the hair stand up on the back of his neck. "You can't do it," he said. "She's not ready. Okay, so she looks eighteen, thanks to you, but emotionally she's twelve. It just isn't time. I absolutely forbid it."

Ginger's jaw slowly descended. For a long moment she stared at him, her golden brown eyes searching his face. And then she giggled. Her hand came up and pressed against her lips, but the giggles bubbled out around her fingers, rapidly becoming a torrent that bent her double and spilled tears onto her cheeks.

"What the hell is so funny?" Craig demanded, but Ginger only sputtered. He frowned at her, scowled, even glared, but she laughed on until the flood subsided.

"As if," she gasped between spurts, "you could . . . keep me . . . from doing . . . what I please."

The truth of that washed over him like cold water poured from a bucket. He'd been a fool to come here, to expect her to be reasonable. Why wasn't he talking to Joan? She was the only female he had any right—or desire—to influence. Feeling like an idiot, he turned on his heel and strode out of the room.

Ginger came after him, her mirth receding to a broad smile. "Craig, wait. Don't be this way. There's nothing to worry about, really. You're just being overprotective."

"Overprotective!"

"It's understandable," she said quickly. "But you know I wouldn't do anything to hurt Joannie."

He shook his head in wonder. "Did it ever occur to you, Miss Brenan, that you might not be as smart as you think? Your judgment could be just slightly off here, you know."

"And yours couldn't?"

Didn't she get it? "I was young once," he told her. "I know what goes through the heads of healthy young men. I know exactly how they think!"

"Well, so do I," she responded. "Maybe better than you, since I was on the receiving end. What's more, I know how healthy young women think, and that's what Joan is rapidly becoming, a healthy young woman. You have to accept that, Craig. She's got to grow up."

"Not overnight!" he exclaimed, throwing up his hands.

Ginger just shook her head, her smile unmanageable again. "All right," she said. "Have it your way. Make a fool of yourself, alienate your sister at this crucial time in her life. Rant and rave, if you want. See what it gets you." She shrugged. "Maybe you'll get lucky."

He glared at her, then stormed out, slamming the door behind him and hearing the glass shudder in its frame. At the edge of the deck, Craig cast one more look over his shoulder. She was smiling still and shaking her head, so sure of herself. That was the moment he began to wonder if he was missing something in all this.

He went on his way, telling himself that it was up to him to protect his sister. Maybe Ginger knew how to make Jo feel better about herself, but he knew a thing or two, as well.

Didn't he? Of course he did. And as his sister's guardian, he should most definitely act upon that knowledge. His mistake was in going to that busybody next-door. He should have spoken to Joan about this in the first place, and that was exactly what he was going to do now.

Be firm, he told himself as he entered the house. *Explain yourself, but be firm.* He went to her room, squared his shoulders and slipped inside. She was standing in front of a full-length mirror, a dress held to her chest. Her bed was strewn with clothing, most of it new.

"What do you think?" she asked. "Is this the kind of dress for an afternoon party?"

Craig felt his shoulders droop a bit and he cleared his throat. "I, umm, wouldn't know, but about that party..."

Joan spun, hugging the dress to her. "I'm so excited! I've never had a party before. I've never had anyone to *invite* to a party before."

His shoulders felt positively weighted, but he pressed them back. "Jo, honey, I'm not sure this party is a good idea."

She stopped, swaying slightly. "What?"

He lifted a hand to the back of his neck. "I don't think you should attend."

Her mouth fell open, and for a moment he felt certain she was about to burst into tears, but the next thing he knew, a belligerent look overcame her and she stomped her foot petulantly. "That's not fair!"

His hand fell away. "I know you're disappointed, but I can't in good conscience let you go to that party."

"It's Aunt Maggot, isn't it?" Jo demanded. "It's because she wouldn't like it!"

"No!" Craig exclaimed, appalled his sister would think him guilty of knuckling under to Maggie's pressure again. "That's not it at all, cupcake."

"Then what?" she cried. "It can't be Ginger." He was not aware of any reaction at all to that remark, but as his sister stared at him, her eyes narrowed knowingly. "Craig!" she exclaimed. "That's not fair! Just because you're afraid of her—"

"Afraid!" he scoffed. "Of Ginger Brenan?"

"You know what I mean!"

"That's the most absurd thing I've ever heard! Why on earth would I be afraid of Ginger?"

Stubbornly Joan met his gaze, her hands going to her hips. It was the most determined stance Craig had ever seen his timid little sister take. He didn't know what to make of it, what to think. Was this the same listless, ineffectual girl who had lived behind the locked door of her bedroom rather than ask a bunch of crass neighborhood kids to leave her home? What had happened to the easily manipulated little waif he'd taken in? Was that her glaring at him with those hard, implacable eyes? She stuck out her newly enhanced chest and squared her shoulders.

"You're afraid you're falling in love with Ginger," she said flatly. Craig was so astonished that he was speechless for a full fifteen seconds, and then he was furious. He knew exactly who to blame for this *aberration* before him.

"Did Ginger tell you that?" he demanded, only to see his sister's lips flatten into an expression of disdain.

"She didn't have to," Joan said. "You know, my head isn't just an anchor for my hair. I've got a brain in here. All she told me was that she likes you and that she made the mistake of telling you she wants to get married someday. The rest wasn't very hard to figure out."

Craig was livid. "Ginger had no right to discuss this with you! She should know better than this! What's wrong with that woman?"

"Not much that I can see," Joan retorted smartly. "Look, Craig, it was Maggie who got me thinking about it, but I'd have to be deaf, dumb and blind not to notice how crazy Ginger is about you. I just asked a few questions, and Ginger was nice enough to answer them honestly, which is more than I can say for anyone else, by the way. For that reason alone, I *have* to go to that party. Ginger's feelings will be hurt if I don't."

"Ginger is an adult," Craig pointed out, more than a little stung by his sister's implication concerning his own honesty. "She won't blame you. I'll gladly take all the heat."

"And you think that makes it all right?" she asked insistently. "What about my feelings, Craig? Don't they count? I'm going to be very upset if we don't go to that party!"

"*We?*"

"That's right, *we*. Did you think either Ginger or I would leave you out?"

In truth, he hadn't thought about that at all. No one had said anything about him going. He had just assumed he wouldn't go. After all, it was his intention to keep Ginger Brenan at a safe distance. On the other hand, if he did go, he could act as a chaperon. Was it possible Ginger had intended that all along?

"Are you sure Ginger intended to include me?" he asked suspiciously.

Joan nodded. "Absolutely. And you two won't be the only adults, either. I told you she was inviting some of her own friends."

Hmm. Now that he thought about it, she *had* said something like that. Still, he hated to give in on this. What if it was just one more of Ginger's brilliant schemes? And what if it wasn't? What if she really was doing this for Jo, and what if Ginger was right and he was wrong about it being the right time for this? *Make a fool of yourself, alienate your sister at this crucial time in her life.* Ginger's words ran through his head, echoing warningly. He rubbed his eyes with his fists, as if attempting to wake up from a bad dream, and licked his lips.

"Well, it sounds reasonable," he muttered. "But I'm still not crazy about this fraternity being invited."

Joan rolled her eyes. "Not the *whole* fraternity, Craig, just Paul and some friends of Ginger's brother." She struck a more relaxed pose. "Let's face it, I'm not the most popular girl in school. Okay, I have made a few new friends lately, but they're all more...well, more experienced than I am. I don't know if they'd even come to this party if Will and his friends weren't. They're like bait, the frat guys. Know what I mean?"

He sighed and pinched his nose. "Yeah, I guess so."

"Then it's all right?" she wheedled. "Please, Craig, this is *really* important to me. Say we can go, *please.*"

Craig looked at his sister's pleading eyes and felt himself giving in. Well, why not? It would be all right as long as he was going to be there keeping an eye on things, Will Brenan included. God, he hoped Will wasn't as predatory as his sister, for all their sakes. And as far as Ginger was concerned, there was no telling what she was going to do next anyway. He sighed in an exaggerated manner and pushed a hand through his hair. Immediately Joan perked up, her hands coming together in an expression of expectant joy. She really was pretty, he realized, in a very delicate, almost elfin way. Suddenly he was very proud of her.

"All right," he said. "Let's party." He smiled and opened his arms. She flew into them, her own slender arms hooking around his neck as she rained kisses on his chin and cheek.

"Oh, thank you, thank you, thank you! You're the best brother! It's going to be so great!" She danced away from him, twirling in circles of ecstasy. He laughed, happy to have made her happy, and it occurred to him that he owed no small thanks for that to Ginger. Again.

She was a mixed blessing, at once infuriating and generous, honest and designing. One thing was certain, though, Jo had definitely bloomed under her tutelage. If it was nerve-racking having a real teenager in the house, well, he supposed it was worth it to see his sister sparkling like this. But he hadn't realized until he'd talked to her just how important this party business was to Jo. He hoped she wasn't being built up for a big letdown, but that result would be on Ginger's head, not his. He'd do his part by being on hand to keep an eye on Will Brenan and his cohorts. There really wasn't much else he could do. It was enough, for the moment, that she was happy. Maybe it would last.

It lasted about twenty-four hours.

As he drove toward his home that next afternoon at the end of a fairly uneventful workday, he spied Maggie's Chevy parked at the curb, and a deep sense of foreboding came over him. Damn her. She would show up just when things were going well for Jo. If she'd upset the girl, he'd strangle her. He parked and got out, hurrying into the house.

The moment he opened the door, his worst fears were realized. Jo and Maggie and Ginger were shouting at the tops of their lungs. He followed the sounds into the living room, which looked at the moment like a closet with furniture. Articles of clothing were strewn all over the place. Some attempt had been made, it seemed, to group them, but his male eye discerned no sense of pattern or congruity.

"What the devil is going on here?" he demanded.

It was Maggie who first let him know that the clothing spread over his living room was somehow at the bottom of the problem. "My sister wouldn't have had such things in her house!" she declared, pointing at what looked like a hot pink knitted tube too big to be a headband, which would have been his best guess.

"Everyone wears them!" Jo insisted. "All the girls have them."

"She just wants to look like other girls her age," Ginger pleaded.

"She wants to look like a common streetwalker, if you ask me!" Maggie said. "I've seen collars longer than that skirt."

Craig took a look at his sister and gulped. Maggie was right. The skirt covered little more than her butt. However, he noted—with some surprise—that his younger sister had been gifted with a pair of rather extraordinarily attractive legs. He was momentarily speechless, trying to remember when last he'd seen her knees. He seemed to recall that one of them had had a nasty scrape on it at the time.

Ginger was talking about style and something called "sixties retro." He closed his mouth and shut his eyes, trying to get a handle on what was happening.

"I don't care what label you put on it," Maggie interrupted. "It's still indecent, and I won't have it!"

He couldn't let that go by. He opened his eyes and fixed her with a level stare. "What you will or won't have is irrelevant, Maggie," he said silkily, and as he had hoped, the tone served him better than a shout. The old girl actually flinched.

"Craig, you can't mean that you're going to allow this child to go to that party with her rear end hanging out!"

"What I mean," he said softly, "is that what Joan wears is no concern of yours. *I* will set the limits on fashion and everything else in this house."

Maggie looked for a moment as if she were having a heart attack. But then she put on that bulldog face of hers, and Craig wearily girded himself for battle. She pulled herself up tight and launched the first salvo.

"I will not stand by and watch my only sister's daughter turn into some kind of strumpet!" she said baldly.

"Joan is not turning into *any* kind of strumpet," he told her, "or the modern equivalent, but that's beside the point. The point is, you don't have anything to say about it. So you might as well *shut up.*"

Maggie's mouth fell open. "How dare you say such a thing to me!"

He shook his head. "Maggie, the wonder is that I didn't say it before."

She looked as if she might cry, and for a brief instant he regretted his choice of words, but good old Maggie had never disappointed him yet, and in a heartbeat she was right back to her usual pushy self. Her expression turned pugnacious, and she puffed up, back arching stiffly. "Craig Russell, I absolutely forbid you to allow this so-called party. Furthermore, I insist that you dress this child in a proper manner *and* that you rid this house of that woman's influence."

It was all he could do not to strike her. He clasped his hands behind him to make certain that he didn't and carefully clamped down on the anger that threatened to overtake his good sense. He made himself smile, not caring that the result was dismal. "Maggie," he said quietly, "we are about to choose a party outfit for my lovely sister, one, I hope, that will show off her fabulous legs, and if you don't like it, well, you can just go straight to—"

"Craig!" Ginger gasped, sounding more nervous than he'd ever heard her. "Wouldn't you like Joan to model these for you?"

He bit back that last word he'd meant to say, took pity on them all and nodded curtly. Ginger snatched up several garments and hustled Joan out of the room while Maggie seethed.

"You mark my words," his aunt told him. "You'll rue the day you let that woman into this house."

Craig didn't tell her that he already had. He wouldn't give her the satisfaction. But any regrets he might have where Ginger was concerned had nothing to do with his sister, and Jo was what mattered most here.

"You're entitled to your opinions, Maggie," he said. "But from now on, I'll thank you to keep them to yourself. And one thing more. Do not ever again come in here and upset Joan. She is my concern, not yours. Remember that."

"Oh, I'll remember every word," Maggie retorted. "And throw them back in your face when she's ruined!" With that she stormed out of the room. The instant the door closed behind her, Joan and Ginger ran into the room, laughing.

"Bravo, Craig!" Joan cried, throwing herself at him.

Ginger was right behind her and just as exuberant. "You handled old Maggot beautifully!"

They wrapped their arms around him and kissed him on both cheeks, squeezing like a pair of boa constrictors. He laughed, silently, vowing not to feel guilty about old Maggot and fearing that he would. But for now it wouldn't hurt a thing in the world to loosen up a bit and simply enjoy himself, and he had every intention of doing so—until he saw what Joan was wearing. That overlarge hot pink headband was apparently a skirt. Worse yet, it came with a matching top, what there was of it. What truly shocked him, however, was that Joan did the outfit justice. His baby sister was a baby no more. He felt his knees begin to buckle and he let himself sink down against the back of the sofa, more or less in a sitting position, while Joan whirled and posed, then ran off to try on another equally shocking costume.

"Bear with us, please," Ginger said gently, and unless he was mistaken, that was pity in her eyes. He nodded, vacillating between dismay and the anger that always seemed so close to the surface these days. Somehow, he managed to sit through the fashion show, alternately biting his tongue and making noncommittal noises. By the time she came out in a lime green jumper that plunged both front and back over a lemon yellow off-the-shoulder T-shirt, he was almost too traumatized to recognize a good thing when he saw it. Ginger, fortunately, was more astute.

"Oh, yes," she said, walking slowly around Joan. "I love it. Simple yet sophisticated, and the colors are so exciting on you. This would go perfectly with those handpainted flats we saw downtown, and do you know what else would be wonderful? A pair of leggings. I think I have some just the color of that blouse. And we'll do your hair in a couple of kicky little ponytails, oh, and a long scarf tied with a big bow. What do you think?"

Joan looked down at herself uncertainly, her lower lip clamped in her teeth. "What do you think, Craig?" she asked.

He thought the sleeves should be pulled up onto her shoulders and that little bit of skin that showed between the bottom of the T-shirt and the "top" of the jumper should be covered up. He thought, too, that the jumper could use another two inches of fabric around the bottom. But he realized that this could be as good as it got, and he wasn't about to louse up his best chance at seeing her decently covered in front of those frat boys. He cleared his throat and made his pronouncement.

"I like it. It's definitely you. And Ginger's right about the colors. Exciting."

Jo wasn't quite convinced, but as she pranced around a bit, looking herself over, she became more enthusiastic. "I think you're right," she said. "I liked the pink, but this is more me." She seemed to have a sudden inspiration. "I have some daisy-chain earrings I've never worn. They were Mother's in the sixties. Do you think they would go?"

Craig was useless with that sort of thing, so he kept silent, but Ginger was encouraging.

"Sounds good to me. Why don't you go try them on and see what you think?"

Joan skipped out of the room, declaring herself suddenly in love with the whole look. Craig wanted to feel relieved, but something told him his simple, rather peaceful existence had definitely come to an end, and he couldn't help feeling a bit resentful about that. He slid over the back of the sofa and onto the seat, groaning.

"God in heaven," he grumbled. "Did you have to pick out the most provocative garments you could find?"

Ginger leaned her forearms on the back of the sofa, smiling comfortingly. "I'm sorry, love, but there is method to my madness. I had to show you that she's not a little girl anymore. They sell those same clothes to other girls her age, you know, but I knew the green jumper was the thing for her the moment I saw it. I just had to convince you, so you could convince her. I thought if you could see the more risqué options, it would be easier for you to go along with the off-the-shoulder look. And I was right, wasn't I?"

He nodded miserably. Hell, yes, she was right. Where Jo was concerned, Ginger was somehow always right, and it bugged him greatly. "I thank you for engineering approval of the least offensive garment," he said tartly. "But I have to tell you, Ginger, that this whole affair reeks of manipulation, and that's not a very attractive trait in a woman."

He hadn't expected her to look so wounded about his comment, but he was not, he decided, going to apologize. Why should he? It was true, damn it, and she had no right to look at him with the eyes of a wounded puppy.

"I'm sorry you feel that way," she said softly, immediately pricking his conscience beyond bearing. Irritated by his own lack of resolve, he got up and paced toward the window.

"Oh, don't mind me," he said. "It's this damned party. It's got me unnerved."

"And that, too, is my fault," she said morosely, straightening. "Well, it isn't such a big deal really. I've given dozens of parties. What's one more? You don't even have to attend if you don't want to." Head down, she walked around the end of the couch and swiftly crossed the room.

"Well, of course I'm going to attend," he said, but she kept on going until she'd reached the door to the deck. "Ginger, wait," he said, feeling like a heel, but she shook her head, smiled and flipped him a wave, then slipped outside. To his utter dismay, her eyes were brimming with tears.

How had that happened? Just because he'd been a little cross? He'd been cross with her before. In fact, he'd been cross with her *a lot*. Why should it reduce her to tears now? And why should he care? He shouldn't, but somehow he did. Hell.

Chapter Eleven

Ginger bent forward, offering soft drinks from the tray she carried on one arm. A few of her adult guests had complained when she'd informed them that she wasn't serving alcohol, but most had merely shrugged and helped themselves to colas. Many of her guests were already in the water. It was a good day for it. The sun was bright. The sky was an unblemished bowl of violet-tinged blue. A cool, gentle breeze blew across the surface of the lake. She couldn't have ordered a finer day for this party, and all seemed to be going well.

Several of the guys were setting up a volleyball net even as she dispensed the remainder of the drinks on her tray, while others were readying grills to cook the hamburgers they would be having for dinner. Hamburgers weren't exactly her first choice, but hamburgers and teenagers were a natural combination, and she had decided to keep this simple. The idea was to get a group together, offer them a variety of activities and let them make their own fun. The goal was a relaxed, entertaining afternoon, during which Joan could polish her social skills and forge some friendly connections. Was it selfish or merely foolish of her to have hoped she could build a bridge of her own this afternoon between her and Craig? Ginger had hoped he'd have loosened up some by now, but he was as prickly as ever, and she was beginning to believe he would never come around. But now was not the time to think about it.

Roland Colgate was at her elbow again. She spared him a smile and went to speak to the musician, Danny, who was setting up his equipment in a corner of the deck. He was very talented and classically trained, but he positively lived for the brittle riffs and shrieking whips of rock and roll. Today he would play the electric guitar, accompanied by numerous tracks recorded on a reel-to-reel tape machine, every one of which he had painstakingly laid down himself, using a rich variety of musical instruments in his own recording studio. He had also recorded several of her favorite pieces of music to be played during his frequent breaks, and at some point she expected to pick up her own acoustical instrument for a more laid-back interlude, and if she could talk Joannie into joining her, all the better. Satisfied, Ginger honestly felt she had all the bases covered, but she had one more brief conversation with Danny to be sure, and then she couldn't resist the temptation to look around for Craig. Maybe he had arrived while her back was turned, but if he had, he'd left right away.

Sighing, she went to answer the doorbell, only to have her brother walk in before she got there, a number of well-dressed, clean-cut young males behind him. She smiled, genuinely delighted to see this younger sibling of hers. Will was a good sort, calm, urbane, sweet natured and self-confident, with a wry sense of humor and a genuine zest for living. But then, how could he be anything else? He was handsome, intelligent, wealthy and much loved, not to mention a first-rate captain of the rowing team and an accomplished polo player on two continents. One day soon she was going to have to look around for the right woman for him. He was already something of a playboy, and she didn't want to see him carry that too far. Besides, he'd be a dyna-mite husband and father.

Will came forward, his arms open, to give her a hug and a kiss. There was a general murmur of approval from his friends, and then Ginger heard someone whisper, "His sis-ter." The murmurs turned speculative. How old? Unat-tached? Will laughed. He loved that his friends found her attractive. She whacked him gently on the shoulder with her hand. Introductions were made. Will had chosen wisely. Of the four young men accompanying him, one was an obvi-ous party animal but seemed harmless enough. He would go along with the flow. The other three ranged from boyish to debonair, but the one she liked best—aside from her brother—was the tall, lanky, quiet son of Craig's business partner. Paul Solis, Jr., had thick blond hair and gentle eyes. He greeted her with a touch of formality, nodding low over her clasped hand.

"Thank you for inviting me, Miss Brenan. I understand Craig Russell will be present."

"I don't know about Craig," Ginger told him, "but his sister is here." She summoned Joan, who came accompa-nied by two of the girls from her school. Both were prone to giggles, but they seemed to know at least the basics of po-lite social behavior. Ginger introduced them. To her delight, it was Paul who immediately took the initiative.

"Joan Russell?" he said. "Little Joan Russell, is that you?" He smiled at her blush, and it made him seem truly handsome. "Why, I remember you at last year's company Christmas banquet, and you were just a child, but look at you now!"

Joan laughed. "I guess I've grown up a bit."

"A bit? I'd say you've crossed over the threshold right into womanhood."

"Well, maybe I haven't come that far," Joan said. Then in an apparent attempt at good manners, she tried to de-flect the conversation from herself. "How is your sister?"

"Spoiled as ever," he answered, grinning. "Actually, she's a pretty good kid. Mother's frantic because she hasn't got a date yet for the spring dance. I suppose I'll have to take her myself."

"I remember your mother made you dance with your sister at the company banquet," Joan said, and Paul laughed outright.

"Actually, it was the other way around. She made my sister dance with me. Mustn't have any wallflowers in the family, you know, even if the band plays *only* polkas. I noticed you weren't dancing that night."

Joan grimaced. "Too shy," she admitted forthrightly.

He took her hand. "You seem to have outgrown that."

They laughed together, as at ease with each other as two young people very aware of a common attraction could be. Ginger could not have been more pleased. This was so much more than she'd hoped for. She passed a conspiratorial look of congratulations to her brother, who shrugged his shoulders. Including Paul hadn't been his idea. It had, in fact, been Joan's, who had recognized the name of Will's fraternity as that of Paul's and suggested that it would be rude not to include her brother's partner's son in the invitation. Watching the two of them together, Ginger now wondered if there hadn't been more to it. Had Joannie been nursing a crush? If so, it was apparently coming to fruition.

The other guys were busy trying to horn in on Paul's conversation with Joan, his interest seemingly enough to spark their own, and Joan's friends were looking on with a mixture of confusion and dismay, as if asking one another, "What has she got that we don't?" Ginger wanted to crow—until she turned and found Craig frowning down on all of them, his glower positively frightening.

Paul noticed Craig at about the same moment as Ginger. Good manners dictated that he acknowledge and greet his father's business partner, but he seemed unwilling to relinquish his monopoly of *Miss* Russell. He solved the problem neatly by slipping his arm about Joan's shoulder and turning her so that she, too, saw Craig.

"Hi!" Joan said, rushing forward and hauling Paul along with her. "Look who's here!"

Paul stuck out his hand. He had to take his arm from around Joan first. "Mr. Russell, it's nice to see you again. My mother sends her best."

Ginger slipped up to Craig's side and surreptitiously poked a finger into Craig's ribs. He jumped slightly and glared down at her. She inclined her head, pleading with her eyes. He got the message. His face smoothed itself out, and he reached for Paul's hand, giving it a strong shake.

"Paul. I, uh, haven't seen your mother in some time. I trust she's well."

"Yes, absolutely. Thank you."

"Ah. Good. So, umm, how's college?"

"Fine. Excellent. I still have two more years."

"Your father says you're studying structural engineering."

"Yes, sir."

"I expect we'll be taking you into the firm one of these days, then."

"I certainly hope so."

"That's wonderful!" Joan said. "I think what Craig does is really interesting."

"You do?" Craig asked. Ginger stepped on his foot, then immediately squeezed his elbow to warn him to stifle the yelp, which he managed just barely to do.

"Joan, dear, why don't you take Paul and the others outside so they can check out the volleyball net. I'll bring you some drinks shortly."

"Sure. Come on, guys. The music's about to start anyway. It's the neatest setup. You've got to meet this musician. He's a genius. I mean, he's a whole band all by himself."

Firmly in control, Joan ushered the group outdoors, Paul at her side. Only Will stayed behind, looking over the painting Craig had helped Ginger hang. Ginger briefly wondered about that. He'd seen that painting before, several times. But she had other things to worry about just now, namely the man at her elbow.

"Why are they doing that?" Craig was saying. "Why is he holding her hand?"

"I would imagine because he doesn't want her to get away," Ginger said calmly.

Craig seemed unable to grasp the concept. He shook his head. "Is that the same little girl who used to curl up on my knee?"

"That little girl is growing up," Ginger said gently. "And about time, too."

He pushed a hand through hair still damp from a recent washing. "One thing's for sure," he grumbled. "She's definitely come out of her shell."

"You sound as if you disapprove," Ginger commented.

He sighed, and the corners of his mouth hitched up into a smile. "Who can disapprove when she's that happy?" he asked, canting his head toward the window.

Ginger followed the line of his gaze and saw Joan leaning a hip against the railing of the deck, her expression relaxed but intent as Paul talked. She seemed very much in her element, neither coy nor flirtatious, just *interested*. Ginger felt a swelling of pride. "She really is handling herself very well."

"Paul seems to think so," Craig said, a slight edge to his voice.

"So?" Ginger asked. "He seems like a nice boy."

"Boy?" Craig scoffed. "That's no boy. If he's not twenty already, he soon will be."

"And Joan's almost eighteen," Ginger pointed out. "Believe me, Craig, she's ready for this."

"Maybe so," he said, "but *I'm* not. Holy cow! That's my business partner's son out there!"

"It's okay," Ginger said soothingly, wanting to point out several reasons why. A look out the door, however, told her that this was not the time. Roland Colgate was headed her way again. She made a mental note to cross him off her list for the next party. He really was turning into a pest. "Try to relax," she advised Craig quickly. "I have to get some drinks. Oh, and thanks for coming."

She gave him a quick kiss on the cheek and hurried off, Roland right behind her. She had hoped the kiss would be a deterrent, but apparently Roland was not going to take the hint. Well, she'd just have to spell it out for him.

Craig watched them go, frowning at the way Roland picked up his pace when Ginger increased hers. He had the distinct impression the fellow was not going along in order to offer his services as waiter. But then it wasn't really any of his business, was it? He turned his head and looked out the window at his sister. She was dancing with Paul, Jr., and managing to carry on a conversation at the same time, despite the volume of the music, if such it could be called. He shook his head. How had that self-conscious little waif turned into the fetching young woman he was seeing? The answer to that was in the kitchen. He turned his head in that direction and caught a glimpse of Ginger pulling away from that guy who'd followed her in there. He frowned, fighting the urge to intercede, and tried to look away—without success.

Ginger had her back to the counter and was smiling at the man. Craig could tell she was speaking, but had no idea what she was saying. Grimly, he turned away, his gut twisting. "None of my business," he muttered. That woman sure had nerve, carrying on like that right under his nose, not that there was any reason she shouldn't—except . . . He slid a look toward his sister. Why, Joan could as easily spot Ginger and her man friend as he could. He gritted his teeth, anger percolating inside him. The compulsion overwhelmed him. With knotted fists, he turned smartly and strode toward the kitchen. As he moved toward her, Ginger lifted a hand and pushed it against the chest of the man who had her pinned next to the counter. It struck him suddenly that she was trying to fend off the character, and he felt his pace quicken.

"Roland," she was saying when Craig stepped into the room. "You have about two seconds to back off and get out of here."

"Now don't be that way," the man said. "You know you like me."

"Once maybe, but I can't for the life of me remember why."

"Why don't I *show* you?"

He leaned toward her, his hands braced on either side of her body, her mouth his obvious aim.

"Why don't *I* show *you* the door?" Craig said, clamping a hand down on the masher's shoulder.

Ginger's gaze jerked up, and Craig almost recoiled from the intensity of the gratitude he saw there. She seemed to know what his reaction would be, for she quickly averted her eyes, but not before she had shaken him to the core.

"Why don't you mind your own business?" Roland said, yanking Craig back to the matter at hand. He had craned his head around and was trying to look threatening. Craig found himself relishing the idea of smashing his fist into that arrogant face. Instead, he wrenched the guy's shoulder back, forcing him to turn away from Ginger, who instantly slipped aside.

"But I am minding my business," Craig said. "See, I'm the official bouncer, and you, my friend, are about to be bounced—unless, of course, you want to just go out that door, turn right and keep going."

Roland slanted Ginger a truly amazed look. Clearly he couldn't believe she was going to let Craig throw him out. She disabused him of that erroneous assumption, however. She raised a hand and trilled her fingers at him. "'Bye, Roland," she said brightly.

Craig squeezed the other man's shoulder as hard as he could. "'Bye, Roland," he echoed.

Wincing, Roland seemed convinced. Craig released him, and Roland made for the door, muttering angrily about being led on. Craig followed and watched the man move down the entry hall and out the front door. Only when the door closed behind him did Craig turn back to her.

"Sheesh! What a creep," he said.

"And what a darling you are!" she replied, hurrying forward. "That was so sweet of you, rescuing me like that. What would I have done without you?"

Craig felt rather flushed with victory at the moment and opened his mouth to voice some appropriate platitude, when suddenly she went up on tiptoe and flung her arms about his neck. For an instant he was too stunned to react, then slowly he became aware of her ripe body pressed to his, from the swellings of her breasts to the rounded firmness of her thighs. Gasping as if injured, he jerked back, reaching up at the same time to close his hands around her wrists, forcing her arms down at her sides. To his ire, they went right back up again the instant he released them. "Cut it out!" he barked, tugging her arms down again and glaring at her.

"I just wanted to thank you," she said with less-than-convincing innocence.

"What for?" he said, struggling to achieve an impassive expression. "I didn't do anything for you. I got rid of that jerk because I don't like having his type at the same party as my little sister."

"Oh," Ginger said, and he relaxed a bit, loosening his grip on her wrists. She turned her arms within the circles of his fingers and slid her palms into place against his. "It had nothing to do with the fact that he was hitting on me?" she asked skeptically.

Craig dropped her hands as if they were hot rocks and brought his own to his waist. "Nothing whatsoever," he assured her gruffly.

She linked her fingers, fighting a smile. "How can I believe you," she asked, "when it was *my* rescue you came charging to?"

"Ginger, I just told you—"

"I don't care why you did it," she said smoothly. "I'm still going to thank you."

Despite his glower, she lifted her arms about his neck once more, went up on tiptoe and carefully placed her mouth against his. Gritting his teeth, Craig refused her a response, but when she pressed close and slowly rotated her head, his lips just seemed to part of their own accord and his teeth followed their lead. Sighing, she licked her tongue along the edges of his teeth, and suddenly his whole body was participating with alarming vigor. He realized with a shock that his arms had come about her and, as before, he jerked back, his hands at her shoulders to push her away, when he found himself staring down into her upturned face, her eyes closed and mouth slightly ajar, a dreamy expression lending her the look of an angel lost in ecstasy.

The poignancy of that expression and the vulnerability it exposed at once angered and enflamed him. How dare she thrust herself into his protection like this? He had told her how sorely he was tempted and exactly what he was tempted to do! But did she listen when he'd insisted that the games stop? Obviously not, or else she didn't believe him, and neither situation was tolerable. It came to him with absolute conviction that he had to teach her a lesson, and the sooner the better. He cleared his throat and, grinning wolfishly, watched with pleasure as her eyes popped open.

"Ah," he said, "so the games are on again. But don't you think we should at least close the doors?"

She gifted him with a moment of utter confusion, during which he excused himself and quickly strode to first one set of double doors and then another, shutting them. That done, he turned back to the woman who had been needling him with her abundant sex appeal since the day he'd taken possession of his house. She made a most fetching picture, her eyes wide and lips parted, leonine hair frothing about her shoulders, her voluptuous body packed into an unusually conservative one-piece bathing suit of shiny purple fabric, a filmy little skirt of floral organza ruffled about her thighs. He walked toward her, hands hanging loose at his sides, and she gulped.

"Cr-Craig," she said, "I have thirty guests out there!"

"They won't miss you for a while," he said, coming closer. "Long enough to play out the game."

"Game? What game?"

"Why, the game of satisfaction," he said. "Mutual satisfaction." He lifted his hands and let them skim down her arms, feeling her skin heat as his rubbed against it. A tightening in his groin warned him that this game carried with it consequences for both players, but he couldn't think of that now. Besides, the fact that a party was going on beyond those closed doors provided certain constraints, a fact of which he intended to convince her he was unaware. "Now," he said softly, "where were we?" Slowly, he took her hands in his and placed them about his neck. "Right about here, was it?" He bent his head, bringing his mouth close to hers, and wrapped his arms about her waist. "Or was it here?"

"Oh, my," she said as he pulled her hard against him and brought his mouth down over hers. He expected resistance of some sort, not kicking and screaming, certainly, but perhaps a stiffening of the neck and shoulder muscles, a firming of the mouth. Instead, he got heat. She just melted, shifting her weight against him and parting her lips, her arms sliding around his neck. It was a jolting, disorienting experience, and he reached up with one hand to clasp the back of her head and keep her from slipping through his arms and puddling at his feet. That proved to be a big mistake, for it deepened the kiss, increasing the pulse in his groin to a whamming throb—and igniting a passion the depth of which he had not begun to fathom even in his dreams.

She was suddenly writhing in his arms, grinding her mouth against his as if she intended to swallow him whole, and with some perversion he hadn't recognized in himself heretofore, he felt sheer joy. Amazed, he captured her head with both hands and thrust his tongue into her mouth. She sucked it deep into the silky cavern, and the automatic response of his body was to press his hips against hers. She answered with more pressure, which was both too much and not nearly enough. He dropped his arms about her waist and crushed her to him, throwing himself off balance and swaying precariously backward, which obliged her to pull in the opposite direction and break the kiss.

Stunned, he stumbled away, gasping, "My God!" while she merely gaped at him, her mouth lush and rosy and wholly delectable. He put a hand to his head, reeling with the aftershocks of such electric contact, and read on her face the same amazement that gripped him. His first instinct was to run. The game was more dangerous than he had supposed, and the sounds of Joan's party spilled through the closed doors of that kitchen as if they were made of air, making him aware that his sister was there on the other side. But even as he pushed his stymied muscles to move, the glow in her eyes pulled at him, and like a magnet to iron, he felt himself moving in the wrong direction. He took one step, and she hurled herself across the space between them and right into his arms, which folded about her as neatly as if they'd done it a thousand times.

His mouth found hers with unerring precision and opened as if by telepathic suggestion. Her tongue skipped past his teeth and licked upward. Thinking he'd burst with need, he bent his head low, giving her back tit for tat and exulting when she moaned pleadingly. She pushed a hand into his hair and splayed the other between his shoulder blades. He slid his arms down her back until his hands cupped her buttocks, holding her as his hips ground against her. She twined a leg about one of his and rubbed her pointed toe into the hollow of his knee. He slid his hands lower and lifted her against him; her legs wrapped around him like ribbons around a maypole.

The game was not satisfaction but torture, delicious, heady torture to which he could see no end but one, and yet he couldn't close out the music, couldn't lose the image of Joan dancing and laughing on the other side of those doors. He wanted to bury himself in this incredible sexy woman and damn the consequences, but he didn't dare. If only it were just the two of them, he'd end this burning ache or imbed it so deeply within him that it could never be assuaged. It had to stop.

Craig possessed more strength of will than he knew, for somehow he found what he needed to coax some distance between them and begin disengagement. Ginger seemed slow to understand that he was forfeiting the match, but gradually her feet slid to the floor and her weight shifted. Little by little, her embrace slackened, and finally her tongue retreated and he parted his mouth from hers, bumping his nose against hers in conciliation. She sighed heavily, and he stepped back, pulling a deep, clean breath. She lifted the back of a hand to her mouth and raised her eyes. They gleamed with triumph.

"One of us proved a point," she said huskily. "If you're bold enough to admit it."

"Meaning what?" he asked, his voice little more than a rasp.

"Meaning," she said, "that it goes far deeper than simple lust."

"There's nothing simple about it," he retorted. "And that's just the problem."

"Don't you see what it means?" she demanded.

"Do you?" he countered.

She placed her hands on his chest and smiled. "It means we're perfectly mated."

"Like hell!" He snatched her hands from his chest and dragged her toward the counter. "You're going to listen to me, Ginger, and get this straight in your head once and for all." He lifted her onto the counter and placed a hand on either side, effectively trapping her. "I am attracted to you, Ginger. In fact, I am wildly attracted to you, but I've been attracted to lots of women, and I haven't married any one of them."

"But this is different," she said. "I know it is."

He shook his head. "No, it's not. It is exactly the same, because I didn't want to get married then and I don't want to get married now. Even if I did, Ginger, I couldn't because I already have obligations."

She arched a slender eyebrow skeptically. "Such as?"

"Such as my sister and my business."

She rolled her eyes. "For goodness' sake, Craig, the world's full of men who have sisters, businesses *and* wives."

"But I'm not one of them," he insisted firmly. "And I'm not going to be!"

"Well, you should be," she retorted. "Even Joan agrees. She's not a baby anymore, you know. Before long she'll be out on her own, then what will you have to come home to?" She scooted to the edge of the counter and slid a hand up his arm to his shoulder, then lifted it to his cheek.

He closed his eyes, saying tightly, "Ginger, don't," but she ignored him and traced the square line of his jaw with her fingertips.

"What you need," she said softly, "is a loving, caring, talented, attractive, *passionate* wife." She slid her hand around to the back of his head and, leaning forward, draped the other arm over his shoulder. "You need someone who can make coming home a very rewarding experience, every day an adventure." She parted her legs and wrapped them around him, pulling him close. "You need me." She bent her head and rubbed her lips provocatively back and forth against his. The effect was absolutely explosive. He ran his hands over her legs and lifted his chin to allow her better access to his mouth.

"Hell," he growled, surrendering to the ache that drew him to her, and yet resisting at least nominally. "You don't know what you're asking for."

"Yes, I do," she whispered, and she pressed her mouth to his.

He responded with ruthless hunger, his hands availing themselves of her body. Deliberately, he cupped her breasts and began to gently squeeze and pluck at the nipples peaked beneath the spandex of her suit. Within moments she was writhing against his palms, the pull of her mouth fiercely intense. She just wouldn't learn, he told himself, and he was tired of fighting it.

He dropped his hands to her thighs and stroked them upward, his fingertips brushing her sensitive apex. She gasped and shuddered, locking her legs around his hips, and he fought thoughts of Jo and the party and the music—but there was no music, only the distant murmur of voices and the faint trill of laughter and a kind of dry grating, which he only belatedly connected with the clearing of a throat. Ginger seemed to make the connection at about the same time, because suddenly the kiss was broken and she was sliding away.

"Don't let me interrupt," said a droll, urbane voice behind him.

Craig spun around to find Ginger's brother, of all people, watching from the doorway. He felt an immediate and intense pique followed by burning embarrassment. He caught a deep breath. "N-no pr-problem," he stammered, bouncing his gaze off of every surface in the room, anything but Will's face. "I—I was..." What? He glanced at

Ginger and swallowed. *About to make love to your sister,* came the thought. Mentally, he reeled away from that and bumped into the word he was looking for. "Going," he said. "I w-was just going."

"Wait," Ginger said. "Let's talk about this. Craig, don't go."

But he couldn't stay, not after what had just happened between them, or what had *almost* happened between them and what Will had undoubtedly witnessed. "I have to, uh, make a phone call," he lied, jerking into motion. "Thanks for..." What? Helping him make a fool of himself? Almost making love with him? *Not* making love with him? He searched hopelessly for a way to complete the thought, then abandoned the effort and simply walked away. He heard Ginger and her brother speaking behind him.

"So that's the one, huh? Not bad, but maybe I ought to tell him to just give up and go peaceably to the altar before someone gets hurt."

"Blast you, Willis!"

Craig didn't hear any more. He was moving too fast.

Will, to his credit, was trying not to laugh, but Ginger was unappreciative of the effort. "What did you think you were doing?" she demanded, aiming her disappointment at the only available target.

"Hey," he replied, "how was I to know you had the guy in a clinch in here? I was just trying to find out what happened to the drinks everybody's asking about."

"The drinks!" Her hand went to her head. Well, they couldn't be too badly watered down by now. How fast did ice melt anyway? Two kisses, two *fireball* kisses, make that three, and an unwelcome interruption. Hardly enough time to melt the polar cap, not that she truly cared at the moment. All she really cared about had just walked out.

No, that wasn't true. There were her parents, Joannie— and Will. No matter how bad his timing was, he was still her brother and she loved him, and because she did, she resisted the impulse to pummel his face. It wasn't him she wanted to pummel anyway.

Sighing, Ginger went to the counter, picked up the tray of slowly warming soft drinks and delivered them into the hands of her smiling brother. "There," she said. "Go calm the natives."

He hesitated, the smile stiffening. "Right. But, umm, sis, mind if I offer a bit of advice?"

As if she could stop him, but then Will was a good kid. She was not only deeply fond of him—when he wasn't interrupting the rare romantic moment—but proud of him, as well. Will was one of the few persons in the world whose opinion mattered to her. She loosened up enough to lose her scowl. "Sure, go ahead, Will."

His handsome eyes grew soft. "Don't push it so hard."

"I beg your pardon?"

"Don't push it so hard with Russell," he said gently.

She lifted her chin. "What do you mean?"

Now his eyes were asking if she honestly didn't know, and she felt herself wilting.

"Gingevine," he said. "I know I'm still a babe in bunting and all that, but I'm old enough to know that if a woman tempts a man with sex, sex is probably all she's going to get."

That hit close to home, too close. She didn't want him to know how close. "Maybe sex is what I'm after," she said. "We girls have to live, too, you know!"

He squinted at her, judiciously shaking his head. "You forget who you're talking to. This is me, the baby brother."

She looked away, sufficiently humbled, and let the despair and frustration surface. "I don't mean to, Will. It's just that he, well, gets to me. He gets close and something just comes over me. I can't think of anything else! But it's the same way with him, Will, I know it is, no matter what he says."

"Probably," Will conceded. "But, honey, that doesn't mean you and he would get the same thing out of it. I mean, you're operating with one motive, and he's almost certainly operating with another."

"I don't care. In the end, I know it would come out right."

"You can't know that," Will argued. "Listen, Gin, guys' minds just don't work the same way as yours. Come to think of it, nobody's mind works the way yours does, but that's beside the point. What I'm getting at is this—as far as sex is concerned, most guys will take whatever they can get, so it's up to the woman to set the limits. That's unfair, no doubt, but that's how it is."

"You think I don't know that?" she asked. "You act like Craig is the first man I've ever met!"

He laughed, then said gently, "Not the first you've met, surely, but maybe the first you've really loved?"

She turned away. "I wouldn't say that exactly. We're still getting to know one another."

"Well, then, you've got to make some decisions."

"Such as?"

"Such as whether or not he's the man you think he is and how far you're willing to go on the chance that he'll reciprocate your feelings and commit."

"He's a good man," she said. "Maybe it's only physical with him now, but it could be more. It *will* be more. Somehow I know it."

"I hope so, for your sake." Will bent and kissed her on the cheek, then left her, bearing the tray of drinks.

She closed her eyes. "So do I, Will," she whispered. "Oh, so do I."

Chapter Twelve

Craig was shaking as he walked across Ginger's living room and out onto the deck. Of all the stupid, harebrained things for him to do, kissing Ginger Brenan had to be the dumbest, especially with all these people around, not to mention Jo! And what had it proved? What had it accomplished? He'd known beforehand that an affair was ill-advised, to say the least, and still he'd let himself fall victim to her allure. It was frightening the way she affected him. And the way she responded to him! Just the memory of it was igniting sexual responses in his body again. A man could get addicted to that—fast. It played with his mind, defeated his good sense. He shuddered to think what might have transpired if Will had not come along when he had. He wanted to think that he would not have actually made love to her right there in the kitchen while the house swarmed with people, but right now he wasn't so sure. He was sure of only one thing at the moment, and that was that he was not ready to "go peaceably to the altar," as Will had suggested. His best alternative seemed to be escape. The problem was going to be Joan.

She was going to be disappointed, but he didn't feel comfortable leaving his little sister with a college guy—never mind that Paul was his business partner's son and well-known to him. Even the best men were susceptible to temptation, mature men who ought to know better, let alone some wet-behind-the-ears Romeo out to prove himself a Don Juan. Joan would just have to understand.

The one-man band Ginger had provided for her guests' listening enjoyment, a relative term at best, was blasting metallic sounds at downtown Orlando. Craig was in no mood to have his eardrums punctured, but he paused at the edge of the deck to look around for his sister. He missed her the first time, but then she moved away from the gang of young people who had surrounded her, Paul, Jr., at her side. The two of them strolled casually down the beach, talking animatedly. It was almost surreal, seeing his sister like that, and he admitted that he was torn about it. Part of him longed for the Joan he had known, a dainty, fragile, shy, helpless little girl, while another part of him lauded the laughing, flirting, socially adept young woman she was now. She had become the essence of femininity, an utter paradox, but she was still his little sister.

He went down the steps and across the sand, past a number of deck chairs and spread towels, all occupied. The music was still loud enough to rattle the fillings in his teeth, but not so loud that he couldn't hear the shouts and hoots of the people playing volleyball at the water's edge and the ripple of laughter coming from the knot of people just abandoned by his sister and his partner's son. Several people nodded and lifted hands as he passed, but he knew none of them and was in no mood to chat. They had to settle for curt nods and fleeting looks, not that anyone really seemed to mind.

Someone behind called out Ginger's name, and Craig had the sudden sensation of being pursued. His skin prickled, and a vision of her formed before his mind's eye. The purple one-piece bathing suit she wore was molded to her slender waist, firm midriff and voluptuous breasts. The filmy flowered skirt she had wrapped around her lower body rippled and floated in the breeze, leaving bare her shapely legs to midthigh and even higher. Her long, thick hair fell about her face and shoulders in wide, silky waves, tendrils of it wafting on an errant breeze. He felt his whole body tighten and impulsively picked up his pace, stumbling over a volleyball that rolled into his path. A moment later he drew up behind Joan and caught her hand. She halted and turned, Paul, Jr., following suit an instant later.

"What's up?" she asked. "Having fun?"

"No," he said. "I'm going home and I want you to come with me."

Joan pushed hair out of her face and just looked at him. "I don't want to go home. Paul and I are taking a walk."

"Jo," Craig said, "we need to talk and—"

"Not now, Craig." Her voice had an edge to it that he had never heard before, a very *mature* edge, firm and even a bit condescending. It took him off guard, left him staring at her with puzzlement. She shook her head and smiled. "I'm sorry. I didn't mean to snap. It's just that Paul and I are taking a walk. Besides, I have friends here, guests. I can't just abandon them. We'll talk later, I promise." She squeezed his hand, and her eyes were filled with something very like ... Pity? That or something so near as to be synonymous. Pity from his little sister? For him?

He backed away, his fingers sliding out of her grasp. She was a stranger standing there, an alien, not his Jo at all. *His* Jo. He knew it was irrational, but he felt betrayed, alone. For a moment he considered ordering her home, but then Paul, Jr., made some movement, a hand lifted to his forehead or temple or the bridge of his nose. It was enough to remind Craig that they were not alone. He wouldn't embarrass her, not in front of an audience, certainly not in front of his partner's son. He turned around and jogged toward home, literally wounded.

"Craig!"

Jo's voice and her hand on his back stopped him. "What?" The word sounded sharp, angry. She stepped in front of him.

"I love you, Craig," she said softly, and his anger just melted away.

He put his arms around her, emotion of another kind swamping him. "I love you, too, kiddo."

She hugged him tight. "I'm going to stay, Craig. I have to and I want to."

He smiled, knowing himself for a fool. "Sure you do. Don't mind me. I'm just tired. Been working too hard. I'm going home to take a nap. You stay and have a good time. Just behave yourself. Promise?"

"Promise."

He squinted down the beach at Paul Solis, Jr., who waited patiently for Jo's return. He had to say it. He just had to. She was his baby sister. "That's guy's too old for you, you know."

She pulled back and shook her head, and there was that look again, as if she had somehow come to understand him better than he understood himself. It cut him to the quick.

"Not anymore," she said, and he knew she was right, and that hurt, too. He pressed a hand to her cheek, turned and walked away, not trusting himself to speak again. Not his Jo anymore, but her own.

He skirted the volleyball net and walked on toward his own private stretch of sand, trying not to hurry. From the corner of his eye he caught sight of Ginger standing at the rail of her deck, arms folded, eyes following him. Will stood at her side, an arm about her shoulders protectively. He surprised Craig by lifting his hand and giving it a jaunty little wave. Likable kid, Craig decided, but he didn't acknowledge the farewell, just put his head down and walked doggedly on. He was trembling again and sweaty.

When he reached the house, he went inside and lay down. After a long while he slept, despite the music coming to him from next door, but his dreams were so erotic they woke him and left him staring at the ceiling in his room. He had never felt so alone in his life, which made no sense at all because, with the exception of a few short intervals, he'd lived by himself nearly fifteen years when Jo had finally come to him. For this, too, he had only Ginger Brenan to thank, and yet he couldn't quite be angry at her anymore.

It wasn't just that he liked her, that she was a gorgeous, sexy, even a charming woman. It was much more. For one thing, she cared. She cared about him and about Jo. He didn't know why. It just seemed part of her nature, caring. Then, too, she was interesting, probably the most interesting woman he'd ever met, not at all the mindless bimbo he'd first judged her to be. Jo was crazy about her. And there was no denying that the woman did things to him physically and sexually no other woman had even approached. So why didn't he just relax and let it happen? He didn't know.

Maybe it was a male thing, a gender-specific aversion to situations that could lead to marriage. Maybe he simply had more marriage-allergic genes than normal guys. On the other hand, maybe it was merely that Ginger's direct, head-on methods offended some deeply ingrained expectation of his. He was honest enough to admit to himself that under other circumstances, he could very well be doing his damnedest to seduce the woman, in which event it could have been a matter of chasing her until she caught him, as the old saying went. Why that seemed preferable, he didn't understand. In fact, he didn't have any answers. He just knew that he couldn't let her run him to the ground like a hunter running down game.

So what was he going to do about it? Again, he didn't have any answers. But some voice in the back of his head was saying, *Why not let nature take its course and see what happens?* Undoubtedly that was his gonads talking. He didn't have any illusions about what the natural course would be with Ginger Brenan and him. On second thought, though, it might not be such a bad idea. Could be that the real thrill for Ginger was the chase. Once she had him—or *thought* she had him—she might not even want him anymore, and vice versa.

It was a risky theory but worthy of some consideration. His other plan was probably doomed to failure, anyway. He

didn't really have much hope of avoiding her, given her relationship with Jo and the fact that she lived next door, not
to mention that Ginger, being Ginger, didn't seem to know
the meaning of the word *defeat*. Still, he would be taking an
awfully big chance. *Might be worth it,* he thought, then
shook his head. Those gonads again. In the end, though, he
found that he really didn't have much choice, short of
moving halfway across the continent. Even then, he knew
that he couldn't escape Ginger Brenan. Joan would never
forgive him, Ginger would always be there between them
and he would still be dreaming, waking to stare at the ceiling. Alone. God, what was he going to do? What could he
do? What did he *want* to do? That was one question, at
least, for which he had an answer, and maybe it was the only
answer.

She didn't know what to think. After the way he'd raced
out of the house and left her party, Ginger had expected the
walls to come up again, and in a way they had, but he wasn't
avoiding her and she didn't know what to think about that.
If she'd had the courage to press the matter, maybe she'd
have found out, but it didn't seem wise for two reasons. One
was the way that last kiss had affected him. He hadn't been
able to run fast enough, and he had gone even after Joan
had refused to go with him, which of itself was proof
enough of his desperation to get away. Reason number two
was a bit more complicated.

Ginger was amazed how greatly *she* was affected by Craig
Russell's kisses. Suddenly she hadn't been in control any
longer, but even knowing that, she hadn't wanted to stop.
Actually, she wasn't sure she could've stopped, and that
worried her because she wasn't sure of something else. She
wasn't sure he was going to change his mind about marriage. She didn't know if she dared risk that. But how could
she not? She loved him. She knew that for a fact now. She
honestly loved him—and Joannie. And it was for Joan that
she went to see Craig nearly three weeks after the party.

He opened the door, stepped back and let her in. It was
raining and she'd gone to the front of the house rather than

the rear for that very reason, because the entry was covered. But here he was playing the gentleman and inviting her in. She left her umbrella on the doorstep and went inside. She felt almost shy about it and was no more eager to touch than he seemed to be. The sensations were too sharp. The very atmosphere around them felt charged. The air almost sizzled. They stood apart in the entry hall, exchanging pleasantries. He asked if she wanted to go into the living room and sit down, but she shook her head.

"I can't stay. I just wanted to have a word with you about Joan."

"All right. Anything special? It can't be a problem. I've never seen her so happy."

Ginger nodded, avoiding his gaze. At that moment, she didn't know what she feared to see there, desire or the lack of it. Perhaps both. She lifted her hair off the back of her neck. It was damp and itched. She wished she had put it up.

"It's about her birthday," she told him. "I thought about planning something, but I know it would mean more to her if you would do it."

He chuckled and folded his arms. "I don't know about *that* but I'm certainly willing to do whatever you suggest."

She was surprised. It wasn't like Craig to give in so easily. In truth, she'd only suggested that he do it instead of her because she had expected him to argue that he wasn't any good at planning celebrations. After a suitable length of time, she'd intended to give in and offer to do it herself. *Hoist with my own petard,* she mused, and it wasn't the first time. Served her right, too. She smiled, stifling the impulse to laugh outright.

"Well," Ginger said, "why don't you talk to Joan about it, see what she wants? After all, a girl only turns eighteen once."

"True. I'll speak to her right away."

"Good, and keep an open mind, will you? I don't know what she's likely to propose, but just remember that at bottom, she's a sensible girl. Whatever she asks for, it's probably innocent enough—and if by some quirk of fate it's not, well, we'll cross that bridge when we come to it. All right?"

She expected a fight now. It was at this point that Craig usually panicked. He didn't yet seem quite able to accept the idea that Joan was gradually achieving independence. She was sure that when he thought over all the possibilities now open to his sister, his feet would start getting cold. She lifted her chin, ready for any argument, and for the first time looked him square in the eye. What she saw there was ... Craig, warmth, a kind of openness. Her heart swelled, her spirit soaring on a rise of new and unexpected hope.

"All right," he was saying. "I'll do my best, but you know how us big brothers are, slow to adapt." He smiled and she found herself laughing.

"You're getting there. In fact, I see real improvement."

His smile widened. "Oh, really?"

"Uh-huh, and I know it's a big adjustment. She sort of blossomed overnight, didn't she?"

"Yes, she did, and we have you to thank for that."

It wasn't meant entirely as a compliment. Craig still had his doubts, which was only to be expected. After all, it had been difficult for him, seeing his little sister become a young woman all of a sudden. Ginger understood. But as he said the words in that slightly scathing tone, he tapped the end of her nose with his finger and she thought she was going to melt. The gesture seemed ... well, affectionate. It was ridiculous, of course, a grown woman getting weak in the knees over a playful little tap on the nose, but she couldn't help it. Only Craig could do that to her. Didn't he know that yet?

She braced herself by pressing her palms against the wall, feeling the rough texture of the paper in enhanced detail. She tried to think of some way to take back her refusal to go into the living room and sit with him, but nothing came to mind, nothing at all. Finally, she gave up and simply smiled.

"Well," she said, gazing up at him with what she feared were worshipful eyes, "I should go now. Er, let me know what Joan says—not that I have anything to do with it. But I do want to know. I want to help her celebrate her birthday, I mean. That's all." She wanted to bite her tongue. What was wrong with her, babbling like that?

But Craig seemed untroubled by it. He just shrugged. "Okay."

Okay? Suddenly it was all right that she automatically included herself in what was normally family domain? Gosh, this *was* improvement, a lot of improvement. Ginger wanted to throw her arms around him, to laugh and hug him and get hugged back, but that would definitely be pushing her luck, and she couldn't bear to cast a pall on all this improvement.

"Great." She groped for the door handle, found it. "Well, I'll be seeing you."

"Absolutely. I'll get back to you quick as I can."

"Great." She'd said that already. "'Bye."

He caught the edge of the door as she pulled it back, so that for a moment she stood beneath his arm. He had only to drop it and fold her against him, but he didn't, and she passed through the door and picked up her umbrella. She hoped he might call her back, suggest she wait until the rain abated, but he just stood there and watched her walk out into it.

When she reached her own house, Ginger paused to look back, and he lifted his hand in a kind of farewell before closing his door, as if satisfied that she had gotten home safely. She hugged herself against the chill of the rain and savored the feel of progress. At last.

Craig stood in the foyer with his hands in his pockets, smiling. She was pleased. She'd made a suggestion and for once he hadn't bothered to argue. It was almost funny how much it pleased her, and it was almost frightening how much *that* pleased him. But what the heck. It didn't do him any good to argue anyway. She usually won, and she was usually right. Besides, if he planned this event, maybe he could control it. Maybe. It was worth a try anyway.

He walked through the kitchen and down the hall to Joan's room, tapped on the door, then opened it and stepped in.

"Ginger was just here," he said.

Joan looked up from the book she was reading. "Oh? What did she want?"

"She wants me to ask you about your birthday."

"Yeah?" Jo closed the book and laid it aside. "What about my birthday?"

"Well, what do you want to do? We can't just let it pass. It's your eighteenth, after all."

She smiled at him in that cool way of hers, a product of the new maturity. "How about a dinner party?"

He lifted his eyebrows. "A dinner party?"

"Sure. Why not? It would be fun, and I'm certain Ginger would help me with everything. I mean, I ought to know how to give a dinner party, don't you think?"

"I guess so. It's just, I thought . . . well, I don't know. Do your friends go in for that kind of thing?"

Jo wrinkled her nose. "Not many of them, but that's okay. It should be something you and Ginger can enjoy, too, because I wouldn't think of having my eighteenth birthday without the two of you there."

The two of them, Ginger and him. Despite the fact that he'd been entertaining such ideas himself, Craig felt a surge of alarm at Jo's casual pairing of them, as if they were truly a couple. Common sense told him that there had to be some level of involvement for him and Ginger between those of speaking acquaintances and marriage, but for the life of him he couldn't seem to put his finger on just what that might be. Had Ginger not been determined to find herself a husband, he felt he might have been able to come up with some mutually satisfying arrangement between them, but as it was, he couldn't seem to just let develop between them what he otherwise would have, no matter that he wanted it. So he found himself drawing her forward with one hand and holding her off with the other, behavior he seemed unable to correct.

"Maybe Ginger would find it an imposition," he said. "I mean, she's already given one party for you." He knew it was an idiotic thing to say, but he was stuck with it.

Jo smiled almost secretively and shook her head. Was he imagining the touch of condescension? "Don't worry about

Ginger," she said. Then softly she added, "Ginger loves us, you know."

Loves us? he queried silently, and immediately he knew it was true. A warm feeling flooded him. Someone loved them. Someone loved Jo; someone loved him. Why? he wondered. Jo was easy to figure. Looking at her now, he saw her as she had been before, so very needy, so lifeless, so lacking in confidence. Ginger's heart had doubtlessly gone out to that fragile, hurting, needing girl. It was that female thing, the nurturing instinct, as well as Joan's innate sweetness, her intelligence, her gentleness. Ginger's affection for the girl was easy to explain. But what about him? Were Ginger's feelings for him more than her very real enthusiasm for marriage, more than passion? Were they truly personal? Could Ginger actually love him just as he was?

He knew he had his faults. He worked too much. He often let matters go rather than confront them. He kept his own counsel, rarely discussing problems or solutions with others. He was beginning to realize, now that he and Joan had been together some while, that he didn't really know how to share. He feared he had even attempted to keep his life carefully separate from hers. And used her to keep him safely separate from others? He closed his eyes and lifted a hand to his temple. He honestly didn't want to think about it. He wasn't even sure he wanted to know how deep Ginger's feelings went. But he could not forget, would never forget how it felt to touch her, hold her, kiss her, desire feeding on desire, his for her, hers for him. His body quickened, blood flowing to his groin. Quickly, desperately, he fixed his attention on Joan.

"It's your birthday," he said, aware that his voice was brusque. "Plan whatever you want and get back to me. We'll work it out." He had purposefully not mentioned Ginger, but he was smart enough to know that she was going to have a hand in this event. He was strangely resigned to it. In fact, it almost seemed right. Ginger was such a big part of Jo's life now, and somehow he had to reconcile that within himself. He had to find a way to integrate Ginger into his own life, not only for Jo's sake, but also his own. He supposed it was inevitable that Ginger come to mean something more than a neighbor to him.

"Thanks, Craig," Joan said. Her smile was soft and generous. He felt a sudden aching need to protect her, cosset her, make her giggle as he'd done when she'd been a baby—but she was no longer a baby. Some part of him wanted to deny that, but he'd have settled for slowing down the process of maturation somewhat. It was just happening too fast, and he couldn't help being afraid for her. Was she truly prepared for the risks, the disappointments, the settlements one made with adulthood? The question nagged at him, harried him, and he knew there could be no pat answer. Troubled, he went out and left his sister to resume her reading and plan her birthday celebration. He only hoped he would find a way to truly share it with her. He just couldn't forget what had happened at the last party that both he and Ginger had attended.

Over the next several days, Joan surprised him with the varying aspects of her plan. She had put together a surprisingly appetizing menu, intending to do the cooking herself, with Ginger's help, of course. Since they didn't have any china, she had arranged to borrow some of Ginger's, but she pleaded to be allowed to buy certain table linens and was given permission. She wanted to serve wine, an idea Craig nixed. Apparently foreseeing this, Ginger had suggested a flavored coffee to be served with dessert, coffee being a very "adult" beverage. He accepted the idea with exaggerated grace.

Then came the problem of the guest list. Joan wanted to invite Paul and Marian Solis to her dinner party—and Paul, Jr.—as well as a friend from school named Nathalie Hotchkiss and a young man whose name Craig did not recognize. He turned out to be a buddy of young Paul's. Joan even had a seating chart drawn up, and a quick look confirmed Craig's greatest concern. It was definitely set up as a couples thing: Paul and Marian Solis; Paul, Jr., and Joan; Nathalie Hotchkiss and the unknown pal; himself and Ginger. Just the idea of it made his collar seem a little tight. He seized upon the only protection that came to mind.

"What about Aunt Maggie?" he argued. "She's bound to feel hurt if you don't include her in your birthday celebration."

Joan bit her lip, clearly disliking the idea, but he held her gaze until she relented, sighing. "Oh, all right. I'll invite Aunt Maggot, but if she embarrasses me in front of my friends, I'm never going to let you forget it."

"I'll speak to her," he promised, knowing full well what Maggie was capable of saying or doing. He would speak to her in no uncertain terms, and she would be on her best behavior or it would be the last time she'd ever embarrass Joan. Was it worth it, he wondered, to feel safe? Or was safety where he and Ginger Brenan were concerned an impossibility? Still, he was rather proud of himself for thinking of Maggie—until Joan shocked him by pairing up Aunt Maggie with Ginger's father. He told himself that Frederick Brenan very likely would not come. Why should he attend the eighteenth-birthday party of his daughter's next-door neighbor? Of course he would not attend.

Craig put the matter out of mind. He watched benignly while Joan painstakingly lettered and addressed simple white invitations, practiced arranging flowers and cooked with newly found enthusiasm and confidence. He nodded helpfully when she modeled the very elegant and—thankfully—modest outfits that she and Ginger brought home on approval from their shopping expeditions. He did his own shopping early, and even acquiesced without argument when Joan requested that he wear his handsome black tuxedo on that all-important evening.

The whole thing had a rather cartoonish feel to him. It was his own sweet Jo playing at being a grown-up, and his role was to portray the indulgent host, to provide the setting for the jewel. He was even enjoying himself. He listened, amused, as the phone calls came, one after another, accepting Joan's invitation. She chatted up each caller, face shining, and to Craig it was as if he were sitting in his mother's clean, modest living room, watching a football game on the television with his father, while little Jo chat-tered in play conversation on a pink toy telephone at his feet. It didn't get real until Frederick Brenan called.

Craig answered the phone himself, the sleek, white cordless model in the den. He was breathless from having pedaled half a dozen miles on the stationary bike, but he didn't have any trouble figuring out who was calling when the clipped, mature voice of a man requested to speak with "Miss Joan Russell," concerning "a very interesting dinner invitation." Craig muttered something in response and slipped down the hall to Joan's room. The door was standing open, so he simply walked in.

"Phone's for you," he said, sitting on the corner of the bed to watch and listen. "I think it's Frederick Brenan."

Joan's eyes widened uncertainly for an instant, but then she swallowed away her nervousness and calmly picked up the receiver on the bedside table. "Hello," she said, then after a moment, "Thank you for calling." She listened attentively for several seconds, then smiled. "I'm very glad you'll be coming, Mr. Brenan. Ginger told me it would be all right to invite you, but I wasn't sure you'd want to bother."

She laughed at something Frederick said, the sound throaty and bubbling and far too mature for Craig's comfort. He fidgeted, trying not to get sweat on her bedspread, and he finally got up, to stand impatiently with his hands on his hips while she finished the conversation. After perhaps another full minute, she hung up.

"That's everyone," she said, hunching her shoulders. "Aunt Maggie called earlier this afternoon." Jo got up and walked toward him almost shyly. "Ginger probably got him to say yes, though, of course, he denied it. He seems very nice."

Craig wondered how nice Frederick Brenan would be to him. Did he know about him and Ginger? *Is there anything to know?* Craig wondered silently. To Joan he said, "I hope this turns out the way you want it to."

She cocked her head. "Me, too."

"Hey," he said, realizing how concerned she suddenly was, "it's going to be fine, really."

She nodded swiftly. "Sure. What can go wrong? I mean, Ginger will be there the whole time."

"And me," he said gently. "I'll be there, too." He reached for levity. "Listen, if everyone gets bored, I'll tell a smutty joke or something."

Joan gasped. "You wouldn't!"

He grinned. "No, I wouldn't, but I could always tell them what an adorable baby you were." Her face broke into a smile and a few giggles escaped her. Encouraged, he went on. "I'll tell them how you used to suck the corner of your blanket and wear that old baseball mitt of mine on your head."

"No, you won't!" she exclaimed, laughing and suddenly swatting at him.

He jumped back an instant before her hand connected, her fingertips fanning his shirtfront. Laughing, he jogged backward toward the door. "I know, I can tell them about the cricket you ate when you were two!"

"Craig Russell, don't you dare!" She chased after him, grinning and slapping at him with her tiny hand.

He fled down the hall, laughing. "Remember when you wore your house shoes to school?"

She gave up the chase, groaned and collapsed against the wall, her hand over her face. Craig stopped where he was, a safe distance between them, and folded his arms. "You'll ruin me with that story," she complained poutily. "And I was only in the third grade!"

He flashed her a grin to show that he wasn't fooled by her dramatic tone. "Oh, and you used to think Edelle Carter from down the street was the *real* Barbie," he teased.

"Any little kid would think that," Joan defended. "She was a teenager with long blond hair, and her boyfriend's name was Ken!"

He laughed at her and saw the wiggling of a smile upon her mouth. Slowly he walked back to her. "I won't embarrass you at your birthday party, little sister," he promised.

"You better not," she said. "Or I'll spike your tea with Tabasco sauce!"

He reached out and ruffled her hair. "You would, wouldn't you?"

She wrinkled her nose and gave him a decided nod, then abruptly she began to shake her head. "Probably not," she admitted, giggling. "But I'd tell Ginger to, and she would!"

He rolled his eyes. "Now *that* I believe."

They both laughed, then gradually sobered. Craig put out his hand and curled his fingers beneath her chin, lifting her face for his perusal. It was a perfect face, delicate, pale, lovely in a classical sense, childlike, yet strangely serene.

"This party is important to you, isn't it, kiddo?" he said gently.

Jo's pale pink mouth turned up slightly at the corners. "Yes," she answered simply.

He waited, but she said nothing more. He supposed it didn't matter why. For whatever reason, it was important to her, and he wasn't about to mess it up. This was for Joan, not Frederick Brenan, not Maggie, not Ginger, not even himself. For her, he would be a relaxed, gracious host. He promised himself that he would be patient and calm, that he would treat her like the adult she was striving so diligently to become. He would keep a tight rein on Maggie and even be charming and accepting of Ginger as a dinner partner. He put his small voices to rest, resolved his doubts and committed himself to it. It was the least he could do for his baby sister, who wasn't a baby at all any longer.

What would happen would happen, with Jo as with Ginger. He had known it for some time now, felt it, but hadn't wanted to acknowledge it. He couldn't keep Jo from growing up any more than he could keep Ginger out of his mind. He was nervous but resigned, and oddly eager for whatever would come. He could only hope that it was not frustration. He'd had his fill of frustration, and it struck him suddenly why. He wanted Ginger Brenan, and he was tired of telling himself that he couldn't have her.

Chapter Thirteen

Ginger was as nervous as she had been back in high school on her first date. Maggie was going to savage her tonight, she just knew it. She only hoped her father could handle it. He could be quite bellicose when one of his children was hurt or criticized in any way. However, the only thing more devastating than Frederick Brenan's temper was his charm, and that was why Ginger had suggested him as a dinner partner for old Maggot. With luck and perseverance, her father's attention would contain Maggie's vicious tongue. Without it, Joannie's birthday party could resemble World War III, and that was the last thing Ginger wanted. But she was forgetting Craig. Craig wouldn't let that happen. Would he? God only knew.

Craig seemed to be making a valiant effort with her lately, and yet it was Craig who had insisted Maggie be invited tonight because, as Joannie related it, he was uncomfortable with the idea of a "couple thing." He seemed to be of two minds about her these days, and Ginger couldn't help wondering which of them was going to prevail. She had the uneasy feeling that she might be about to find out.

Determinedly, Ginger put Craig and herself out of her mind. Joan should be the focus of attention tonight.

Not for the first time, Ginger wished Joan had chosen another form of celebration, but the girl was understandably eager to achieve maturity. She had missed so much and was now trying to make up for it. She had such high hopes for this dinner party. Joan seemed to think that she could prove herself an adult to Craig, a woman of talent to Paul and a person of consequence to her school friend all in the same night. And perhaps she could. Ginger certainly intended to help her in every way that she could.

Ginger had intended to be early, but styling her hair had set her back, so by the time she started across her yard toward the Russells' house, her father's gold Mercedes was already pulling up at the curb. Frederick Brenan got out of his car and came along the walk to take his daughter's arm and accompany her. His pale gray suit was the same color as the highlights in his salt-and-pepper hair. With it he was wearing a striped burgundy-on-white shirt and a hand-painted silk tie.

"Smashing," he said, drawing level with her. "But then you always are."

Ginger laughed and clutched his hand to her side. "And you, as always, look wealthy and dignified, which you are." He inclined his head in acknowledgement of her compliment. She briefly laid her head upon his shoulder. "Thank you for doing this, Dad. It means a lot to Joan—and me."

"Mmm," he mused. "She sounds like a charming young lady. I don't blame her for not wanting her birthday ruined by an old dragon of an aunt."

Ginger laughed again. "That was exactly my first impression of Maggie. The problem is, you see, she likes to impose her will—and Craig has difficulty handling her. He tries to sit on his temper because she's family, and she takes advantage of that. To make matters worse, she hates me." Ginger put her nose in the air. "She disapproves."

"Ah," Frederick said, "the righteous sort. Never fear, Gingevine, I can handle dear old Auntie. One has merely to agree with her and fawn a bit."

"I know you'll do your best," Ginger told him. "Just promise me you won't lose your temper with her."

He gave her the look that she had so dreaded as a small child, eyebrows drawn together, lips compressed, eyes intense. She laughed, knowing how false was his disdain, and after a moment he laughed with her. Then they were standing at the Russells' front door.

Ginger tugged at her skirt and pushed the bell button. The door opened almost instantly. Craig, in a black double-breasted tuxedo of Italian design, took her breath away. He wore a black silk bow tie and a crisp, white-on-white embroidered shirt. At his wrist were onyx cuff links set in silver. His dark hair had been swept straight back, a single wispy lock falling forward, and his jaw was freshly shaved. The fragrance of mint and lime hung in the air.

"Come in," he said, smiling, and his eyes swept over her with obvious approval.

"Craig, I'd like you to meet my father, Frederick Brenan." She stepped into the entry and moved past him.

"Of course. Mr. Brenan, thank you for coming."

"Oh, call me Frederick, please, and it is my pleasure to be here."

The two men shook hands, then Craig ushered them into the living room. Maggie was seated on a sofa, a glass of iced tea in her hand. She looked frumpy and cross in a two-piece suit of off-white bouclé knit. She had a pink grosgrain bow pinned in her steel gray hair and pink buttons clipped to her ears. A string of multicolored glass beads hung around her neck. Craig immediately made the introductions.

"Aunt Maggie, this is Ginger's father, Mr. Frederick Brenan. Frederick, my aunt Maggie."

Frederick reached for Maggie's hand and bowed low over it, brushing his lips across her knuckles. "Madam, I am charmed. You must call me Frederick. I swear, you put me in mind of my own dear sister, a saint of a woman, generous, caring, upstanding. May I call you Maggie?"

The poor old thing hadn't a chance. Maggie literally batted her prickly eyelashes as she gave her assent. Frederick took up a post at her side.

"What can I get you to drink, Frederick?" Craig asked, clearly amused. "I didn't much like the idea of Joan serving alcohol with dinner, but I think we adults can be allowed one cocktail prior to."

"No, no, not for me," Frederick said. "I'll just have what the charming Maggie is having. Iced tea, isn't it?"

"Iced tea it is." Craig moved toward the bar, but just then the doorbell rang. Joan, as yet, hadn't put in an appearance, but Ginger denied the impulse to go in search of her and offered her help instead to Craig.

"I'll pour that if you like."

He smiled, his dark eyes sparkling, and a shock wave of warmth swept through her. "Thank you," he said quietly. "I'll only be a moment."

She nodded and lowered her gaze, her pulse beating pronouncedly in the hollow of her throat. Craig moved toward the foyer, and Ginger poured tea from a pitcher into a glass already filled with ice cubes, then carried it to her father, who gave her a wink as he chatted up Maggie adroitly. Craig brought Paul and Marian Solis into the living room and made the introductions. Joan showed up about then, a little breathless and apologetic, but looking elegant in a tea-length sheath of black smocked crepe, her hair piled softly on top of her head. Ginger's diamond ear studs and a simple gold chain were her only accessories. The effect was perfect. Ginger smiled encouragement and took a seat, leaving Joan to perform the duties of hostess. The girl was nervous and a little slow, but managed well enough, despite Maggie's scowl, which Frederick Brenan did his best to distract.

The drinks were hardly dispensed when the remainder of their party arrived together, Paul, Jr., his friend, Skip, and Nathalie Hotchkiss, who looked out of place with her severely spiked bangs and metallic blue minidress and, to her credit, had the grace to know it. Joan saw them seated, seemed to breathe a sigh of relief at their refusal of drinks and excused herself to fetch the appetizers. Thereafter, the evening went smoothly.

Joan's simple assortment of toast points with cheese and shaved pickles, whole water chestnuts wrapped in crisp bacon strips and celery sticks filled with sesame paste and pâté were an instant hit. When they moved into the dining room, Marian Solis exclaimed over the lovely table setting while Craig lit the candles and the others eagerly found their places. The water glasses had already been filled and were frostily chilled. Small crystal plates of pressed-butter patties and tiny silver salt- and pepper shakers added sparkle and matched Ginger's silver-rimmed white china with crystal gores. The mingled scents of fresh flowers filled the room. Soft music played in the background.

Craig sat at the head of the table, Ginger on his right, Marian Solis on his left. Marian's husband had the chair next to Ginger, then came Maggie and Frederick. Joan's chair at the end of the table opposite Craig remained empty while she put the final touches on her dinner. Paul, Jr., sat to her immediate left, with Nathalie Hotchkiss at his side, and between Nathalie and Marian was Skip.

The steady flow of three conversations being conducted at once ceased the moment Joan carried her perfect crown rib roast into the room. The aroma was absolutely heady. Mouths began immediately to salivate. Joan literally beamed as she placed the carving tools in front of Craig. He stood, steadied the dressed roast with the fork and went to work. The knife cut through the tender meat as if it were butter. Ginger looked around the table. Every face was rapt and expectant. Success. Ginger sent a spare, proud smile in Joan's direction and with a barely perceptible nod, sent her happily on her way. By the time the roast had been carved and served, Joan had produced the rest of the meal, twice-baked potatoes, asparagus steamed with white wine, mushrooms and lemon, glazed carrots with mint and crusty yeast rolls.

Every bite was perfect. Joan seemed confident and gracious. Her guests were suitably impressed. Craig was urbane and, as the evening wore on, increasingly attentive.

Once he leaned across the corner of the table and whispered into Ginger's ear, "Did she really cook this?"

Ginger looked into his eyes. "Every morsel—more or less."

His chuckle was husky. "You're a miracle worker." His hand covered hers and squeezed. Fire licked through her body.

Another time he leaned close and under the table his hand came to rest lightly on her knee, but he said nothing, merely smiled into her eyes before withdrawing his hand and turning his attention to Marian Solis, who wanted his opinion on the most practical types of engineering degrees. He kept his answer short and deftly turned the conversation to art. Ginger had the distinct impression he had done so for her benefit, and she tingled with pleasure—and hope.

By the time dessert came around, key-lime pie piled high with whipped cream and served with candied raspberries, Ginger was so aware of Craig that his every nuance seemed significant. His every look seemed to be telling her something, the tone of his voice, the whisper touch of his leg against hers beneath the table. It was all she could do to swallow and maintain a casual air, let alone participate in actual conversation.

At the end of the meal, having agreed to take their coffee in the living room, they were about to leave the table. Craig got swiftly to his feet and stepped behind her chair. As she rose, his hands fell to her shoulders and slid down her arms to the elbows. The breath caught in her throat. "I haven't told you," he said softly, "how incredibly beautiful you are tonight."

She turned swiftly to stare into his eyes and discern his intention. Was he actually flirting with her? She almost asked, but the next instant he had stepped away and was waiting for her to precede him, which she did reluctantly.

They had their fancy-roast coffee with conversation. Only Craig remained silent. Perched on the arm of the sofa next to her, he seemed to be hovering, waiting, but for what? Desperately, she attempted to ignore him, but her awareness of him was too intense, too sharp. She made a decided effort to talk with Marian Solis and anyone else who seemed inclined to listen. Presently, she noticed Joan was giving her a frankly puzzled look. Then slowly it came to her that no one else was saying a word. Moreover, everyone was looking at her. Suddenly she couldn't even remember what she had been talking about. Her mouth was open and nothing was coming out. She closed it, smiled gently and said, "Forgive me. I didn't mean to monopolize the conversation."

There were some polite protests, after which Frederick Brenan cleared his throat, glanced at his watch and announced that he had to be on his way. Maggie made a face and, with a hand grasping his arm, urged him to stay, but he politely refused and reminded Ginger with an apologetic look that he was leaving early the next morning for Japan. Joan spoke up to thank him for attending her party. He replied that it had been his pleasure and rose to leave. Ginger also stood up, intending to have a word with her father before he left, but Craig's hand suddenly clamped on to her arm, the grip almost painful. She looked up and found on his face the most stubborn, dogged expression she had ever seen there. Her heart turned over. Tonight. Tonight her dreams became reality—or nightmares. She could scarcely breathe, scarcely recall what was happening around them. Her father. Japan. Only with great difficulty did she manage to turn her head to address her father.

"H-have a good trip, Dad," she said a little breathlessly. "Call me."

He nodded and bent to kiss her cheek, his slight frown the only evidence that he had noticed the host's grip on her arm. "Craig, I trust you'll see my daughter home," he said smoothly, but Ginger heard the edge beneath the silky tone.

Craig's hand slid away as he came to his feet. "Absolutely."

"Don't be silly," she heard herself saying. "This is a protected neighborhood, after all."

Craig's hand came up again and fastened on to her wrist. Her heart sped up alarmingly. "I insist."

Frederick Brenan nodded with satisfaction. "Goodbye, all." He strode elegantly toward the door, but before he got there, the Solises were saying that they ought to make an early evening of it, too. Craig seemed to relax. In fact, he seemed almost eager to see them gone. He released her and saw them out along with Frederick. Ginger sat down again. Then Paul, Jr., said that he was certainly willing to help Joan clean up if it meant that she and Nathalie could join him and Skip for a late movie. Skip said that he had been known to wash a dish or two in his time, as well, but Nathalie wrinkled up her nose, looked down at her dress and complained that she would have to change before she could either clean or go to a movie.

"Well, that's no problem," said Joan. "Come on with me and you can borrow something." The two girls were leaving the room just as Craig was returning, and it was Maggie who informed him, rather imperiously, what they were planning.

"A late movie?" Craig mused. Then he shrugged. "I suppose that's all right. After all, it is her eighteenth birthday."

"Humph!" said Maggie. "I don't see what that's got to do with it."

Craig and Joan exchanged a look, then Craig sat down next to Ginger, and Joan skipped off to get Nathalie changed. Several seconds of silence followed.

Finally Maggie spoke up. "Frederick Brenan is a charming man," she said to no one in particular.

It seemed to Ginger that some acknowledgment of the compliment was in order as he was her father, so she merely said, "Thank you."

Maggie ignored her. "Very well mannered," she continued, "and richer than the government, one supposes."

Ginger was slightly embarrassed. "He's a very well-known businessman," she mumbled.

Suddenly Maggie impaled her with a direct look, the hostility of which was patently obvious. "Was your mother of...common stock?" she asked innocently, rushing on in the stunned silence that followed. "I mean, your father seems such a refined, urbane person, and you're...well, you're...not."

"Holy cow," Craig muttered, while Ginger's face turned a deep shade of crimson and Paul and Skip developed sudden interests in their hands and laps and the plaster on the wall.

Maggie was all too aware of the effect she was having, but she blinked as if uncertain why it should be so. "I don't mean to offend," she said lightly. "It's just that I can't imagine a man like Mr. Brenan producing such a—"

"Shut up, Maggie." Craig's low, steely voice cut through the heavy atmosphere like a knife.

Ginger's gaze rose, caught Maggie's tight, smug little smile. She turned to Craig.

For a moment he seemed to teeter on the edge of true rage, but then he glanced at her, clamped his jaw and backed away. "I'll walk you home now," he said softly, gripping her elbow and lifting her up with him as he rose from the sofa.

Ginger had meant to help Joan with the cleanup, and it had occurred to her that she could take care of it and let Joan and her friends go on their way, but something in the sound of Craig's voice when he had said he'd walk her home forestalled any argument on her part. Besides, she wasn't fool enough to stay around and let Maggie get her claws in one more time. Another insinuation about her mother, who was ironically one of the world's greatest snobs, and Ginger knew she would lose her own temper and make a terrible scene. For Joan's sake and Craig's, she didn't want that to happen. She meekly allowed Craig to steer her toward the door that led onto the deck.

They stepped out into a still, cool night that smelled of ocean breezes and freshly mown grass. Craig released her arm and slid the door closed behind them. They stood for a moment, letting the silence envelop them, then Craig strolled to the rail of the deck, leaned against it and sighed, staring out across the dark, moon-streaked mirror of the lake. Ginger felt the weight of his regret and followed, instinctively seeking to relieve his mind.

"It's all right," she said. "I don't let the Maggies of the world bother me—too much."

He shook his head. "You don't understand."

She smiled at that. "Yes, I do. You're feeling guilty because you made Joan invite Maggie."

He turned around, put his back to the rail and folded his arms. "So you know about that, do you?"

She nodded, looking down at her feet. She heard him pull in a deep breath and lifted her gaze. He was staring up at the sky.

"You never fail to amaze me," he said gently.

Ginger laughed. "How's that?"

His gaze fell on her, his eyes so warm and dark and sparkling that she felt them like a physical caress and reacted accordingly. "By ignoring my ill-mannered aunt," he answered, "and my own stupidity. By helping Joan be what she wants to be. By working so hard to make tonight's dinner a success and then sitting back and letting Jo take all the credit. In other words, by just being you."

Such sweet words. They were almost too sweet to bear. They went right to the heart of her, right to the deep core of longing that Ginger had felt for this man ever since she'd first laid eyes on him. She turned away, afraid for him to see how his words affected her, afraid he'd regret them. "You didn't have to say that," she told him lightly.

"Yes, I did," he stated, then his hand closed on her elbow again. "Come on, let's walk."

She nodded and together they walked to the steps, went down them and started across the fine sand. At once the tiny grains filled her shoes. "Wait." She paused to step out of her shoes and snatch them up.

"Won't you ruin your stockings?" Craig asked.

She shook her head. "Not wearing any."

"Oh." He laughed. "Of course."

"What does that mean?"

He smiled and shook his head. "It means you're delightful."

She gazed at him with wonder. Could this really be happening?

They resumed their casual pace, she carrying her shoes, he with his hands clasped behind his back. They walked in silence for a bit, but as they were drawing toward the hedge separating their properties, Ginger searched her mind for something to say that might prolong the contact.

"The Solises are nice people," she said at last.

Craig nodded. "Yes, they are. Paul's been a good partner, easy to work with, very intelligent, knows his stuff. I don't know Marian very well, but she's always been nice to me, and Paul speaks highly of her. That's good enough for me."

"They've certainly done well by Paul, Jr.," Ginger went on, and again Craig agreed, but with reservations.

"He's okay, I guess."

"I think he's more than okay," she stated easily. "I think he's very bright, very stable. I like him, and that they've done well with him is part of why I like his parents so much."

Craig frowned. "I don't see why you have to champion him."

Ginger stopped and stared at Craig. "Have you noticed the way those two kids look at one another?"

He craned a frown down at her, eyebrow cocked. "I've noticed."

"Good," she said. "Then you know they're absolutely smitten."

"No doubt about it."

"I think it's just what Joan needs right now," she said.

Both eyebrows went up this time, and Craig yanked at his tie, freeing it. "I don't see why."

"Well, to boost her ego, of course."

"Is that what you think it's about?" he asked gruffly. "Men are ego boosters?"

She blinked up at him. "Sometimes, though not ultimately."

"Ultimately?" he said. "Just what is the ultimate, Ginger?"

She knew what he was thinking, that for her the ultimate relationship with a man was marriage, but that wasn't true, not with every man. Only with one. She licked her lips, aware suddenly that they were dry. "It depends, Craig," she said tremulously, "on the man."

He stared down at her, a kind of anguish in his eyes, and when next he spoke, she knew they were no longer talking in generalities. "But what if the man can't be, ultimately, all that you want him to be?"

She thought that over, wanting very much to give him an honest answer and finding one. "I think you are everything I could want," she said softly, casting aside all pretense. "And if you're not, well, you're the closest thing I've found."

His fingertips lightly skimmed her cheek, his eyes studying her face, and she saw that he came to some kind of decision within himself, but before she could decide what it was, his focus shifted to her mouth and then away. He lifted a hand to loosen his collar, and when his hand came again, it found hers. "Come on," he said.

They walked on past her house and another, until they came to the curve of the shore. He paused and looked down at her, moonlight reflected in his eyes. "Do you want to go back?" he asked, his voice barely above a whisper.

Her heart in her throat, Ginger shook her head. She wasn't certain what was happening, but desire was melting her from the inside out, and she sensed that it was the same for him. He linked his fingers through hers, squeezed and they went on, around the end of the lake and down the other side, halting finally almost directly across from the very spot where they'd started. "I've seen this hut," Craig said, pointing to a small thatch-roofed structure on the beach. "I know you can buy them like this. I just don't know why you'd want to."

"Oh, that's easy," she told him. "It's the Petries', you know, the brothers. Their parents put the hut here so their friends could change out of their bathing suits without tracking sand in the house."

"Ah. Makes sense." He pushed aside the striped canvas curtain that functioned as a door and peered inside. "Do you think they'd mind if we borrowed it for a bit?" he asked, his voice soft and husky.

Her heart began to pound in her chest. "I don't think so," she whispered.

He looked at her; what he intended was plain on his face. *How far,* she asked herself, *are you willing to go?* But she already knew the answer. For his love, for just a chance at his love, she was willing to go all the way to the end of the road. She gripped his hand, telling him so the only way she knew how, and he slipped inside. She followed.

There were hooks in the posts holding up the walls and a cheap plastic towel bar with a beach towel, still slightly damp, folded over it. Craig took off his coat and hung it on one of the hooks, then spread the towel and sat down upon it. He removed his shoes and poured the sand out of them, then peeled off his socks and stretched out on his back, his arms folded beneath his head. He said nothing but merely waited, letting her know that he wouldn't push, wouldn't demand, and because he wouldn't, he didn't have to. Ginger could no more have walked away in that moment than she could have ceased to exist.

She dropped her shoes and went down on her knees beside him. Slowly, Craig twisted to the side and pushed up, his upper-body weight braced on one arm. He brushed a lock of hair away from her cheek, caught it, and rubbed it between thumb and forefinger. She could barely breathe, and her heart was hammering so hard, it rocked her with every beat.

"Help me," he whispered. "I want you so badly it hurts. Help me make love to you."

Tears filled her eyes. Joy welled up in her. She reached out with trembling fingers and unbuttoned his shirt. When it was opened, she brushed her hands lightly across his chest and felt him shudder at her touch, his pulse beating rapidly in the hollow of his throat. Then his arms came around her and he pulled her down on top of him, his mouth finding hers, and her hair slid forward, curtaining them in whisper softness. He turned her into the fold of his arm, holding her against his side as he slowly, thoroughly plied her mouth.

Tasting, exploring, his tongue slid around inside her lips and filled her mouth, curling and stroking until it seemed her whole being was centered there and she felt the invasion to the tips of her hardening nipples and the pit of her belly.

His hand lay lightly upon her hip and as he kissed her, it slid into the curve of her waist, flexed and paused, heating her flesh through the supple fabric of her dress. Then, as he continued to plumb her mouth, his leg came over her, his knee sliding up the outside of her thigh, parting the veils of her skirt and carrying them upward. She hardly noticed that his hand moved to her back and slipped beneath her hair until she felt the hook at the top of her dress give and the zipper slowly part. No longer could she lay quiescent and meek while the cool night air nipped at her spine and silk whispered against her skin.

She reached out for him, seeking the warmth she knew he could give her and finding fire. When her fingertips touched the skin of his chest, he flinched and made a sound low in the well of his throat, and suddenly he was crushing her to him, his arm and leg winding about her, his hand pressing and kneading and pulling until the dress lay puddled between her breasts, one arm freed of the strap. He rolled her into a sitting position and gently pushed the other strap over her shoulder and down her arm. The dress slid to her waist. His gaze moved to her breasts, and he began to tenderly stroke them, first one and then the other. His light, stroking touch was slowly driving her mad, and she closed her eyes, letting the sensations flow through her, feeling her body swell and tauten beneath his fingers.

"I've wanted this from the beginning," Craig told her in a raspy whisper.

"So have I," Ginger admitted, opening her eyes to gaze up at him. His expression was rapt as he gently stroked one taut, rosy peak. Her stomach clenched, and hot liquid seemed to pour downward.

"I fought so hard against it," he said. "And now I know it has to be."

At last! she thought, his words music to her ears. "Yes," she said, her voice breaking. *Oh, yes.*

He bent his head and engulfed the peak of her breast with his mouth, sucking and nipping with his teeth. Suddenly she was caught up in a whirlwind of sensation. She could not think or speak, only feel. When he drew back to throw off his shirt, she knew only that he had left her, and she reached out to pull him back, but he resisted and instead pushed her down upon the sand and eased the dress over her hips, tossing it away. Then his fingers curled beneath the lacy elastic of her panties, and she felt those peeled away, too. What followed was ecstasy in its purest form. He probed first with his fingers, and then he was naked and between her legs, bare skin igniting bare skin. His mouth was everywhere, at her breast, throat, ear and finally mated to her own again as the long, hard length of him parted her and filled her, driving and thrusting, propelling them both toward that moment of mindless euphoria that was the core, the essence of human existence, that instant when nothing could separate them, when they were one together, whole, complete, when no one ever remembers that a moment never lasts.

Chapter Fourteen

"You're sorry," Ginger said, combing her fingers through her hair. Craig shook his head and pulled her close once more. He wasn't sorry. He was afraid. When he looked into those golden eyes and saw the love shining there, he was very much afraid that he was going to hurt her. She wanted a husband, the promise of a lifetime, eternal commitment. And what did he want? Her body. God, yes. Even now when he had just loved her, emptied himself into her tight warmth, he wanted to burrow into her body and forget everything else. But forever? Who the hell knew what could last forever? He certainly didn't, and he feared—was terrified—that he just didn't have forever in him.

"It's all right," she said, a hint of bitterness in her tone. "I don't blame you any more than I blame myself."

"Well, I do," he told her gruffly. "We both know I made it happen."

"What difference does that make?" she asked, sighing. "I wanted you to make love to me. Not that it was wise."

"No," Craig said, oddly stung. "It wasn't wise, but it happened, and I take full responsibility for it."

"Damn you," Ginger said, springing up to her feet. "I don't want you to take responsibility. I want you to love me. I want you to be happy that I love you. I want," she finished lamely, "too damned much." With that she pushed through the curtain and left him. He could hear her steps plowing through the sand, and he thought briefly of going after her, but no. He had to think.

The funny part of it was, he thought he probably did love her. How could he not? There was her beauty and the attraction of her body, of course, but it was more than that. It was her generosity, her acumen, her wisdom. Already she knew his sister better than he did and had more influence with her. And who could deny that Ginger would be an exemplary wife? Plus she was honest, too honest, if there was such a thing. It was a part of her eccentricity, and that eccentricity was a part of what made her so very interesting. The truth was that if he was going to get married to anyone, he'd want it to be Gingevine Brenan—*if* he was going to get married.

Why couldn't they just live together? he wondered frantically. Ginger was always saying how grown-up Joan was now. He would simply explain it to her. *I love Ginger, and I want to be with her. I want to sleep with her and wake up with her. I want the warmth she would add to our home, the excitement she would bring to our lives. I just don't want to marry her because... Because I might regret it later, because she might regret it later, because divorce is so damned sticky these days, because I'm selfish as hell and I know it. I just don't know what to do about it, and even if I did, Ginger wouldn't agree to this! She's made it pretty plain that she wants a husband, not a live-in boyfriend.* Disgusted with himself, Craig got up and put on his jacket.

Ginger had left her shoes, so he took them up in one hand and his own in another. He had buttoned his shirt but left the tie undone. He knew he was wrinkled and sandy and that anyone who had seen him leave with Ginger would surely guess what he'd been up to, but he wasn't particularly worried about it. Jo would still be out at the movie, and Maggie religiously went to bed early. Besides, Maggie didn't usually wait for evidence to make her judgments. She'd have pinned him with this even if he hadn't done it.

He stepped out of the little hut and started around the lake, taking the route opposite the one that had brought him there. It was probably cowardly of him, but he didn't want to pass Ginger's house. He didn't want to have to argue himself out of going inside. The route seemed longer than the one he'd taken with Ginger, but that walk had been filled with quiet acceptance and anticipation. This one was filled with regret and worry. Why couldn't he have just kept his hands off her? It had seemed almost predestined to happen, but he knew it was only his own desire that had made it seem so. And the worse part of all was that he still wanted her, deeply, desperately. The sweetness of sex with her had only increased his appetite, and he wondered if he would ever be free of the craving.

When he reached his house, he sat down on the steps of the deck for a minute to wipe sand from his feet and stick them bare into his dress shoes. His socks he stuffed into a pocket. Then he picked up Ginger's shoes again and went inside. Just as he opened the door to his bedroom, Maggie appeared, wearing her old pink bathrobe, rollers in her hair. She flipped on the hall light and looked him up and down pointedly.

"Just as I thought," she said righteously. "You don't care about your sister."

He shook his head in warning. "Don't even start, Maggie."

She ignored him. "You're allowing that woman undue influence on the child for your own base purposes."

"I'm warning you—"

"Look at yourself. You're positively disgusting. And to think you've exposed your sister to this!"

"Enough, Maggie!"

"Well, Joan will just have to come back to live with me. It'll be a sacrifice, naturally, but I know my duty."

It was all Craig could do not to shake his aunt until her teeth fell out, but neither would he defend himself to her. Instead he took a deep, calming breath and reached for the doorframe in order to steady himself. That was when he remembered that he carried Ginger's shoes. Maggie gasped as if the shoes themselves were shameful. He raised them defiantly, rubbing her face in it.

"I don't care what you think of me, Maggie," he told her harshly. "In fact, I don't care what you think, period, so we'll go right to the important stuff. Joan will never be subjected to you again, and if I'd had any sense, she never would have been. Furthermore, Ginger Brenan has done more for Joan than you and I put together, so I don't want to hear you bad-mouthing the woman, *ever.* And finally, my life is none of your business. I'll thank you to keep your opinions to yourself, and if you can't manage to do that, well then, just don't come back."

"How dare you!" she gasped, bowing her back and sticking her nose in the air.

"I dare, Maggie," he said flatly, "because Joan is *my* sister and this is *my* home and *my* life, and as far as I can tell, you've never added a damn thing to any of it that we wouldn't have been better off without. Now if you can manage to keep your mouth shut, you can stay the night, but you'll be gone bright and early, and if you say so much as a word to Joan about any of this, I'll *throw* you out on your sanctimonious butt."

He left her standing there and went into his room, slamming the door behind him. It was dark, but he didn't turn on the light. He was so angry, his chest was heaving, but his anger was not reserved exclusively for his self-righteous aunt. He was as angry with himself as he was with her. What had possessed him to think he could get this past her? What in God's name was he going to say to Joan if she got wind of this? Surely Ginger wouldn't say anything, and Maggie had damned well better not. But that didn't really change anything. Only now did he understand what he'd done to Ginger and to himself. Maybe Joan wasn't a child any longer, but that didn't mean he shouldn't protect her, and now the only way to do that was to conceal the truth, which was just another way of lying. He dropped Ginger's shoes onto the bed and sat down heavily beside them.

When Joan came home some time later, he was still sitting there. She came to his door, opened it a crack and told him that she was there. He knew she thought he was in bed already, and he didn't bother to correct the assumption. He just asked if she'd had a good time, heard that she had and sent her to sleep unaware that he'd hurt someone they both loved. Only then did he undress and lie down, though sleep was still far away.

"I have your shoes," Craig said, his voice sounding strained over the phone.

Ginger bit her lip and thought that she dared not see him, then in her brightest voice suggested he leave them on her doorstep. "I'll bring them in later when I'm not so...busy."

"You're avoiding me," he said softly, and she closed her eyes against the sound of pain.

"No, I'm just busy. I—I have a deadline, you know. My publisher's anxious to get his hands on this particular cookbook, and I don't want it to be late."

"Ever the thoughtful one," Craig said in a near whisper. "I'm sorry I've hurt you, honey."

"Don't be silly." She tried to sound upbeat. "You haven't done anything to me that I didn't want you to do. I'm just busy."

Silence. Then, "I'll leave the shoes on the doorstep."

"Thanks."

She hung up before he could say anything else and dashed sudden tears from her eyes. He really wasn't to blame, and she hated that he felt he was, especially as there was no reason for it. She had known all along that they wanted different things, and it wasn't as if he'd seduced her with lies. He hadn't said he loved her, after all, or that he wanted to marry her. She had no one to blame for the pain she was feeling except herself, and she really ought to see him and make him understand that, but she just couldn't. She didn't trust herself to see him, speak with him, not now, not knowing that it was hopeless for them. She saw now that it was hopeless, because if what they'd shared hadn't convinced him they were right together, then nothing could. Once she had accepted that, really accepted it, then maybe they could be friends and neighbors. But not now.

He left the shoes on the doorstep that afternoon, and she brought them in soon after she was certain that he was gone. When Joan dropped by later to chat, Ginger gave her a few minutes, then insisted she had to get back to work. Joan gave her a funny, probing look, but Ginger put on a smile and did her best to deflect the girl's concern.

Things got easier after that because Joan was wrapped up in Paul Solis, Jr. They seemed to be dating often, and when they weren't actually together or at school, they were spending a good deal of time on the phone. She still dropped in from time to time during the next week, but her conversation was all about Paul and what they'd done or were planning to do together. She talked about Craig, too, but Ginger soon learned to turn off the sound of the girl's words and simply make interested noises until the subject was exhausted. The up side was that Ginger was really getting a lot of work done. The book would be ready for the publisher sooner than expected.

After the book was done, though, she didn't know what she was going to do. Perhaps she'd take a trip. Her father was always talking about Japan. That could be interesting, and she knew she'd be welcomed in any of a dozen other places by friends she hadn't seen in a good while. Joan would be all right without her, and she was truly glad of that. If her enthusiasm was somewhat lacking, it wasn't because of Joan. It was because . . . It was because her enthusiasm was somewhat lacking. But that explanation wasn't good enough for Joan the day she came home early from school and dropped by to find Ginger still in her nightclothes, her hair uncombed, her face drawn and bare of cosmetics.

"You're depressed," she said, striking an authoritative pose.

Why deny it, Ginger wondered, when it was so obvious? She pushed her hair out of her face and nodded. "I suppose I am, but it's just one of those things, you know? Happens to everybody sooner or later. I'll snap out of it."

Joan looked at her thoughtfully for some time. "Are you too depressed to come over for dinner tomorrow night?" she asked. "I don't want to spend the whole evening alone."

So Craig was leaving his sister on her own for a change. Ginger couldn't help wondering why. Was he seeing someone else? She scolded herself for even thinking such a thing. It wasn't any of her business. She had no claim on him whatsoever, a fact she knew only too well. She sighed, feeling strangely hollow. Now what about Joan's invitation? She really didn't want to have dinner with anyone right now, but if Joan needed her... Ginger forced a smile, but knew there wasn't much cheer in it. "Let's not do anything too extravagant tomorrow evening," she said. "I'm just not up to that."

Joan clapped her hands together. "You'll come. Great! And don't worry. I'll take care of everything. Maybe I'll even order in. What do you think?"

Her pleasure was uplifting. Ginger felt her smile soften. "Ordering in will be fine. Get whatever you want—burgers, pizza, chicken, Chinese...."

"Pizza," Joan said. "They deliver."

Ginger actually laughed. "Pizza it is, then, but no anchovies."

"Right. Gotcha. Tomorrow, about six-thirty?"

"Fine."

Joan grinned and patted Ginger's shoulder. "Don't worry," she said consolingly. "Everything will be fine."

Ginger nodded and made an effort to sit up straighter. She wished she could believe all would be well, but there was much Joan didn't know, and Ginger hoped she never did. It was hard to admit to herself that she'd been a fool, but harder still to admit such a thing to the person who thought the best of her, and she certainly didn't want to lower Craig's stature with the girl in any way—for all their sakes. Besides, how could she tell this lovely young woman just now daring to live her own life that sometimes, despite all her best efforts, a woman could still wind up with a broken heart?

Craig walked into the house and was greeted by the raucous sound of rock music. It was strangely welcome, though jazz and easy-listening were more to his taste. He would hate to come home to silence just now. With Ginger so much on his mind, he didn't really want to spend a lot of unstructured time alone. Besides, home was more *homey* when you had someone with whom to share it. He wondered how he had forgotten that in all those years alone. He wondered if it didn't get to Ginger sometimes, living alone, then immediately he sought to put her out of his mind.

He went into the living room, his suit jacket draped over one shoulder, briefcase and blueprints in hand. Joan was stretched out on the sofa, the phone crammed up against her ear, foot bobbing in time with the music. He bent over and kissed the top of her head, smelling the mingled fragrances of hair spray, cologne and shampoo. She covered the mouthpiece with her hand and smiled up at him.

"Hi."

"Hi, sweetie. What's for dinner?"

"Ordering in," she said before going back to her conversation.

Ordering in. That meant pizza. He hoped to high heaven she'd left off the anchovies this time. He hated anchovies. He moved toward the hall, wanting to change into more comfortable clothing, but Joan popped up off the couch and called him back.

"Craig?"

He stopped and half turned. "Yeah, hon?"

"I, uh . . ."

He cocked his head. "What?"

"I, uh, have to go out later," she said quickly. "Paul's coming by for me."

He tried to stop his frown. "You're seeing an awful lot of that boy," he said. "Maybe too much."

That tiny chin went up a notch, then came right back down. "I like Paul, and anyway, this is important. It's a recruitment seminar at the college.

"Oh." That was different. He was delighted to hear her moving in that direction finally. He'd brought it up a time or two, but she hadn't seemed interested and he hadn't wanted to push. If Paul had gotten her to thinking about this, then he was grateful. It was past time she did something about college. "Ah, should I go with you?" he asked.

"No!" Joan backed up a step and shook her head, seemingly regretting the outburst. "What I mean is, I want to show them I'm mature enough to do this on my own, you know? Besides, there's not anything for you to do at this point. This thing is just to meet the registrar and various deans in person. Paul already knows them, see, so he can introduce me. Anyway, I figured I'd better make the best possible impression because I'm getting such a late start. Most of the kids in my class have already applied and everything."

"Sounds reasonable," he commented. "I'm glad you're taking this seriously."

She took a deep breath, seeming nervous, and licked her lips. "Well, like I said, it's important. I feel kind of bad about it, though, because I wanted to spend some time with Ginger this evening. She's kind of depressed right now, and I don't think she really needs to be alone, but I can't help it. Tonight's the last time they'll be recruiting this year."

So Ginger was depressed. Craig knew well enough who was to blame for that, and guilt prodded him sharply. He might even have succumbed to it and called Ginger himself if guilt had been all it was, if the desire to be with her had not been so strong. Too strong. He dared not give in to that, even though the alternative at this moment was an evening alone, consumed with thoughts of her. He shrugged at Joan.

"Well, I, ah, had better get moving myself. I brought home a lot of work."

"Oh, sure." She nodded. "You go ahead." She stepped forward and kissed him on the cheek, her smile oddly sly. How much, he wondered, did she already know about him and Ginger? He didn't even want to think about it. He smiled and got out of there. Maybe he'd have a beer with his pizza, watch a bit of television and get down to some serious work. The evening would pass and he'd keep Ginger out of his mind.

He stood in the shower for twenty minutes, streams of stinging hot water pounding his body, and tried not to think of Ginger naked beneath him. When he felt drained and lethargic, he turned the water off and got out. He took his time toweling off and dressing, finally pulling on comfortable old jeans and a soft, faded rugby shirt, the sleeves of which he pushed up to the elbows. He stuck his bare feet into ragged canvas shoes curled up from a recent washing and combed back his shiny wet hair without bothering to watch himself in a mirror. He'd just slipped the comb into his hip pocket when the doorbell rang.

He wondered if Joan had the money to pay for the pizza and decided she probably didn't when the bell rang again. He picked up his wallet and stepped out in the hall.

"Jo?" No answer, just that darned bell going off again. "Coming!" he shouted, knowing he couldn't be heard at that distance, and starting down the hall. "Coming," he called again from the living room. He jogged down the entry and wrenched the door open.

Ginger physically recoiled. "Sorry, I must be early," she said. "I'll come back later."

She started to turn away, but somehow he couldn't let her. "Wait! It's all right. Come on in. Please."

She shook her head. "No, really, I should come back."

"There's no point in that. I mean, if you're here to see Jo, you better do it now before she—" He broke off as a delivery van pulled up into the drive. "There's the pizza. I ought to get that." He stepped outside and moved toward the van. "You go on in. Jo's probably in her room getting dressed. I won't be a minute." Ginger shrugged and went in.

Craig met the delivery man, forked over fourteen bucks and took two large pizzas with everything, minus the anchovies. Who was this kid feeding? Was she expecting Paul to eat with them? If not, he'd better be prepared to eat a whole pizza by himself, Craig decided. He carried them inside, stowed them in the oven and headed down the hall toward Joan's room. He knocked, waited a moment, then opened the door only to find Ginger standing next to the bed, a folded piece of paper in her hand.

"She's gone," she said, confusion thickening her voice.

"Already? That's strange. I thought she wasn't going out until later."

Ginger looked at him with clear distress. "I thought *you* were the one who was going out. Joan and I were supposed to have dinner together."

"Well, that's funny." Or was it? "I didn't have any plans for this evening, but when I came in, she told me that Paul was taking her to a recruitment seminar at the university. She also said something about not wanting you to spend the evening alone."

Light dawned in Ginger's tawny eyes. "Oh, my."

He nodded and leaned against the doorjamb, folding his arms. "We've been set up."

"Well, I'll just have to go then, won't I? And later I'm going to have a long talk with that young lady, a very—"

"Don't," Craig said, stepping into her path and blocking the doorway. "Please don't. God, I can't stand this anymore. We have to talk. We have to work this out. I need to be with you." He reached for her hand, but she jerked back, shaking her head.

"I can't. Not again."

"We can find a compromise," he argued. "If we really want to, we can find a way—"

"For what?" Ginger broke in suddenly. "We don't even want the same things!"

"We both want one thing," he reminded her.

"And you think we can accommodate that? How? By sneaking around? Or shall we just announce to Joan that we're sleeping together? Is that what you want for her, to think that it's okay to have the sex even if you don't want the love that goes with it?"

"You're putting words in my mouth."

"But they're the right words!"

"No, they're not. They're not the right words at all. I do love you."

Hope flared and died in her eyes. "I want to believe that, but how can I when you don't want to make a commitment to me?"

"Don't you understand?" he all but shouted at her. "I'm afraid to make a commitment to you!"

"But that's what love is, Craig! Without that, all we have is sex! And that's not enough for me."

"I know that," he told her. "But if you could just give me some time to figure out what I'm capable of... I want to *try*, damn it, doesn't that mean anything?"

She turned away and back again, closed her eyes, then opened them. "Yes," she finally said. "But you have to understand that I must protect myself from you. I have to, Craig. I can't let happen again what happened the other night. It wouldn't be fair to either of us."

"I know." And he did. Strangely, it didn't even seem important. For days, weeks, all he'd thought about was making love to her, and now that somehow seemed far less necessary than just *being* with her. What did that mean if not love? "Look," he said, "we can start over again. We'll put all that aside and just be friends for a while." He saw the doubt on her face. "No, I mean it. Let's do this. Let's take a couple of beers and the pizza and sit in front of the TV and just . . . hang out. All right?"

"I want to Craig, but—"

"No buts. You have to have dinner anyway, and there's enough pizza to feed the Miami Dolphins."

"I don't know. . . ."

"Please. Let's just try." She was weakening, he could tell. "No anchovies," he added hopefully, and she actually smiled.

"I *hate* anchovies."

"So do I! See, we've already found something else we have in common."

She chuckled. "All right. As long as I'm here anyway."

"Great! Well then, I'll get the plates and the pizza, if you'll get the beer and the glasses. Deal?"

She nodded. "Deal."

He grinned. "Come on."

They walked down the hall side by side, but Craig was careful not to touch her. He didn't dare if he meant to keep sex out of it. Later maybe... But no. He wouldn't think of that. They were friends again, and that was enough for now.

They got things together and carried them into the den. He turned on the television, found something they could both enjoy at least minimally and sat down on the couch beside her, keeping as much distance between the two of them as he could without making a point of it. If things were tense, well, that was to be expected. It would get better, he told himself. They'd learn to relax again and just let nature take its course. Uh, no. Better to leave nature out of it. If this was going to work, he had to learn to think of her as a friend, a buddy.

He glanced her way as he leaned forward to help himself to a slice of pizza. She'd pulled the top part of her hair back in a sedate ponytail that lay flat against her head, and she was wearing a faded pink T-shirt with her blue jeans. No jewelry. No makeup. She was still beautiful, achingly so, but there was something vulnerable and almost tepid about her. Jo was right about her being depressed, and it was all Craig could do not to take Ginger into his arms and kiss her until she came alive again. But he couldn't. He had a feeling he was going to miss the old Ginger, her flamboyance and excitement, her flirtatiousness and unpredictability. But she would come back. She had to. He needed her. Jo needed her.

He tried to concentrate on the television, but he was so painfully aware of her and her sadness that he couldn't fix his mind on anything else. He kept grabbing pizza just to get a look at her, and before he knew what was happening, he'd eaten darn near the whole thing. Ginger, on the other hand, hadn't finished even her first piece. This wasn't working and he knew it, was sick about it, but what else could he do?

The program they were watching ended and it was no surprise to him that Ginger said she was tired and ought to go. He didn't argue. He didn't want her to leave, but he didn't want her to stay when she was so obviously uncomfortable. He walked her to the front door and fought the urge to kiss her goodbye.

"Thanks for the pizza," she said, and slipped outside.

He put his forehead to the wall and closed his eyes, aching for the woman he'd made love to out there on the sand. He went back to the den and sat through another program that couldn't hold his interest. Then he listened to the news, and finally he made himself clean up after their meal. He gathered up everything they'd taken to the den and carried it back to the kitchen. A whole pizza was still in the oven, and he decided not to leave it there. He left it to cool, and later he would wrap it up and put it in the freezer. If Jo was hungry when she came in, he could heat it up in the microwave. Or maybe he'd let her take care of that. He wasn't sure he wanted to see her, because she was going to ask what had happened with Ginger. Then again, he might as well. He was going to have to talk to her anyway. She obviously knew something was wrong or she wouldn't have dreamed up this scheme to get him and Ginger together for the evening.

But what could he say to her? They had worked nothing out, really, and the bald truth didn't seem wise. It would be better for them all if he and Ginger could work something out. But what? If he could just make Ginger understand what he was feeling, then maybe he'd know what to say to Jo. Suddenly he knew he shouldn't have let Ginger go without hashing out this thing. But did he dare go over there? Anything could happen. Was he ready for that? Yes, because he couldn't go on this way, none of them could. He got up and ran next door.

Ginger answered his knock but obviously wasn't happy to see him. "Go away, Craig. I can't talk to you now."

"No. We've got to nail this down."

"I thought we were going to be friends and put the rest of it behind us."

"I was stupid to say that. Let me talk to you. Don't make me say it out here on the sidewalk."

She bit her lip, a flicker of interest brightening her eyes. "Say what?"

"Let me in and I'll tell you."

She backed away from the door reluctantly and walked into the kitchen. He followed. Suddenly the fax machine on her counter signaled and starting spitting paper. She stepped over to it and read the copy as it came out of the machine. It seemed her father was getting ready to leave Japan and wanted to do some shopping before he left there. Could she make some comments about a long list of suggestions right away?

"I have to take care of this," she told Craig. "Maybe we ought to postpone whatever you were going to say."

He shook his head stubbornly. "I'll wait."

She wasn't happy about it, but she let him stay. While she formulated a reply for her father, Craig thought over what he wanted to say. Finally, Frederick was satisfied and the fax machine was silent.

Ginger faced Craig and folded her arms. "Let's get it over with."

"That's just it," he told her. "I don't want it over with. I want us together. It may not be all that either of us wants right now, but eventually I know we'll come to some sort of—"

"What do you mean by 'together'?" she cut in, and he took a deep breath.

"What most people mean by *together*. Us, as a couple. Seeing each other, spending time together, going out, staying in." He swallowed and fought for the right tone. "Maybe even living together."

"Ah."

"Joan's not a child anymore. You're right about that. Before we know it, she'll even be going off to college. And eventually, more than likely, almost certainly, we'll be..." She stared at him, waiting. "Exactly what you want us to be," he finished.

She smiled, but it was cold, brittle. "You can't even say it," she scoffed, shaking her head. "Go away, Craig. For God's sake, just go away."

"Ginger, please—"

''No,'' she said firmly. ''I don't want you like this. You needn't feel responsible or guilty or anything at all. I made a mistake about us, Craig. We're not right for one another.''

He was wounded, perhaps mortally. *Now* she decided she was mistaken about them? He loved her. He was going crazy because of her, and she had decided they weren't right for each other after all? Anger flared up in him, but he was too hurt even to give it vent. She walked ahead of him to the door, and he followed dumbly.

''I'm sorry, Craig,'' she rasped, and opened the door. He was slow moving, heavy of limb and he kept looking at her face, trying to understand. She was staring out the door, apparently at something in particular, and then suddenly she slammed it shut again. ''Ah, wait, maybe we'd better talk about this some more. I don't want you to go away...''

What? he wondered.

'' ...confused,'' she said.

He knew suddenly that she was stretching, stalling. ''What's wrong with you?'' he said. ''What's out there?'' He reached past her for the doorknob.

''No, Craig, wait!''

But the door was already open and he was standing there staring at a car parked at the curb. Paul, Jr.'s car. So? There was movement of some sort, and then he realized he was watching the tops of two heads disappear below the line of the seat, the *back* seat. He took off without thinking, Ginger at his heels.

''Craig, don't do anything you'll be sorry for. A scene won't help. We have to be rational about this.''

''*You* be rational,'' he snapped, yanking open the door of Paul's car.

Jo and Paul popped up like frightened rabbits, and in the painful glow of the interior light, Craig saw his little sister scrambling to get her arm back through the sleeve of her top and the hem pulled down. He was mad enough to wring her neck—or, better yet, the neck of Paul Solis, Jr. Instead, he reached inside and hauled Joan out onto the sidewalk.

"What in hell do you think you're doing?" he bawled at her. Then he bent over and fixed Paul, Jr., with his most baleful glare. "Mister, you just tore it with me. I can't believe this! I'm so disappointed with the two of you."

Paul shoved his way out of the car and stood at Joan's side. "Now wait a minute, Mr. Russell, we weren't really doing anything—"

"Not doing anything! You were undressing my sister practically in my own front yard!"

"Well, where would you have us go?" Paul demanded. "Some back alley somewhere? We figured this was the best place."

"The best place!"

"It's a secure neighborhood," Joan argued. "And we thought everybody else would be in bed by now."

"Well, you thought wrong!" Craig roared. "Get in the house, now, before I throttle you where you stand!"

"Now wait a minute," Paul said, stepping in front of the girl. "You hurt her, man, and you'll answer to me."

Craig was dumbfounded. Him hurt his own sister? This from the guy who was about to seduce her in the back seat of his car!

"Paul, I think you should go," Jo said quietly. "It's all right, really. He didn't mean that. He'd never do that. Just let me talk to him."

The kid wavered a moment, but then he turned, kissed her firmly on the mouth, got into his car and started it up. It was all Craig could do to control himself while the boy drove away. No sooner did the car turn the corner than Jo attacked him.

"You don't have to throttle me, Craig! Why don't you just embarrass me to death!"

"Embarrass you? Me? Looks like you were doing a pretty good job at that yourself! What were you thinking? Were you thinking at all?"

"Well, I wasn't thinking about you barging into something that doesn't concern you!"

"You're my sister! How could it not concern me? I'm supposed to just let you make the biggest mistake of your life?"

"Yes, if that's what I want to do! It's my life!"

"No way! I'm not going to stand by and watch you ruin your chances for happiness!"

"I wasn't doing that! I'm in love with Paul!"

"You don't know what love is!"

Jo turned away suddenly and rushed to Ginger, who was hanging back, trying not to interfere. "Ginger, tell him how stupid he's being! I'm not a kid anymore."

Craig started to demand that Ginger be kept out of it, but she lifted her hand pleadingly, and he bit back the words.

"You're not a kid," Ginger agreed quietly. "But neither are you fully an adult, Joan. I'm sorry, but Craig's right this time. Not in the way he's going about it, maybe, but that's just because he's so concerned and frightened for you."

"But I love Paul!" Joan cried, tears coming now that her best source of support was being denied her.

"I'm sure you do," Ginger said. "And no doubt he feels the same way about you. But is it going to last, Joan? That's what you have to ask yourself. Sex is dangerous, even for adults. There's great risk emotionally, giving yourself to someone only to realize later that you shouldn't have. Besides that, you're setting yourself up for all kinds of other problems, not the least of which is an accidental pregnancy, and you weren't prepared for that, were you?"

"We weren't going to let it get that far," she said tearfully. "We didn't plan anything."

"I understand that, Joan, and that's just the point. These things require a great deal of thought and preparation, and two people have to trust each other completely to be frank enough to deal with that. You and Paul just aren't there yet. I don't think you can get there without a commitment like marriage. That's something I've learned the hard way. So please, promise me you'll be more careful, more thoughtful and wiser in the future."

Joan nodded, smearing tears around her face. "All right."

Craig stepped forward and put his arm around her shoulders to let her know that he loved her and was again in control of his temper. "Go in the house, honey," he said gently. "We'll talk again in the morning. Talk, not shout."

She sniffed and nodded. "You won't blame Paul, will you?"

He looked at Ginger and remembered. "I won't blame anyone," he said. As Joan walked toward the house, her shoulders slumping, Craig held Ginger's gaze.

"We really messed up, didn't we?" he said softly, and she nodded.

"Yeah. We really did."

"I'm sorry, sweetheart."

"I know."

"Thanks for what you did. I was about to blow it but good."

"Craig, you have to talk to her about birth control," Ginger said ardently. "Promise me you'll do that."

"Right," he muttered. "Okay. Sure."

She spun away then and hurried into her own house. He stood there watching her, his hand coming up to cover his mouth. Why hadn't he thought of this before? Dear God, could it be? Was that why Ginger was so very upset? A baby? He closed his eyes and tried to think, to feel the possibilities. A baby. *His* baby. *Their* baby. Hell.

Chapter Fifteen

Craig could not remember ever leaving work in the middle of the day, but somehow he couldn't concentrate. He just kept hearing over and over in his mind the things Ginger had said to Joan. *You're setting yourself up for all kinds of problems, not the least of which is accidental pregnancy. Accidental pregnancy.* Was the result of their lovemaking an accidental pregnancy? He simply had to find out, and he knew no other way to do so than to ask her.

The clock on his dashboard read 1:17 when he pulled up into his drive. That gave him nearly three hours before the bus dropped off Joan from school—provided Ginger hadn't gone out for some reason. It occurred to him that he really didn't know what she did during the day besides dabble with her paints and test recipes for her cookbook. Perhaps that was enough to keep her busy and at home. On the other hand, she could be going out for something like an aerobics class several times a week. She had to keep that gorgeous body in shape some way. But did expectant mothers do that sort of thing? He really had no idea, not that it mattered. She could have gone out for any number of reasons. She could have gone to the hairdresser or the post office or the grocery store—or the doctor. His hands trembled as he shut off the engine and got out of the car, leaving his suit jacket behind.

He looked at Ginger's well-landscaped yard and hoped she'd be home. He had to know if he was going to be a father. He just had to know. And yet, how did one ask a woman if she was carrying his child? Straight out, he supposed. How else?

Bucking up his courage, he walked down his drive and along the sidewalk, then up Ginger's beautifully decorated walkway to her front door. He actually closed his eyes and took several deep breaths to calm himself before pressing the doorbell button. Within moments he heard her sandals on the stone floor of the entry hall. She was home. Twin waves of relief and despair swept over him, one warm, the other cold. She opened the door, smiling.

"Hi," he said brightly. "Can I come in?"

The smile wavered and settled into a lower-wattage version of the original. "You're home awful early. What happened, Congress outlaw cars?"

"Ha-ha. No, actually the business is fine. This country runs on highways, you know."

"If you say so."

It occurred to him that she hadn't answered his question. "Do we have to talk out here?" he prodded gently. The pause that followed displayed Ginger's reluctance clearly. He bowed his head, desperation burning the back of his throat.

"Want a cup of tea?" she asked. "Dad brought back a special blend from Japan."

Craig smiled at her. "Thanks."

Ginger backed up and turned away, her hips swaying gracefully side to side as she walked down the hall. She was wearing blue jeans and an orange-and-yellow striped blouse, the tapered and elongated tails of which wrapped around her slender middle, crisscrossing to tie in front. On her feet were yellow beaded sandals. He noticed that she'd painted her toenails orange and had pulled up her hair into a slightly off-center ponytail that seemed to have been ratted with frayed orange ribbon. These small eccentricities made his smile widen, but when he walked into the living room and saw Frederick Brenan sitting on one of the sofas with a cup balanced upon his knee, the smile faded.

"Sit down," Ginger said. "I'll get another cup and be with you in a second."

Craig disciplined a frown and moved toward the center of the room. Great. Just the sort of audience he needed for the delicate matter at hand. Maybe Frederick would be leaving soon. If not, perhaps he could move the man himself. *Pardon me, sir, but might I have a private moment to ask your daughter if I accidentally impregnated her on the beach a few weeks back?* Was Frederick Brenan enough of a gentleman, Craig wondered, not to deck him? He wouldn't bet on it. Well, he could take his medicine, the very least of which might be a hard right to the jaw. He walked to the sofa opposite Frederick, intending to take a seat, but the entire length of the thing was covered in various sizes of bundles wrapped in tissue paper. He stepped around the coffee table and took a seat on the end of the couch on which Frederick sat.

"How are you, Craig?" Frederick asked, lifting his small, handleless cup.

"Well enough."

"Hmm." That sounded skeptical, but Craig had no time to explore its meaning as Ginger returned with the cup. She knelt on the floor beside the coffee table and poured greenish, strong-smelling tea into the tiny cup before passing it to Craig. He sipped at the tea, found it bitter but not undrinkable and nodded satisfaction.

"Look at what Dad has brought me from Japan," she said.

Turning over the first package, she carefully peeled back the paper and lifted from it a pair of black lacquered wooden platform sandals with red velvet thongs. Intricate scenes were carved into the sides of the thick soles and handpainted in vibrant colors. Next she unveiled a slinky pair of black embossed silk pants, then a long, grass green kimono heavily embroidered with winged dragons in black, red and gold. A gold obi a foot wide and fully ten feet long was displayed next, followed by a floor-length coat, heavily and intricately embroidered, of white and gold silk lined with black. There were other exotic items—a kind of wire headdress that resembled a tree with tiny gold leaves hanging from it; a saffron yellow dress with green frogs up the front and side slits piped in black; a jade-and-black lacquered brooch in the form of a writhing dragon pierced with a golden sword, its ruby eyes glittering somehow with sadness. Last came a sandalwood box, carved and inset with jade, its many trays lined with red velvet and rimmed with gold beading. From them Ginger took many differently shaped pieces of pierced metal, tin perhaps or pewter, and snapped them together. The finished product was a child's toy, a kind of stick puppet in the form of a geisha. Ginger manipulated it, making it bow, kneel and dance.

A child's toy, Craig thought. His child's? He put down his tea cup with a loud crack against the glass top of the table. "I have to speak to you."

Ginger looked at him with surprise. "About what?"

He opened his mouth, then slid a glance at the man at his side and closed it again. But he couldn't let it go. Agitated, frustrated, Craig got to his feet and bending, caught Ginger by the arm. "I need to talk to you," he repeated, hauling her up.

"So talk!" she exclaimed, looking at him as if he'd lost his mind.

"Not here," he retorted crossly. But where? His eyes swept around the room until they came to the bedroom door. "Come on." He pulled her across the floor, aware only when she slipped from his grasp that she had been struggling against him.

"What is wrong with you?" she demanded, anger flashing in her golden eyes.

He sent a glance toward her father, who was sitting forward, intent upon their exchange. "I need to talk to you," he repeated yet again, adding this time, *"alone."*

She rolled her eyes and said between her teeth, "I have company."

"This is important," he insisted.

"So is this!" she hissed at him, flinging an arm in her father's direction. "He just got back from Japan. Besides, I don't want to talk to you *alone* right now."

"Well, that's a fine thing to say!"

"What are you so angry about?"

"You won't talk to me!"

"You don't want to talk, you want to unload your conscience!"

"How the hell would you know when you won't listen to anything I have to say?" The words fairly bounced off the walls, resonating like the tolls of some enormous bell. He was shouting. He was shouting at her in front of her father. Craig looked at Frederick Brenan and saw that his eyes were large and protruding and his face was red. Only with effort did the older man keep his seat. Suddenly Craig knew it was useless. He whirled and strode out of the house, boiling with impotent rage.

God, oh, God, what a mess he'd made of everything. How big a mess he still didn't know, but the likelihood remained that he had fathered a child. Somehow he had to find out. And then what? That was a question he did know the answer to. There was only one option, really, as far as he was concerned, and Ginger had to know that, too. She had to have guessed, and if it was what she wanted, what she had wanted all along, then why wouldn't she talk to him? Didn't she know that she had already turned his life upside down? *Yeah, and if you're right, it isn't going to get anything but worse, buddy.*

Craig went into his own house and did something he had very rarely ever done at that time of day. He poured himself a tall, stiff drink, and by the time Joan came home, he was well on his way to a deep, silent, brooding depression.

He woke the next morning in a calmer state of mind. *Big deal*, he told himself. So what if he was going to be a father? He was practically that now with Jo. He could handle it, and Ginger would be a dynamite mother. Hey, he might even get to like the idea. Sure. Other guys did it. Why not him? Now he had only to convince Ginger. But this time he would remain serene at any cost and carefully frame what he wanted to say in his mind before he spoke.

He dressed, and downed a cup of coffee, his thoughts full of words and intonations. His hands were shaking, but he paid them no mind as he considered what had to be done. First, he had to be sure that Ginger was, indeed, pregnant, then he would agree to marry her. Nope. Wrong approach. Ginger was too direct to have planned this. She wouldn't like the idea of trapping him. She'd want to know first of all that he cared for her. All right, he could do that. He'd simply tell her, truthfully as it turned out, that he loved her, then he'd find out about the baby and *ask* her to marry him. She'd accept, of course. Or would she?

What if she didn't want him after all? What then? Could he just turn his back on his flesh and blood and pretend he had never happened? *He?* Yeah, he. A boy. A son. Wouldn't *that* be something. Then again, girls were nice— but difficult. Very difficult. A boy would be better. Unless he turned out to be some kind of punk. Yikes! No kid of Craig's was going to shave his head, put a ring in his nose and smoke dope. He wouldn't have it. He absolutely would not have it—provided he had anything to say about it. And he would. Ginger had wanted him once, and by God, she was going to want him again if he had to... What? How?

A cold shudder shook him. *You're getting ahead of yourself. You don't even know for sure that she's pregnant. So find out. Now. Right now.*

Craig walked out his back door, across the deck, down the steps and across the sand to her place. She was wearing something pink and slinky beneath a white, bell-shaped robe of sorts that she had tied with a big fluffy bow at the neck. Neither garment came anywhere near her knees, making a very fetching costume. He could see her through the patio door, swigging coffee and massaging her temples. Morning sickness? Only one way to find out. He rapped on the glass, saw her look of dismay and rapped again, harder.

She came to the door. "What now?"

"I have to talk to you."

"Oh, Craig, this just gets worse and worse. And what could there possibly be left to say?"

"I love you."

That rocked her back. She pushed the door wide and stepped aside. "When did you decide *that?*" she asked skeptically, but he knew she wanted to believe him. Otherwise he wouldn't be standing once more in her living room.

"I've known it for a while."

"Really? I suppose you knew it that night on the beach."

"I did."

"So why tell me now?"

He reached out for her. "You have to know up front that I love you very much," he said. "Because I have something very important to ask you."

She was holding back, resisting the pull of his arms, but her eyes were wide and soft, and her voice, when she spoke, was very small. "You do?"

"Yes, and it's something I couldn't ask you in front of your father. You understand that, don't you?" She nodded.

"It's just that you were very rude."

"Yes, I was," he admitted. "But forget that now. I have a question to ask you, and your answer is very important, so you must be honest with me. Promise?"

"Craig," Ginger said, stepping forward, "I've never been anything but honest with you."

He folded her close and held her against him. It felt so good, so very good. "You do love me, don't you?" he whispered into the cloud of her hair.

"Of course I do." She tilted her head back. "Is that what you wanted to ask me?"

"No, but that helps."

"Good." She lifted her mouth to his, and he couldn't resist.

Kissing her was the next best thing to heaven. Maybe marriage wouldn't be so bad with her. One thing about it, he'd never stop wanting her. He was practically certain now that she was expecting his baby. Why else would she have pulled back, tried to push him away, when she so obviously did love him? The answer could only be that she hadn't wanted to trap him into this—not that he would have suspected her of it. She was too honest for that. He had no doubt about it, and he wanted her to understand that. He broke the kiss and hugged her tight.

"You should have told me," he whispered, enjoying the feel of her large, firm breasts against his chest with only the thin layer of her nightclothes between them.

"I did tell you," she answered dreamily. "I told you in every way I could think of how much I love you."

It was true. He saw that now, and it thrilled him in a way he hadn't thought possible. "Yes, you did tell me that," he said, holding her away from him so he could gaze into her eyes. "It's the other thing I'm talking about."

She cocked her head slightly. "What other thing?"

He lifted a skeptical eyebrow. Was she so intent on protecting him? Well, he wasn't going to let her, not when there was so much else at stake. He smiled at her understandingly and just laid it on the line. "You're pregnant, aren't you?"

Her mouth fell open, then curved into a smile, only to grow round again. "You...you..." She shook her head and blinked her eyes, then suddenly her eyebrows drew together and her forehead creased. "Is *that* what you wanted to ask me?"

Her tone surprised him. From it he deduced that something was wrong here. Maybe he hadn't said it right. Whatever the reason, he had best step carefully. He lifted one shoulder. "Well, of course, I had to ask, but I wanted you to know that I understand, and it doesn't make any difference to me. I mean, it makes a difference, a huge difference, but it's all right. I love you, and it goes without saying that I'll marry you."

She stared at him hard for several seconds, then half turned her head to stare at him from the corners of her eyes. "You'll marry me," she said, "as long as I'm pregnant."

He *hadn't* said it right. Craig licked his lips, silently imploring her to understand. "I'm not very good at this kind of thing, Ginger, but I've thought about it a lot, and I want to marry you.''

''Because of the baby,'' she said, and her voice was flat, entirely too unemotional.

''And because I love you.''

''*And* you want to do the right thing?''

No shame in that. He nodded. ''Absolutely. You must have known I would or you wouldn't have kept it from me.''

''This supposed pregnancy, you mean?'

''Yes.''

''Ah-ha.'' She pulled away from him and walked to the dining table, her hand reaching out for a glass bowl colored with wavy lines. ''I suggest you go, Craig,'' she said. Her voice, deceptively cool, suddenly heated. ''Before I split your stupid skull!''

''*What?*'' She couldn't have meant that the way it sounded. Could she?

She smiled mirthlessly and shrugged. ''Can't say I didn't warn you.''

He watched disbelievingly as she picked up the bowl and heaved it at him! ''Ginger!'' She reached for another one, never mind that it was filled with flowers. He raced for the door. ''Damn!''

''My sentiments exactly!'' she yelled, showering the room with flowers, water and shards of bright glass.

''What'd I do?'' But he couldn't wait for the answer. She was walking toward the coffee table—and a large jar of crystal marbles. He bolted through the door and ducked just as it flew over his head, landing with a crash on the deck beyond, and she was coming toward him with a chunk of lava rock as big as a grapefruit. ''What's wrong with you?'' he yelled, ready to restrain her if she attempted to heft that rock at him.

''Not a damned thing!'' she told him sharply. ''And for your information, *if* there *were* something wrong with me, *if* I were *stupid* enough to get myself pregnant, *you* would be the last person I'd want to know! The very damned last!''

He stared at her, mouth open. She chunked the rock away, turned around and fled back into the house, slamming the door so hard, he thought the whole wall of glass would come sliding down in shards. He could see her stalking around in there and fuming, talking to the ceiling, shaking her fist.

Slowly it came to him. She wasn't pregnant! There was no baby. He didn't have to marry her. He was free of any obligation to the woman and... He felt rather deflated. He watched her pacing and fuming and told himself he was well rid of her. It was only that he'd accepted the notion of her carrying his child, and yet how terribly odd it was to be feeling this way. He wasn't going to marry Ginger and never again would he make love to her.

Suddenly a picture of Ginger flashed before his mind's eye. He saw her naked beneath him, her butterscotch blond hair fanned out to one side and curling softly about her long, slender neck. He remembered putting his mouth to the curve of that neck and inhaling the musky nutmeg perfume of her hair and, as he did so, feeling himself throb inside of her. That single sensation flushed him, sweeter and hotter and more intense than any other like memory he had experienced. *Never again,* he thought. She had chased him from her house, throwing things at him. Never again would they make love. Dear God, what had he done? He put his hands to his head and said words he hadn't said in years, if ever.

What a chump! What a prize goof! The woman wasn't even pregnant! How in hell had he convinced himself that she was? No wonder she had thrown things at him! He'd as much as accused her of carrying his baby and keeping it a secret. He'd ruined it. She had wanted him, loved him, and he had ruined it.

But wait a minute. Didn't it matter to her at all that, had she been pregnant, he was willing to do the right thing? He'd told her that he loved her. What else did the woman want? He put his hands on his hips. Throw rocks at him, would she? Well, they'd just see about that! He wouldn't marry her now, no matter how much he wanted to! That was it. He had come to her with his heart in his hand, and she'd thrown things at him! Disappointed? Hell, no, he wasn't disappointed! He wasn't going to let a woman like that make him pine, no sir, not now that he knew how callous she could be. Talk about a near thing, a close escape!

He stalked back to his own house, a free man. That was it, then. Done. Everything could go back to the way it used to be. That wild woman had seen the last of him. She wouldn't have *him* to hang her claws in anymore, no sirree bob, and any minute now he was going to feel this incredible rush of relief.

Any minute.

Right away.

Just as soon as the shock wore off, he'd feel the bright lift of relief. Sooner or later. When he'd worked it all out.

All right, so it was going to take working out. So what? Eventually, he was going to be glad about this.

Ginger was so angry, her chest was heaving. The floor was slick with shattered glass, water and crushed flowers, but still she paced back and forth across it, the soles of her satin-and-lace slippers crunching the debris beneath her feet. The nerve of that man! Should she be stupid enough to let herself wind up carrying his child, he would deign to marry her. How magnanimous! She supposed she was expected to be grateful. But what woman wanted a man to marry her out of duty? Oh, he said he loved her, but he would only marry her if she was pregnant! That was hardly her idea of an appropriate foundation for a successful marriage. She wished fiercely that she had hit him just once. Just once. And if he came back, she would.

The doorbell rang and Ginger smiled thinly. On her way to answer it, she caught up a large piece of driftwood, which she grasped firmly by one of its smooth, gray branches.

"All right, Craig Russell," she said. Cocking the driftwood like a club with one hand, she reached out with the other and opened the front door.

Her father peered at her from beneath a wrinkled brow. At his side stood her brother.

Will frowned. "Ginger, are you all right?"

"Of course not!" Frederick Brenan barked. "Look at her. Does she look all right to you? Now then, girl, just what has that Craig Russell done?"

Ginger lowered her makeshift club. "Nothing."

"Don't give me that guff again!" Frederick said in his sternest father's voice. "Something is going on between you two, and I intend to get to the bottom of it right now." With that, he pivoted on his heel and strode away. Only when he turned up the sidewalk toward Craig's house did she realize what he intended—and what he would learn.

She looked at Will with desperation. "Oh, no!"

She sprinted after her father, losing her slippers in the process. Behind her, Will bent to pick them up. They were wet. He turned them over in his hands, saw the pieces of glass and crushed flowers imbedded in the soles and shook his head.

Craig opened the door to a very curious sight, Ginger's back, against which she held an unwieldy-looking piece of driftwood. Beyond her stood her father.

"No, Daddy, no," she was saying. "It's nothing, just a silly misunderstanding."

"Then it's about time it was cleared up," Frederick Brenan huffed, and with a sweep of his arm, he brushed her aside. "Now then, young man," he said, stepping up into Craig's foyer. "What's this all about?"

Craig sent Ginger a murderous glare, which she returned. As he switched his attention back to Frederick, he caught sight of Will coming up the drive, Ginger's house shoes in his hands. What was this, a lynching? But why? Because he *didn't* get their darling Ginger pregnant? Craig cleared his throat and attempted to sound stern. "I'm sure you understand, sir. It's a private matter."

"Craig's right, Dad," Ginger put in. "It's private."

"Not anymore!" Frederick asserted doggedly.

"Craig?" It was Joan. He closed his eyes and gritted his teeth.

"Not now, hon. We're kind of busy at the moment."

"What's going on?" she asked.

"Precisely what I would like to know," Frederick Brenan
stated, forging past Craig and down the hall.

The look Craig sent Ginger was desperate, but there
wasn't time for more as he hurried after her father. She
hopped up into the house on her bare feet and followed right
on his heels.

"What's going on?" he hissed at her.

"You should know! You're the one who made the scene
yesterday!"

"And you're the one who made the scene this morning!" he retorted.

She stopped where she was, gasping. "*I* made a scene?"
she exclaimed. "You're the one who came in throwing
around meaningless marriage proposals!"

"Did you say 'marriage proposal'?" Will strolled unin-
vited into Craig's house without a qualm. "Good for you
darling. Come tell us all about it." He pecked Ginger on the
cheek, dropped her shoes onto the floor and continued on
into the living room. "Nice house," he muttered.

Craig put his balled fists to the sides of his head. "I don't
believe this!"

"Oh?" Ginger said in that querulous tone of hers. "You
don't believe my own family could be concerned about me?
Well, believe me, they are! Now let me tell you what I don't
believe. I don't believe I once wanted to marry you! *That's*
what I don't believe!"

"Well, you did, lady!" Craig shouted, even though he
was talking to her back as she marched into his living room.
He stalked after her, determined she wasn't going to pin the
blame for this mess on him. "And as far as I'm concerned,
it's the only intelligent thing you've done since I've known
you!" he went on. "What's more, you made *me* want to
marry you, too! And you did it *on purpose!*"

She halted and spun around, her driftwood swinging out
at her side as she did so. "Then I take it all back!" she told
him smartly.

"Oh, no!" he roared. "You made your bed, now you're
going to lie in it! You wanted me to love you, and I do! You

wanted me to marry you, and I'm going to! And that's final!''

"Is that right?"

"That is exactly right!"

For a long moment she glared at him, her jaw working side to side, then she tossed her head back and narrowed her eyes at him. "All right," she said. "But you know something? You were right. You stink at this. Luckily you won't have to do it again, *ever*."

"Fine!" he snapped.

"Fine!" she snapped back. Then, with a smug look over her shoulder, she dropped the driftwood onto the carpet, dusted her hands together, lifted her chin and walked out.

Craig stood with his hands on his hips, staring after her, feeling oddly as if he'd missed something. Then the clearing of a throat reminded him there were other matters needing his attention. He turned on the lot of them, both eyebrows lifted in challenge. Instantly Joan dissolved in giggles.

"What's the matter with you?" he demanded sharply.

"Nothing," she squeaked, clamping her hand over her mouth.

He noticed that Will was going through some sort of gyrations with his facial muscles, first pursing then thinning his lips. Craig glared at him. "I take it *you* have something to say."

Will lifted a shoulder and broke out in a grin. "So much for champagne and candlelight."

"What's that supposed to mean?" Craig growled.

It was Frederick Brenan who replied. "Don't take offense, dear boy," he said, spots of color high on his cheeks. "It's just that one seldom hears a proposal delivered in such...strong tones."

Proposal? Yes, he supposed it could be called that. He just hadn't realized they had overheard. But, of course, they had. They were standing right there, weren't they? He felt himself color slightly. All right, so he wasn't Don Juan, what of it? He'd laid down the law to that woman, and he was going to go right on doing so until he got the message through her thick skull. After all, he had a right to a little happiness, didn't he? Of course he did. He folded his arms.

"Well, if you're waiting for an apology..." he mumbled, but Will chuckled.

"No, I wouldn't think an apology was called for," he said. "I should think congratulations were more in order. I wonder if you realize that?"

Congratulations? Craig looked at the younger man in puzzlement, then at Frederick and finally at his own sister, all of whom were quite literally beaming.

"You did hear Ginger accept, didn't you?" Joan asked around a smile.

Accept? he wondered. Then it hit him. Good heavens, she had! At least, he supposed one could call it an acceptance, about as much as one could call what he'd had to say a marriage proposal, anyway. *More like a marriage edict,* he thought, and that wasn't how he wanted to leave it at all. He loved that woman. He was going to marry her and make babies with her. They were going to spend the rest of their lives together, and it was what he wanted more than anything else in the world. If he hadn't told her that, it was only because he had just realized it himself! But she ought to know. She had a right to know. And he was the only one who could tell her. He went to her without so much as a thought for the three people who subdued their smiles as they watched him go.

Ginger plucked impatiently at the bedspread. Had he meant it? Had he really meant it? Or was she jumping to conclusions again? *If he meant it, he'll come,* she told herself, *and if he doesn't, this time I'll just die.* She got up and paced the floor, the hem of her peignoir swirling about her thighs. On the third lap she decided she was a fool. He wasn't coming. And then she heard the bell, followed immediately by the opening of the door. She held her breath.

"Ginger?"

The sound of his voice rolled over her, warm and welcome. For a moment she could do no more than stand there, basking in the joy of it, then suddenly the tears started.

Quickly, she dashed them away, a smile coming in their place as she padded on bare feet to the bed. She slid beneath the covers, moving almost to the center of the wide mattress. Rolling on her side, she took a deep breath and combed her hair away from her face with her fingers. Finally, she licked her lips.

"Here," she said.

His footsteps grew louder as he moved down the entry hall toward the open bedroom door. Her heart pounding, Ginger waited, but the footsteps halted. She bit her lip. Had he changed his mind? She sat up, suddenly panicked. As if on cue, he stepped into the doorway, looking as tense and desperate as she felt. Unaccountably, that relaxed her somewhat. She smiled tentatively and smoothed the bedcovers around her. His own smile was a bit shakier.

"That's quite a mess I made in the other room," he said.

She thought of hurling the bowls at him and sighed. "We," she corrected. "That's quite a mess *we* made. But we can always unmake it, can't we?"

He nodded slowly and moved on into the room. "We can unmake all our messes," he told her softly. "If you only love me half as much as I love you."

She lifted her chin, quaking inside. "Even if we're not having a baby?"

Craig looked mildly surprised. "We're not having a baby *now,*" he said. "But sooner or later we will. Won't we?"

Ginger's eyes slowly closed. "I hope so," she said fervently, savoring the moment when the last doubt left her. They were neighbors no more, but lovers, and soon, husband and wife. She opened her eyes again and got to her feet in the middle of the bed. Very deliberately, she slipped the bow at her neck and peeled away the frothy peignoir, revealing the lacy little nightie beneath. "We have a lot of unmaking to do," she said. "I think we ought to get started." She held out her arms to him in invitation.

He stepped out of his shoes and, a moment later, up onto the bed. "Promise me two things," he said, the bed sinking and rolling as he walked to her.

"Anything."

He grinned and slid his hands beneath the tiny, delicate straps of her gown. "First," he said, pulling one of the straps over her shoulder, "that you'll wear something absolutely outrageous to the wedding."

She smiled and lifted that shoulder coquettishly, her whole body glowing with happiness. "Of course."

He pulled down the other strap. "Second," he said, his voice soft and husky with emotion, "that it will be soon."

"Very soon," she promised him breathlessly, and as his mouth found the curve of her neck, he began to slide the gown down her body. "Very, *very* soon."

He lifted his head and gazed down at her, his eyes soft and appreciative. "How did you know?" he asked gently.

"That we were right for each other?" He nodded, and she slipped her arms up and around his neck. "The same way you knew, I suppose. It was so easy to imagine us together, and afterward, so difficult to imagine us apart."

"Yes," he said. "Exactly the way I knew—finally."

She put her forehead to his, silently giving thanks. "At least you know now. That's all that matters."

He kissed her, lovingly and deeply, and it was like no other kiss he had given her. In it was knowledge and commitment and certainty and a wealth of desire, everything she could want, all she had hoped for, and much of which she hadn't even guessed, the icing and the cake, a whole lovely feast, the finishing of fulfillment. In it was love and family and wholeness. The hunt was over, and she had found her mate, and as he pulled her to her knees and lowered her onto her back, they were both laughing and both whole. Together.

* * * * *

VOWS
A series celebrating marriage
by Sherryl Woods

To Love, Honor and Cherish—these were the words that three generations of Halloran men promised their women they'd live by. But these vows made in love are each challenged by the tests of time....

In October—Jason Halloran meets his match in *Love* #769;
In November—Kevin Halloran rediscovers love—with his wife—in *Honor* #775;
In December—Brandon Halloran rekindles an old flame in *Cherish* #781.

These three stirring tales are coming down the aisle toward you—only from Silhouette Special Edition!

NORA ROBERTS

Love has a language all its own, and for centuries flowers have symbolized love's finest expression. Discover the language of flowers—and love—in this romantic collection of 48 favorite books by bestselling author Nora Roberts.

Two titles are available each month at your favorite retail outlet.

In November, look for:

For Now, Forever, Volume #19
Her Mother's Keeper, Volume #20

In December, look for:

Partners, Volume #21
Sullivan's Woman, Volume #22

THE LANGUAGE of LOVE

Collect all 48 titles
and become fluent in

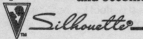
Silhouette®

What a year for romance!

Silhouette has five fabulous romance collections coming your way in 1993. Written by popular Silhouette authors, each story is a sensuous tale of love and life—as only Silhouette can give you!

SPRING FANCY

Three bachelors are footloose and fancy-free... until now.
(March)

to Mother with Love

Heartwarming stories that celebrate the joy of motherhood.
(May)

SILHOUETTE
SUMMER Sizzlers

Put some sizzle into your summer reading with three of Silhouette's hottest authors.
(June)

SILHOUETTE
Shadows

Take a walk on the dark side of love— with tales just perfect for those misty autumn nights.
(October)

Silhouette
Christmas
Stories

Share in the joy of yuletide romance with four award-winning Silhouette authors.
(November)

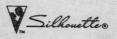

Silhouette®

A romance for all seasons—it's always time for romance with Silhouette!